THE QUANTUM CHILD

A MATT HUNTER MYSTERY

BY CHARLES AYER

ALSO BY CHARLES AYER

WALTER HUDSON MYSTERIES:

A Deadly Light

Placid Hollow

Dutch River

The Iron Range

MATT HUNTER MYSTERIES:

Finding David Chandler

God As My Witness

"But at my back I always hear
Time's wingèd chariot hurrying near."

Andrew Marvell

"To His Coy Mistress"

CONTENTS

CHAPTER ONE

T HE ONLY REASON the phone rings at 3:30 in the morning is because someone is dead.

My phone rang at 3:30 in the morning.

I was in the deepest part of my sleep cycle, and I answered the call while I was still dreaming, about what, I'll never know.

"I thought I had my pants on," I said, sounding alert and confident.

"Matt? Matt?" came the reply. "It's Steve, you know, Detective Goldfarb. Do I need to give you a minute?" Steve Goldfarb had been promoted to Detective when the Washingtonville Police Department had merged with the Devon-on-Hudson Police Department the previous year in an effort to increase resources and save precious budget money for both small towns. He'd deserved the promotion, and he also provided a convenient buffer between me and Chief of Police Eddie Shepherd, which was a good thing for both Eddie and me. We'd both basically gotten past our youthful conflicts over the years, but Eddie and I still had our good days and our bad days, and I was glad to have Steve around.

"No, that's okay," I said, the cobwebs rapidly clearing. I swung my feet off the bed and quickly left the bedroom, hopefully before I disturbed Doreen. "Who died?"

"It's Ada Danforth," replied Goldfarb. "You know, Professor Ada Danforth."

My heart skipped a beat.

"How?" I said, probably a little too quickly.

"We're still working on that," said Goldfarb, but he'd obviously heard the shock in my one-word question. "Why?"

"Because I'm thinking you wouldn't have called me in the middle of the night if she'd died in her sleep."

"Any other reason?"

"I don't think so," I said, but I'm not a good liar, and I didn't even believe myself.

"Okay," said Goldfarb. "Look, I know it's the middle of the night, but do you think you could swing by? I think we're going to need you on this one, so you might as well get in on the ground floor."

On the surface it was an innocent request. I drew a healthy percentage of the income from my private investigating business from contracting out to the Devon-on-Hudson police department. Despite the consolidation, it was still understaffed and underfunded, and hiring me on an hourly fee to cover peaks in their workload was a lot cheaper than hiring another full-time detective. Besides, I was good at what I did, and my history with the New York Police Department gave me a lot of credibility with the full-timers. But I also sensed that there was more to this request than met the eye. Goldfarb wasn't pushing me for the moment, though, so I wasn't going to push him.

"Sure," I said. "Where are you?"

"We're at her house," said Goldfarb. "Do you need an address?"

"No," I said, "I have it."

"Oh," said Goldfarb, letting the word dangle.

"Look," I said, "I'll see you in about twenty minutes, okay? We can talk then."

"Good," was all Goldfarb said before he hung up.

Yes, good.

I slipped back into the bedroom and into the bathroom to splash some water on my face, brush my teeth, and run a comb through my hair. The image that stared back at me in the mirror wasn't reassuring, but vanity and a shower would have to wait. I threw on the pair of jeans and the red "St. John's Law" sweatshirt that I'd tossed on the floor the night before. The four miserable years I'd spent struggling through law school at night while working full-time as an NYPD cop were a distant memory now, but I'd hung on to the sweatshirt, just like I'd held on to my law license. Some bridges just shouldn't be burned. I looked over at Doreen, but she was still sound asleep, so I snuck back out of the room and went downstairs. I laced up the old pair of New Balance running shoes that always waited for me by the door that led to the garage like a faithful dog. It was early December, but the weather was uncommonly mild, so I just threw on a light jacket over the sweatshirt. I almost tripped over Doreen's son Donnie's pair of running shoes on the way out, a reminder of the other mystery in my life that I was going to have to deal with at some point, but I'd have to think about that later.

I hopped into my silver '05 Honda Accord, shoved the stick shift into reverse, eased out the clutch, and backed out of the garage. The car's odometer had just turned over 250,000 miles, but I wasn't even considering giving it up, even though at this point in my life I could afford just about any car I wanted. The fact of the matter was I didn't want another car; I wanted my Accord.

I swung by the local Dunkin' Donuts that I knew was open all night and picked up a Box O' Joe and a couple of dozen donuts. I figured if Ada's death was as suspicious as Steve Goldfarb's call made it sound, there would be hungry cops at the scene desperate for a sugar and caffeine hit. I put the coffee and the donuts on the passenger seat, thanked the tired looking young man at the takeout window, and rolled back into the night.

Ada Danforth's home was in the high hills overlooking the west bank of the Hudson River, just a couple of miles from the village of Devon-on-Hudson, the little upstate New York village where I'd been born and raised, and where I now once again lived and worked. It was also just north of West Point, home of the United States Military Academy, and one of the most beautiful spots in the country, if not the world. Under normal circumstances I would have looked forward to the drive, but these weren't normal circumstances and, besides, it was still pitch black out. I knew the area well but I'd never visited Ada's house, so I'd punched the address into my Garmin and let it guide me to my destination.

* * * * * *

The flashing lights and the four police cars parked along the narrow lane, one a new Ford Explorer Police Special that I hadn't seen before, guided me to Ada Danforth's house long before my Garmin had the honor of announcing that I'd arrived at my destination. A young cop, obviously drawn by the smell of the coffee and donuts, was at my car door, offering to help me with the precious sustenance before I'd had a chance to get out of the car.

"Don't forget the house is a crime scene," I told the kid, whose nameplate said "Beth Gardner," as she pulled out the boxes of donuts while I grabbed the Box O' Joe and the bag of paper cups, utensils, creamers, and napkins that came along with it.

"I'll just put everything in the back of the Explorer and leave the tailgate open," she replied. "I'm pretty sure everybody will find it."

Smart kid.

"You're Matt Hunter, right?" said Officer Gardner. She was small and trim, with a pretty face and a few stray strands of dark hair peeking out from under a cap that looked too large on her. She looked like a high school student to me, but then again, they all do these days.

"That's right."

"Pleased to meet you," she said. "I've heard a lot about you. My name's Beth, Officer Beth Gardner."

"Pleased to meet you Officer Gardner," I said, not out of formality as much as to give the young officer, clearly a rookie, the dignity of the position she'd earned through dedication and hard training. Having been a rookie cop once, I knew how much that meant.

Sure enough, by the time Officer Gardner and I had poured ourselves a cup, a half-dozen young cops had surrounded the Explorer like squirrels laying siege to a pile of acorns.

"Way to ruin my crime scene investigation," said a voice behind me.

"Don't worry, Steve, it'll sharpen their senses," I said, turning to face the large man who had spoken to me. I'm six-one, but I had to look up at Detective Steven Goldfarb. The ex-Navy Seal probably had twenty pounds on me, but it was all lean muscle. It was odd seeing him in mufti now that he'd been promoted to detective, but there was still no mistaking him for anything but a cop.

"Right now I'm not going to argue with you," he said, as he poured his own cup of coffee and grabbed one of the donuts, which were disappearing at a frightening rate. "We've been here since midnight."

"Leave your coffee cups and your crumbs out here!" he shouted to the assembled cops, "and put on fresh boots and gloves! We're done with the inside of the house, but I need you to scour the area around the house. Whoever did this had to have left something behind. You too, Matt. The boots and gloves are on the front seat."

Goldfarb polished off the donut and downed a couple of slugs of coffee while I grabbed a pair of plastic boots and latex gloves for myself, as well as a fresh pair for Goldfarb.

The ground beneath our feet was crunchy with fallen leaves as we walked to the house, a modestly sized bungalow with a spectacular view of the Hudson River that flowed beneath us in the dark, its river voice whispering to us on the night air, making it seem alive. The Hudson was breathtakingly wide at this point, technically a fjord more than a river, the broad valley having been carved out by glaciers during the last Ice Age. The house may have been small, and it sat on a parcel of land that was surely modest, but the view doubtlessly made it worth a small fortune.

The front of the house was dominated by a spacious verandah, furnished with two large Adirondack chairs and a small table, all covered for the winter. A short, paved driveway led to a covered parking space that sat to the right of the house. A dark-colored Toyota RAV4 that looked older than my Accord sat on the concrete slab.

The small home was constructed in the shotgun style, the front door opening into a living area. Behind the living area was a dining space, and beyond that, partitioned off from the dining area, a tiny kitchen. Off to the left were what I guessed to be two small bedrooms and a bathroom. The living room was sparingly furnished with a sofa and two chairs of the Scandinavian design so popular in the 70's, upholstered in a monochromatic pale oatmeal-colored fabric. A low teak coffee table sat in front of the sofa, and a small table stood next to one of the chairs, the only piece of furniture that showed any signs of use. An out-of-date, non-flat screen television sat off in a far corner. It was plugged in, but I didn't see any cable wires attached to it.

Four chairs were placed around a beautifully carved solid maple table in the dining room, but there was a place mat in front of only one of the chairs. A credenza constructed of the same wood was placed against the dividing wall between the kitchen and the dining area. A small, decades old black and white photo of a young couple standing in front of a 50's vintage car sat in a rectangular silver frame atop the credenza. Probably grandparents. We were all young once, I thought, with an unexpected shiver. It appeared to be the only photo in the house: none of Ada with friends, family, or colleagues that may have helped to identify possible suspects. The tiny galley style kitchen contained a white, four-burner gas stove, a white, European-sized refrigerator, and a stainless-steel sink. There was no dishwasher. The counter tops were covered with burnt orange Formica. Home renovations clearly had not been at the top of Ada Danforth's to-do list.

"Any sign of forced entry?" I said.

"None," replied Goldfarb. "And as you can see, there are no signs of any struggle, and nobody ransacked the place looking for valuables. We swept the place from top to bottom for any telltale evidence, but we came up empty. And we dusted the entire place for fingerprints and shoe prints, but all the prints were clustered in the places that you would expect the occupant to be touching and walking on in the course of daily life here, so I'm not hopeful. It's like the killer was never here."

"Any tire tracks out front?" I asked.

"We stopped the police units a couple hundred feet from the front of the house when we got here, of course. But the only tire tracks we found were made by Professor Danforth's car. We took impressions just in case, but the tires on the car are pretty new, and the visual match was pretty obvious."

"So are you guessing the killer got here on foot?"

"I don't know what else to think. We'll see what my team finds on the perimeter search.

"Okay," I said, "can we take a look at the body?"

"Let's go."

Goldfarb led me over to where the two bedrooms were located on either side of the bathroom. I peered into the bathroom. The drainpipe underneath the sink had been removed, as had the drain cover in the tub, obviously by Goldfarb's search team, but otherwise the bathroom appeared spotless.

"We took samples from the drains," said Goldfarb, following the direction of my glance. "No obvious signs of blood or other residue, but we'll see what turns up in the testing."

"But you're not optimistic."

"No, I'm not. Whoever did this clearly knew what he was doing."

"Or she."

"You're right," said Goldfarb, "or she."

I peered to the left into the larger of the two bedrooms. It was simply furnished with a twin-sized bed, carefully made, a dresser, and a nightstand.

"She never went to bed last night," I said.

"No, she didn't," said Goldfarb, "but the M.E. put the estimated time of death at about ten, so that's nothing surprising."

"How sure was she of the time of death?" I'd had to deal with the county medical examiner, Dr. Patricia Heath, on more than one occasion over the past couple of years, and you couldn't ask for anyone better.

"Pretty sure. The body was still warm and rigor hadn't set in yet when she got here."

"Okay," I said, "let's take a look."

The second bedroom had been furnished as a home office, with a desk that looked like it could have been purchased at IKEA. An Apple Macintosh computer that I guessed was at least a decade old sat on the desktop. There was no printer. The desk chair was a simple, wooden affair that clearly had not been designed with comfort or ergonomics in mind. A file cabinet sat beside the desk, and a small loveseat, upholstered in utilitarian beige fabric, was placed against the wall opposite the desk.

And the woman who had lived her life in this home in such monkish simplicity lay still on the floor.

I'd been at a lot of murder scenes in my life, and you can often learn quite a bit simply from first appearances. Sometimes you'd see what you'd expect: Dead eyes wide open, still full of fear and panic; mouths open, teeth bared; bloodied hands and fingers curled into claws as once sentient human beings had reverted to their mindless, reflexive, animal essence in their final struggle. Or sometimes there was simply an expression of surprise, the victims learning only at the last instant of their fate.

And then there were the victims like Dr. Ada Danforth, who had seemingly departed this earth in blessed ignorance of what had been done to her.

She lay on her back, having quietly slipped to the floor after suffering a deadly blow to the back of her head that she had never sensed coming.

Her eyes were closed and her expression was placid, as if a peaceful dream had overcome her just as she'd fallen asleep.

The awkward fall to the floor had left her wedged between the desk and the chair, her arms prayerfully folded across her chest. Her legs were slightly bent at the knee. She wore a brown woolen sweater over a white blouse, khaki slacks, and brown slippers.

With the exception of the brown slippers, it was the same outfit that she had been wearing when she had come to visit me in my office back in July.

* * * * *

"No blood," I said, as I crouched down next to the body.

"It was blunt force trauma," said Detective Goldfarb. "And it was something with a large surface area, not a hammer. I'm guessing maybe a small frying pan or a wooden mallet, something like that. Skull fragments would have pierced the dura, and then the brain itself. Death would have been almost instantaneous."

"Did you find anything like that in the house?" I said, standing up. It seemed like an invasion of privacy to remain crouched down next to the body when there was so clearly nothing else to see. We moved back into the living area.

"We found a set of cast iron frying pans in one of the kitchen drawers, and the smallest one of them could have done the trick. It looked clean, but we had it taken away for printing and testing anyway. Problem is, if it was something like a mallet, the killer probably brought it with him and took it away."

"And we'll never find it. Too many places to ditch something like that around here. Did you have a chance to interview any neighbors?"

"Neighbors? What neighbors? There's a cottage a hundred yards south of here, but it's only a seasonal home and there was no one there. There's another cottage a hundred yards the other way, but it's owned by an older couple that was sound asleep when we knocked on the door. It took ten minutes of pounding just to wake them up, and they'd fallen asleep with the television on to boot."

"So, if there weren't any neighbors, who called in the crime?"

"Funny thing about that," said Goldfarb. "It was an anonymous call to 911."

"Male? Female?"

"Hard to tell, just from listening to it. You know how 911 tapes are."

"Yeah. So what was funny about it?"

"It came from this house."

"There's a land line in this house?"

"Yeah, it's in the bedroom. I'm willing to bet she had it installed so that she could get internet back in the AOL days."

"What was the time of the call?"

"10:32 PM."

"Right about the estimated time of death."

"Correct."

"Are you going to have the tape analyzed?"

"I guess so," said Goldfarb, "but so what? Unless we have another voice to match it up against, it's worthless."

"Okay," I said, looking out one of the front windows of the house. The eastern sky was starting to brighten, giving the Hudson a glow. "Look, Steve, your guys won't be finished with their search of the area here for a couple more hours at least. I'm going to swing home for a shower and a bite to eat, and then I'm going to head into my office. I'd like to drop by the station to see you any time you're available." It had been a long night for Steve, but I knew he would go straight to his office once he was finished here. The Seals had taught him to go without sleep, and he would have a lot to do.

"Why?" he said.

"Why what?"

"Why do you want to stop by my office later?"

"There are some things we need to talk about, Steve, but it will probably be a much more productive talk if I have a chance to stop in at my office first."

"Why is that, Matt?"

"Look, Steve, I'm not trying to be evasive here, but I'm not even sure I know what I'm talking about yet. Please, bear with me."

"Could it have anything to do with this?" Steve asked, as he drew a carefully folded piece of paper from his breast pocket. He handed it to me and I read it carefully.

"Where did you find this?" I asked Steve when I was done reading.

"It was underneath the keyboard of her computer."

"Yes, Steve," I said. "This is what we need to talk about."

"You want to give me a hint?" he replied, sounding just a little exasperated.

"Steve, please," I said, knowing that I was trying his patience.

"Okay," he said after a brief pause. "But here's what we're going to do. I'm going to stop by your office around noon, and you're going to have a kosher roast beef sandwich with lettuce, tomato, and mustard on rye from Sally's waiting for me. And a bag of those Utz pretzels."

"Done," I said. Sally's was a deli located almost directly across the street from my office in town. It was owned and operated by a guy named Salvatore Bongiorno, ably assisted by his daughter, Clara. His sandwiches were outstanding, and they were huge.

"And a can of Doc Brown's Cream Soda."

"Didn't even have to ask."

"And one more thing."

"What's that?" I said, anxious to get out the door before he changed his mind and started grilling me right there.

"You're going to stay here for an hour while I run off to morning prayers. A couple of the guys are out of town, and they won't have a minyan without me."

Steve was an Orthodox Jew, and morning prayers at his synagogue meant a lot to him. I also took it as a compliment that he trusted me to supervise the crime scene investigation while he was gone. I'd come a long way.

"No problem," I said.

"Thanks," he said, heading for the door.

I waited until his car was heading down the narrow lane back to town before I looked back down at the piece of paper that I still held in my hand. It was dated July 23rd of this year, the same day that Ada Danforth had come to visit me at my office and left me with the sealed envelope that I still hadn't opened: the one that said "*To be opened only in the event of my death*" on it. The note that I held contained a simpler message:

"*Please contact Private Investigator C. Matthew Hunter at 245 Main Street in Devon-on-Hudson. Thank you. Ada Danforth.*"

Detective Steven Goldfarb was being patient with me. Damned patient. I'd make sure Sally put extra roast beef on his sandwich.

* * * * * *

CHAPTER TWO

"WHO DIED?" said the love of my life before I'd even had a chance to take off my jacket. It was nine o'clock by the time I got home, and Doreen was already showered, dressed, and ready for the day. Her thick, wavy auburn hair, cut short, shone, her hazel eyes glistened, and the high color of her clear complexion radiated well-being. I would have hugged her and given her a kiss, but my unshaven mug felt like sandpaper, God only knew what my breath reeked of, and I stank. She handed me a cup of coffee and wisely kept her distance.

"Thanks," I said, taking a long sip that scalded my throat. I didn't mind; I was in a state of extreme caffeine deprivation, and this already long day was going to get a lot longer before it was over.

"Well?"

"Ada Danforth," I said, "Professor Ada Danforth."

"Oh, no."

"Oh, yes."

"My God, Matt, that's terrible! Have you told Steve Goldfarb about the envelope yet?"

"Not yet," I said. "It just didn't seem like the right time, especially since I haven't even opened it yet. But he knows something's up, so he's going to stop by my office at lunchtime."

"How did he know something's up if you didn't tell him about the envelope?"

"He found this on Dr. Danforth's desk, so he knows something's going on." I handed her the note.

"You're going to have an interesting lunch," said Doreen after she'd glanced at the note.

"Yes, I am; but I won't even know *how* interesting until I open that damn envelope."

"Look," said Doreen, "why don't you go get cleaned up and I'll make us a little breakfast."

I knew that I was going to be having a Sally's sandwich with Detective Goldfarb in just a few hours, but I was starved, and I wasn't going to make it to lunchtime without something in my stomach. And besides, I wasn't about to pass up the opportunity to spend a few moments with Doreen. Time, I had learned the hard way, is something that we can't take for granted.

"Sounds great," I said, promising myself that I'd only get a half sandwich at lunchtime. "I'll be right down." I didn't want to ask, but I felt as though I had to. "Have you seen Donnie yet?"

"He's already up and gone."

"Have you had any chance to talk to him yet?"

"When would I do that? Ever since he got home last week he's up early and out the door, and then he doesn't come home until midnight. He hasn't had a single meal here, never mind being around long enough to talk."

"So no clue as to what's going on?"

"None. As far as I knew, he was doing just fine until he showed up back here. But Donnie and I have always been close, and we've always been able to talk. I'm sure when he's ready he'll open up to me. So, let's not worry about it, okay?"

"Okay," I said, but it really wasn't, at least to me.

The previous summer Donnie had started to date my daughter, and I didn't want to see her getting hurt. But I wasn't going to bring that up with Doreen right now. When we'd gotten married, we both knew that we would eventually have issues with our new blended family. All four of our kids, my son and daughter and her fraternal twins, had endured the divorces of their parents, and no matter what they tell you, that is a life changing event for a child. And Donnie in particular, had been forced to face the fact that his father, his hero, had been a fraud in so many ways it was difficult to fathom. Of course there were going to be problems.

"Good," said Doreen. "Now get that cute butt of yours into the shower and hurry back down, okay?"

That was fine with me. More than anything, I didn't want anything getting in the way of the happiness and contentment that Doreen and I had found with each other after so many years of loneliness for both of us.

Twenty minutes later I was back downstairs and tucking into my half of the cheese omelet that Doreen had made for the two of us, along with an English muffin. Doreen makes her cheese omelets with Gruyère, and they're irresistible.

"Will I see you tonight?" I asked while we were cleaning up the dishes after the meal. Doreen had recently been elected the mayor of Devon-on-Hudson with almost one hundred percent of the vote. It had been over twenty years since she'd been elected Homecoming Queen, but she was still the most popular girl in town, not to mention the smartest. I was glad she'd been elected; she liked the job, and she was awfully good at it, but it kept her out nights more than I wanted.

"Yes, you will," she said. "No more Town Council meetings until after the Holidays are over. I should be home right around five."

"So, maybe we could play Santa and Mrs. Claus tonight," I said, putting down my dishtowel and drawing her close to me. "Perhaps you and the elves could dream up a little pre-Christmas surprise for me."

"Jesus, you're such an idiot," she said, but she was smiling when she said it and she didn't push herself away from me. "And leave the elves out of this, you'll just corrupt them. Now let go of me; I have to get to work." But she gave me a kiss anyway.

We both left the house at the same time, and I was heading to my office by ten. As I drove, my mind wandered back to the little I'd been able to learn about Ada Danforth, Ph.D., since our strange meeting last summer.

CHAPTER THREE

A DA RACHAEL DANFORTH had not been forthcoming about her own life when she had come to visit me on that warm, wet July day. So what I had learned, I'd had to stitch together from information on the internet gathered for me by my sister Lacey, and from discussions with Doreen, my old friend and teammate Richie Glazier – who, as the owner of the always crowded Latitude Pub and Grill, knew everything that went on in our small village – and my office mate and landlord, Harvey Golub, who was an attorney by profession but who seemed to know more than a little bit about a lot.

Ada had been born and raised in Devon-on-Hudson, but she'd never really lived here. Her father, Vincent, was a machinist at a local automotive component manufacturer, and her mother, Barbara, was a C.P.A. at a small accounting firm. They were both devout Catholics, as was Ada herself. Ada was only five years younger than Doreen and me, but I'd never really heard of her until she had achieved national fame.

Because when Ada Danforth was twelve years old, she achieved a perfect score on the math portion of the Scholastic Aptitude Test, and also scored 100 on the Calculus and Physics AP exams. What was largely overlooked was that she had also attained a near perfect score on the verbal portion of her SAT, and that she wrote lovely poetry as a way of relaxing from her scientific studies. She was an autodidact who kept to herself, and neither her parents nor her elementary and middle school teachers had been aware of her gifts.

Her parents had wanted to remain quiet about their young daughter's accomplishments to protect her from unwanted publicity. But both her parents and the small group of educators who had become aware of her rare gifts knew that something had to be done, and whatever that was, it was well beyond the capabilities of the Devon-on-Hudson public school system.

They found the Tappan School, a small private school for gifted children in nearby Newburgh, New York. It was close enough so that her parents could drive her to and from school every day. The tuition was well beyond their means, but young Ada was offered a full academic scholarship. Even though it was a secondary school, most of the faculty held doctorates in their areas of specialization, and they seemed unintimidated yet excited at the prospect of working with the young prodigy.

All seemed to go well for a while, but at the end of her first semester at Tappan, Ada's teachers arranged a meeting with her parents to tell them that there was simply nothing more they could offer her. They said they had been in contact with the faculties of both Stanford University in California and Cornell University in Ithaca, New York. Both schools had small cadres of brilliant young scholars like Ada, so she wouldn't feel isolated there, they said.

Young Ada may have been a genius, but she was also still a thirteen-year-old child, and the prospect of living a continent away from her parents frankly frightened her. So they chose Cornell, an outstanding Ivy League school only a few hours by car from her folks, at least when the notorious upstate New York winter weather allowed. She was enrolled in the doctoral program in Physics, and that autumn, just six weeks shy of her fourteenth birthday, her parents drove her out to tiny Ithaca, New York, and settled her into her dorm room on one of the loveliest college campuses in the country.

Three years later, at the ripe old age of seventeen, Ada Rachael Danforth was awarded her Ph.D.

Her specialized field of study was quantum mechanics, in particular, the behavior of subatomic particles in dense gravitational fields.

I never even took physics in high school, never mind at the college level; and since I hadn't seen or spoken to her since that summertime meeting, and since I had no idea of the contents of the envelope that she had so mysteriously left with me, I hadn't felt any burning need to educate myself on the subject, if that was even possible.

What I did know, what everyone soon knew, was that after a few short years on the faculty of the University of Chicago and performing what was apparently ground-breaking research at the Fermi Labs, quiet, reticent young Dr. Ada Danforth became controversial within the elite scientific community that was her world.

Rumors had begun to float around in academic circles that Ada, at the unheard-of age of twenty, was about to be awarded the Nobel Prize in Physics. The *New York Times* got wind of this rumor, and decided that it might be a good time to do a profile on the young prodigy and publish it in their weekend edition. They sent their talented young science correspondent, Brent Skowron, out to Chicago to interview her.

All went well during the interview, still available on the internet where Lacey found it for me, until the *Times* correspondent innocently asked a throwaway question at the end: What does it feel like to understand the universe?

Brent Skowron clearly expected some modest reply, something like, "I couldn't have done it without all the people who came before me." You know, the old "I've stood on the shoulders of giants" routine. It would have been a great way to wrap up the interview, and Skowron would have been delighted. But Ada didn't say that.

What she said was, "Oh, for heaven's sake, I can no more comprehend the nature of the universe than a termite can understand how the house that it's eating was built."

"What do you mean?" asked the slightly stunned Skowron.

"I mean that human beings simply don't have anything approaching the intellectual capacity necessary to understand the true nature of the universe, and we never will."

"But what about Steven Hawking? What about Einstein and Nils Bohr? What about *you*? What have all of you been doing if you haven't been figuring out the universe?"

"We've all been sniffing around the edges, leaving little scratch marks here and there, that's all. We've all been doing what humans do: we've been trying, because that's our nature. And that's all we'll ever do."

"So, I guess I have to ask you," said a baffled Skowron, "how do you think your colleagues are going to react to being called termites?"

"I guess you'll have to ask them," Ada had replied, an innocent smile on her face.

And suddenly, the interview was over.

The *Times* published the interview, but it was pushed to the back pages of a weekday edition where it went largely unnoticed, except by the tiny, elite scientific community.

As it turned out, Ada Danforth's colleagues didn't find being called termites amusing. Not one bit. Perhaps they should have given her a break because of her youth, but they didn't.

Shortly thereafter, rumors started to surface that the quality of Dr. Danforth's research had begun to deteriorate, that she had, as another leading researcher was rumored to have said, "lost her fastball."

There really wasn't much more in the written record. But from that point on, there was no longer any talk of a Nobel Prize for Ada Danforth, and not long after that she quietly disappeared from the Fermi Labs. There were no outright denunciations, no highly publicized firing, but neither did anyone come to her defense. Nor did Dr. Danforth herself make any attempt to defend herself. She was simply gone, and no one cared to explain why. The only thing that was clear was the Dr. Ada Danforth was finished.

So, she came home to Devon-on-Hudson for much the same reason I had: she had nowhere else to go. She was able to get a job teaching freshman physics at Orange County Community College, and she purchased her beloved little cottage overlooking the Hudson River with the royalties she had earned from a wildly successful popular book she'd written called *"Q Is For Quantum."* There she had lived quietly for the past fifteen years, invisible and largely forgotten.

Until she was murdered in that lovely home, leaving me with a message telling me to open an envelope in the event of her death, a death that she had so plainly foreseen.

* * * * * *

CHAPTER FOUR

W HEN I GOT BACK TO MY OFFICE the first thing I did was pull the envelope that Ada had given me out of my desk drawer. After she'd given it to me I'd taped over the lid of the envelope so that the strip of tape was attached to both the lid and the envelope itself, and then scribbled my initials and the date so that my writing covered both lid, tape, and envelope. Not perfect, but it would have made it tough for anyone to tamper with it. Everything was intact, just as I had left it, but I didn't open it. Instead, I stared at the photo that my sister Lacey had downloaded from the internet and that I'd clipped to the outside of the envelope.

It was an 8"x10" black and white print of young Ada and her plainly proud, slightly bewildered looking parents at her graduation from Cornell. To her father's right, standing slightly apart, was an adolescent boy whom I knew to be Ada's younger brother, her only sibling. Ada was seventeen at the time of the photo, but the ensuing years had been kind to her, and it was essentially the same woman I had met last summer.

There was nothing extraordinary about her appearance. Her short hair was straight and dark; it barely covered her ears, and it had clearly never received the attention of a hairdresser. Her dark eyes were lively and intelligent, looking directly into the camera. Her other features were pleasant but unremarkable. Her body was hidden from the camera by her academic robes, but from meeting her I knew that she was slim, and by no means voluptuous. She was the type of person most people would walk by without ever noticing.

There was something compelling about her, though, both in the photo and in my memory of her. She was so young, and for all her intellect she looked even younger. But there was a timeless quality to her. I remembered thinking when I met her that I must have seen her face somewhere before, or that she could have been a model a Renaissance artist would have used for a Madonna, or perhaps Eve before the Fall. Her youth, her innocence, and her remarkable intelligence all shone forth, and I found it hard to take my eyes off her.

My attention was finally diverted by a light knocking on my doorframe. I expected to see Steve Goldfarb when I looked up, but I was wrong.

"Jeremy?" I said, looking up at the short, slightly chubby man standing in my doorway. I knew he was a few years younger than I was, somewhere between my age and Ada's, but he'd already lost most of his hair, a fact he tried to cover up with an embarrassingly severe comb-over. "How are you?"

"Hi, Matt," he said, in a voice so quiet I could barely hear him. He was one of those people who shifted his weight from foot to foot when he was nervous. He was nervous. "Do you have a minute?"

Like me, Jeremy Carter was a graduate of Devon Central High School, but that was about all we had in common, and I had only vague memories of him from our school days. I think he'd been a freshman when I was a senior. By that time I was locally famous as the three-time All-County wide receiver on our undefeated high school football team. Jeremy, to the best of my recollection, was then what he was today: a short, quiet nebbish of a kid who tended to hug the wall as he walked down the hallway between classes. He'd gone on to major in English and secondary education at SUNY Potsdam in upstate New York, and had returned to Devon Central, where he now taught English.

"Sure, Jeremy, come in and sit down," I said, waving to the nearest of the two chairs that sat on the other side of my desk. He hesitated at the door for a couple of seconds, then came in and sat down in the seat I'd offered. "What can I do for you?"

Before he had a chance to answer, we both heard the sound of large shoes walking toward my office, and a few seconds later the immense form of Detective Steven Goldfarb was looming in my doorway.

"Where's my sandwich?" he said, before he noticed Jeremy sitting there.

I stood six-one, and Goldfarb was probably an inch or two taller. Between us there were well over four hundred pounds of mostly muscle. Poor Jeremy stood maybe five-foot-five with his shoes on, and despite his chubbiness probably didn't weigh more than one-forty. He looked scared as Goldfarb took a seat beside him, and I didn't blame him. It's the burden of big men that we intimidate people, and it's not fun watching someone shrink back from me just because I walk up to shake his hand.

"I'm sorry," said Jeremy, almost in a whisper, "I probably shouldn't have shown up like this without an appointment."

"It's okay, Jeremy," I said. "What can I do for you?" But then I saw him staring at the photo of Ada Danforth lying face up on my desk, and I suddenly knew. Goldfarb saw the same thing, and our eyes briefly met.

"Hi, Jeremy," said Goldfarb, as quietly as he could. "I'm Detective Steven Goldfarb of the Devon-on-Hudson Police Department." He held out his hand, and there was a brief, awkward moment as Goldfarb's enormous paw enclosed Carter's small hand.

"Look, Jeremy," I said, "we were just about to order sandwiches from Sally's. Would you care to join us?"

"Oh, that's okay," he said. "I actually have a class to teach in twenty minutes, and I really have to get back to school."

"Then how can we help you?"

"I, uh, I heard people talking at school about Ada Danforth this morning, that maybe something bad had happened to her. One of the other teachers has one of those police scanners, and he was saying that he was hearing stuff. So I called the police department, but they said I should call you. I don't know why, but I was between classes, so I just got in my car and came over here. I guess I didn't want to hear anything bad about Ada over the phone."

"Steve?" I said, looking at him.

He nodded to me. It was his signal that the next of kin had been notified, and the murder was going to be all over the news by the time lunch was over in any event.

"Did you know Dr. Danforth, Jeremy?"

"Actually, I've known her for a long time."

"How long?"

"We were, you know, in elementary school together, and she lived on the next block over from me. She was a year behind me in school."

"Were you friendly?"

"Not really. Not until middle school, at least."

"And in middle school?"

Jeremy hesitated and squirmed in his seat, clearly uncomfortable. I waited.

"Well, you know," he finally said, "I, uh, started to, you know, like her in eighth grade."

"And did she like you back?" I asked.

"I guess I never really got to a chance to know."

"Why was that?"

"Because then she disappeared. Nobody ever told me anything. Just, one day, she was gone. I eventually learned about what happened and everything she did, but by then it was way too late."

"What about when she came back?"

"I didn't know for a long time that she *was* back. Everybody kept everything so quiet. But a couple of years ago she visited Devon Central for a science day, and we reconnected. I'm sorry, Mr. Hunter, but are you asking me all these questions because it's true that something happened to Ada?"

"I'm afraid the answer is 'yes,' Jeremy."

"Can you tell me what happened?"

"I'm sorry to say that she was murdered last night."

All the color suddenly drained from Jeremy's face as tears welled up in his eyes. His mouth fell open, and sweat started to pop out on his pale forehead. His body started to list to the right, and for a few seconds I thought he might faint. But he slowly straightened himself up, and the color began to return to his face.

"How?" he said.

"That's not something we're going to discuss right now," said Goldfarb. "But if it's any comfort to you, we don't think she ever knew what happened to her, and she died before she ever felt any pain."

"Do you have any suspects yet?"

"No, we don't, Jeremy," I said, "and that's why it's so important that people like you tell us anything you can about Ada. She was a very reclusive person, and we know very little about her. The more we learn, the better we'll be able to establish a motive, and then match the motive with a perpetrator." I annoy myself when I hear myself talking like a cop, but sometimes it just can't be helped.

"I'll tell you what I can, but I'm afraid it's not much."

"Anything you can tell us would be helpful."

"Look, like I was telling you. I didn't even know she was back in town until a couple of years ago. That's how private she was."

"Did that bother you?" I said.

"Did what bother me?"

"That she had been back in town all that time and you didn't even know about it."

"You know," he said, "it would be easy to say, 'of course not.' I mean, the most you could call whatever I felt for her all those years ago was puppy love, and I'm not even sure she ever even noticed. So why would I expect her to remember me, never mind try to contact me?"

"But it did bother you, right?"

"Why do you say that?" said Jeremy, sounding annoyed, which would have surprised me if I hadn't learned from hard experience that nothing should ever surprise me in a murder investigation.

"Because you said it would be easy to say that it didn't. So I'm guessing the hard thing to say is that it did."

He hesitated for a couple of seconds. I got the impression that he hadn't realized what he'd said.

"We're all human," he finally said. "And I guess the old saying is true: You never forget your first love. So I guess on some level it bothered me, but it wasn't like it was a big deal or anything."

"Okay," I said. It wasn't like I could disagree with him about first loves. Doreen had been my first love, and I'd certainly never forgotten her. "But in any event, you reconnected with her when she showed up at a science fair at the high school."

"Yes, that's right."

"Did she remember you then?"

"Yeah, she did, right away."

"That must have been nice."

"Yeah, it was."

"Did you have any time to talk to her?"

"Not really. She was pretty busy. But at the end of the day I caught up with her and we exchanged contact information."

"And so you eventually got in touch with her?"

"I actually wrote her an email that night, and she got back to me the next day. I was pretty surprised."

"Did you ever ask her to go out with you?"

"Yes, I did, that same week."

"And did she accept?"

"I was kind of surprised, but yes, she did."

"What did you do on the date?"

"Is all this really relevant to a murder investigation, Mr. Hunter?" said Jeremy, annoyance once more creeping into his voice. I guess I could understand that, but right now it wasn't my job to worry about who I was annoying.

"Please understand, Jeremy," I said, trying to sound reasonable, "this all just happened, so we're just trying to learn everything we can about Ada's life right now. We'll figure out what's relevant later."

"Okay, I guess I understand," he said, sounding at least a little bit mollified.

"So what did you do?"

"It was hardly even a date. We went to lunch at the Latitude."

"Why did you go to the Latitude?"

"Actually, Ada suggested it. She said she couldn't resist the steak sandwiches and onion rings."

Neither could I. Suddenly, Ada started to seem like a human being to me. "How did it go?" I said.

"It was going okay," Jeremy said, "but then Kevin Waldron showed up and kind of ruined things."

"Who's Kevin Waldron?"

"He teaches history at Monroe Woodbury High School, and he also teaches night classes at OCCC, you know, Orange County Community College, where Ada teaches. Ada told me afterwards that he'd been bugging her for a date for a long time, but she'd been putting him off."

"Did he make a scene?"

"I think he might have, but he never really got the chance. Richie Glazier, you know, the owner of the Latitude, noticed what was going on right away, and he moved Kevin on before anything could happen. Richie's good at that."

Yeah, Richie's good at that. Richie was a teammate of mine on the high school football team, where he'd played tackle both ways. He was even taller than Steve Goldfarb, he wore a retro Afro that made him look seven feet tall, and he looked like he could still play. For a lot of reasons, Richie had passed up an opportunity for a pro career, and instead had transformed the Latitude Pub & Grill from a pest infested gin mill buried under code violations into one of the most popular eating and drinking destinations in the area, and nothing happened there without Richie knowing. Doreen and I spent a lot of time at the Latitude, and Richie and Doreen had been close since we were all kids. Richie liked to joke that she knew that he was gay before he did, and he and his husband, Henry, were frequent guests at our house.

"But still," I said, "nothing was quite the same after that, right?"

"I felt so bad," said Jeremy. "Ada seemed so shy, and I don't think she knew how to handle situations like that."

"Did you continue to see each other?"

"That's what was so sad," said Jeremy. "It was like that whole episode at the Latitude kind of burst the bubble, you know? I asked her out a couple of times after that, but nothing ever worked out."

"So you haven't seen her since then?"

"Oh, I've seen her here and there, and we've chatted a couple of times, but nothing beyond that."

A buzzing sound started to come from Jeremy's pocket. For a second he looked puzzled, as he pulled his iPhone out of his jacket pocket. But before he even looked at the phone he blurted, "Oh, shit!" then looked at his watch.

"What?" I said.

"My class started five minutes ago!" he shouted, as he furiously started tapping on the phone. "Shit!"

"Sorry, Jeremy," I said. "Get to your class. We'll contact you if we need anything more from you." But I wasn't sure he heard me as he raced out of the office.

"That was kind of odd," said Detective Goldfarb, who had sat silently throughout my entire discussion with Jeremy Carter.

"What was odd?" I asked.

"Well, here you had this guy who had a brief childhood crush on Ada Danforth, then doesn't see her for twenty years, then had one disastrous date with her and that's it."

"Yeah? So?"

"And then he gets in his car and drives over here when he hears a rumor that something's happened to her, and breaks down when he hears that she's been murdered? Why would he do that?"

"I hadn't thought about it that way," I said, thinking the people I'd known who did things like that were usually psychopaths who'd murdered their wives or mothers, and who had a weird desire to follow the investigation of the murder they'd committed. You meet all kinds when you're a cop. "But now that you mention it, I guess that was kind of strange."

"And I'll tell you something else," said Goldfarb. "I don't care how harmless he looks, that guy's got a temper, and it's on a hair trigger."

"Yeah, I got that impression, too."

"A couple of years ago," said Goldfarb, "I had to answer a call one night at Napoli's pizzeria in Washingtonville. There'd been an altercation in the parking lot there between two guys, and one of the guys had gotten the shit kicked out of him. I mean, he was a real mess by the time I got there. And you know what that guy's name was?"

"Let me guess: Jeremy Carter?"

"No: Kevin Waldron."

"And who was the other guy?"

"Nobody knows. Napoli's doesn't have any lighting in its parking lot, and nobody except for the three guys it took to drag him off Waldron saw the assailant, who was gone before I ever got there."

"And what about those three guys?"

"They said it was dark out, and they were too busy breaking up the fight to get a look. I think they just didn't want to get involved. But all three of them said that if they hadn't broken up the fight, the guy would have killed Waldron, and from the looks of Waldron, I didn't think they were exaggerating."

"What about Waldron? He didn't know who attacked him?"

"I think he did," said Goldfarb, "but he wouldn't tell me. I checked back with him a couple of months later, and he still wouldn't tell me."

"Did he say why he wouldn't tell you?"

"No, he didn't, but I think that he was afraid that if he talked it would get back to the assailant, and he'd be risking his own life."

"And you said this was a couple of years ago?"

"Yep."

"You know, Steve," I said, "one of Richie Glazier's steak sandwiches is suddenly starting to sound good to me. What do you think?"

"I'm thinking that Richie's steak sandwiches are kosher, and he keeps Doc Brown's cream soda in stock."

"You're not going to miss those Utz pretzels?"

"It's hard to miss pretzels when you've got Richie's onion rings sitting on your plate."

"You've got a point there," I said as we both grabbed our jackets and headed for the door.

As I walked out of the office, I realized that I'd never had a chance to read the contents of Ada Danforth's mysterious envelope, and I'd never even told Goldfarb about it. But as we got out to the parking lot, Goldfarb turned to me and said, "Why don't we ride in my car. We're coming straight back here anyway."

"We are?"

"Sure we are," he replied, "so that we can both look at what's inside that envelope that's sitting on your desk."

"Good plan," I said.

*   *   *   *   *   *

CHAPTER FIVE

"**T**ELL ME IT AIN'T SO."

"I'm afraid it is, Richie," I said, as Richie Glazier seated us at a quiet table in the far corner of the Latitude Pub & Grill. I usually sat at the bar to eat my lunch when I wasn't with Doreen, but as soon as Richie had spied Goldfarb and me, he caught our eyes and led us over to the table. He took our lunch orders and passed them on to a waiter, ordering a glass of iced tea for himself. Despite being a pub owner and a terrific bartender, I don't think I'd ever seen Richie touch a drop of alcohol in his life. He took a seat at our table, turning his chair around as he always did, and rested his enormous forearms on the back of the chair.

"What a damn shame," he said.

"Yes, it is," I said. People with really good social skills, like Doreen, always seem to know the right thing to say at moments like that. I'm not one of those people.

I was saved by the arrival of the food. Despite the somber occasion, Goldfarb and I were both famished, and Richie sat patiently while we tucked into our lunches. He must have sensed that we were both exhausted and hungry, because the sandwiches we were served were huge, and we both got a heaping serving of onion rings.

"So," said Richie after a decent interval, "I'm supposing you're here because you heard somehow that Ada used to drop by here for an occasional meal."

"Actually," said Goldfarb, between bites, "we heard it from a guy named Jeremy Carter. He stopped by Matt's office a little while ago after he'd gotten wind of what happened to Ada."

Richie Glazier is one of those people with the rare gift of stillness. His expression didn't change as he seemed to focus his attention on the salt and pepper shakers on the center of the table.

"Guy's got balls, I'll give him that," he finally said.

"Could you help us with that, Richie?" said Goldfarb, after another awkward silence.

"Between him and that little shit Kevin Waldron, they basically drove Ada out of here," said Richie, a man for whom "heck" was an expletive.

"Maybe you should take us back a little here, Richie," said Goldfarb.

"Yeah, maybe I should," he said. He went silent again, but we waited, our now empty plates sitting on the table in front of us. We sipped our drinks. "You guys want some dessert? I baked a couple of apple pies fresh this morning."

"Sure," we both said in unison.

Richie looked up and nodded his head at the waiter, and in a matter of what seemed seconds two huge servings of apple pie à la mode and three cups of coffee appeared at the table.

"Okay," he said after taking a sip of his coffee. "Six or seven years ago I started teaching a couple of seminars on restaurant management and entrepreneurship at Orange County Community College. Coming from where I came from, I really support OCCC's mission of offering people of all ages good, solid, practical training that will help them lead useful lives. So one day I was walking from my car to the campus, and I saw this woman staring at me from about fifty yards away. I'm used to getting stared at, so I didn't think much of it. But I thought I recognized her, so I started to walk her way. She didn't run away, so I thought she might have recognized me, too. You know how it is, Matt, even after all these years people still recognize us from our football days."

It was true. Well over twenty years later, I still occasionally get stopped on the street by people who want to thank me for all the great memories that my teammates and I had given them.

"So, anyway, as I got closer, I realized it was Ada Danforth. I'd seen her picture in the news a few years back, when she got into all that mess with the scientific community. To be honest, I didn't know she was living in the area, and I had no idea that she'd spent her childhood in Devon-on-Hudson. As I got closer to her, I nodded my head in her direction just to be polite, and she nodded back. So now it would've been rude to just walk by, so I walked over to her and introduced myself. "She said, 'I recognize you. You're one of the football players. The *Journal-Record* just did a fifteenth anniversary story about that great football team you were on. You and David Chandler, and Matt Hunter, and Kenny Cooper.' I said, yeah, that was us, and then she introduced herself, but all she said was 'I'm Ada Danforth,' like that was all she wanted to say, so I just said, 'Pleased to meet you, Ada,' back. And then she mentioned that she heard that I owned the Latitude now, and how I'd turned it into a great place. I asked her if she'd ever been there, and she said, no, she didn't eat out much. I said she should come on over sometime. I gave her one of my cards and told her to call me in advance and I'd make sure she got a nice, quiet table and excellent service from the owner himself. She laughed at that; it was a really sweet laugh, and she said she might take me up on that. Then we went our separate ways.

"But I'll tell you something, Matt, and you, too, Steve. You know me: I'm gay. I spend about as much time looking at women as you guys do looking at other men, but there was something about Ada. I mean, I'm no judge, but I'm pretty sure you guys would agree that she wasn't exactly a looker; pleasant looking, but that's about it. But none of that mattered. I simply couldn't take my eyes off that young woman. After a while I started to feel self-conscious about it, though Ada didn't really seem to notice. So anyway, like I said, we said our good-byes and that was it."

"Did she ever take you up on your invitation?" said Goldfarb.

"Yes, she did," said Richie. "I'd actually pretty much forgotten about the whole thing, but then one morning my phone rang and it was Ada. She asked if the invitation to come and eat at the Latitude was still good, and I said of course it was. I asked her what she liked to eat, because I was afraid she might be one of those crunchy vegan academic types, but she surprised me by saying that she heard I made the best steak sandwiches and onion rings in Orange County, and she'd really like to try them. So, I asked her when she'd like to stop by, and she said, 'How about today?' which in a way didn't surprise me, because even back then I was pretty sure she was shy, and sometimes shy people do stuff like that just so they don't give themselves a chance to back out."

"And she came over?" I said.

"Yeah, she did. I sat her at the corner table right over there," said Richie, pointing. "I sat with her with my back to the room so that nobody else could see her, and we had a really nice lunch."

"What did you talk about?" said Steve. "Our impression is that she was kind of a hermit."

"We mostly talked about the restaurant business," said Richie. "It was really odd. Remember, she wasn't even thirty yet when I met her, but she was even younger than that. There was something of the child in her, I guess, like everything in the world was new to her, and she wanted to learn all about it."

"Was that the only time she came here?" asked Goldfarb.

"No, it wasn't," said Richie. "Maybe three or four times a year, I'd get a call, and it would be Ada. It was always the same thing, always last minute, and it would always be just the two of us. I think that's how she felt safe."

"And you never saw her in here with anybody else?" I asked.

"Not until that one time a couple of years ago with Jeremy Carter."

"So, tell me," said Goldfarb, "what's your beef with the guy?"

"Let me tell you something," said Richie, putting down his cup of coffee, "he may not look the part, but that little creep has a mean streak in him, and once he's got a couple of beers in his belly there's no telling what he's going to do. He came in here one time and got into a scuffle with another customer, and I had to ask him to leave. I run a respectable place, and I told him I can't be having that, and if it ever happened again I was going to ban him from the premises for good."

"Was he okay after that?" I said.

"Yeah, for a while," said Richie, "but then one night he came in and he really got into it with another guy. The other guy was a lot bigger than he was, but Jeremy didn't care. I literally had to tear him off the guy, lift him off his feet and carry him to the door, and let me tell you, that was work. He never gave up, and he was totally fearless. I told him I never wanted to see him in my place again."

"Did he leave peacefully?" I said.

"Yeah, he did," said Richie. "But he gave me a look before he walked away that told me he wasn't afraid of me, and he wasn't finished."

"And was that the last time you saw him until he came in with Ada?"

"That's right."

"So," said Goldfarb, "Jeremy told us that everything was going okay until Kevin Waldron showed up and started causing problems."

"Well, that's half the story."

"What's the other half?" asked Goldfarb.

"Look," said Richie, "like I said, I had told the guy I never wanted to see him in my place again, and then he not only shows up, he shows up with Ada, and that to me wasn't going to add up to anything good for anybody. And then, just to make things more fun, I see Kevin Waldron sitting at the bar, trying to impress some young woman who didn't look like she was in the mood to be impressed, at least not by him."

"So you already knew who Kevin Waldron was," I said.

"Yeah, he came in here now and then."

"Was he a troublemaker like Jeremy Carter?" Goldfarb asked.

"No, not like Jeremy. He was just somebody I needed to keep my eye on, that's all."

"Was he a drunk?" I said.

"No, he wasn't. He wasn't really that much of a drinker. The problem with Kevin Waldron was that he fancied himself a ladies' man."

"And the ladies didn't, I'm guessing," I said.

"No, they didn't," said Richie. "I would have felt bad for him if he wasn't interfering with my business."

"Was he harassing your women customers?" asked Goldfarb.

"I wouldn't call it 'harassing,' exactly, but you know how it is sometimes with guys. Whatever it is that women are looking for in a man, Kevin didn't have it. I have a lot of young women coming in here. Some come in with dates, some don't. Some come in here looking for something, and some of them aren't. None of my business. But I've got to make sure they feel safe here, and guys like Kevin just don't help."

"But you said he wasn't harassing them," I said.

"Words are funny things aren't they?" said Richie. "You know, I don't know anything about legal definitions, but in my business definition, I know harassment when I see it: It's behavior that makes the other party feel threatened, intimidated, or frightened."

"And Kevin wasn't doing that?" I said.

"No, he wasn't," said Richie. "He was just being, you know, annoying."

"The old 'how do you like me so far' routine," said Goldfarb.

"Yeah," that's right," said Richie. "He'd always be sitting down next to some young woman, offering to buy them a drink when they already had one, trying to engage them in a conversation they didn't want to get into. That kind of thing. I'd had to talk to him a couple of times, and I'd already told him that I would have to disinvite him from my place if he didn't straighten out. Young, single women are an important part of my clientele, and I just can't be having it getting around that the Latitude isn't a safe place for them."

"So you had a potentially combustible situation on your hands," I said.

"Yeah, I did. I was already heading over to the table where Jeremy and Ada were sitting. I was just going to stop over and say hi, just to make sure Jeremy knew I had my eye on him. He wasn't supposed to be in here in the first place, and he knew it, but he probably figured I wasn't going to make a scene if he had a date there. And I also wanted to let Ada know that I was keeping an eye on things, just in case."

"But he didn't know that you were friendly with Ada, right?" I said.

"No, he didn't, but I was going to make sure he knew. But then all of a sudden, I see Kevin Waldron heading over to their table, and I didn't know what that was all about. Ada told me later that every time Kevin saw her over at OCCC he'd try to get her to go out with him, but I didn't know that yet. All I knew was that the second Jeremy Carter spotted Kevin coming over to the table, he got that look on his face, and I knew there was going to be trouble."

"The way Jeremy told it to us, Kevin was the only troublemaker, and you took care of it," said Goldfarb.

"In a way, that was true. I got there before Kevin got to the table, and I was able to head him off. He knew he was on thin ice with me already, so he kind of veered off as soon as he saw me."

"That's funny, though," said Goldfarb, "because the way Jeremy told it to us, Kevin kind of ruined the entire date."

"What ruined the entire date," said Richie, "was that Ada saw the same look on Jeremy's face that I did, and it scared her. By the time I got over to the table, she was already telling Jeremy that she was really sorry, but she didn't feel well, and that she had to leave."

"How did he take that?"

"Not well, but he behaved himself. I walked Ada out to her car, which is when she told me about Kevin bugging her for dates, and then she thanked me and left. That was the last time she came to the Latitude." It was one of the few times in my life I'd ever seen a bitter expression on Richie's face.

"And did Jeremy leave too?" asked Goldfarb.

"By the time I got back in to the restaurant, Jeremy was already at the bar with a beer in his hand, giving Kevin Waldron the evil eye. I caught the bartender's eye, and she gave me one of those, 'you better get over here fast' looks. I went over to Jeremy and reminded him that he wasn't supposed to be here. He said, 'What are you going to do about it?' I told him that he knew what I was going to do about it, and it was his choice whether he wanted this to go down easy or hard."

"What did he do?" I said.

"Luckily, he hadn't gotten too far into his beer yet, so he went quietly, but he stared at Kevin all the way out the door. I waited until I saw Jeremy pull out of the parking lot, then I went over to Kevin and told him that I wanted him to leave, too, and that I didn't want to see him in the Latitude anymore. He just nodded at me and left. And that was the last I saw of either Jeremy or Kevin."

"Richie," I said, 'do you remember about when this all happened?"

"It was sometime in mid-August, year before last. I can check my calendar if you want. I usually leave notes to myself on it if something happened that I want to make sure I remember."

"Okay," I said. For the time being, it was just a data point.

"Oh," said Richie, "and before I forget to mention it, Ada asked me once if I could recommend a good private investigator, and I gave her your name."

"Did she say why?" I asked. "That must have seemed like kind of an odd request."

"No, she didn't, and I didn't ask. The last thing anybody needs is a nosy barkeep."

"Okay," I said. "Thanks for the heads up."

We were getting up to leave when Richie held up his hand in the universal "just one more thing" sign.

"Yeah Richie?" I said.

"Look," he said, sounding uncharacteristically hesitant, "I'm not really sure how to say this..." He hesitated long enough so that it was starting to get awkward, but I waited. I knew Richie well enough to know that he'd say whatever he had to say when he was good and ready, and not a minute before. He finally nodded to himself, and said, "Okay. Let me tell you something about Ada Danforth. On one level, sitting down to talk with her was like talking to anyone else. She was friendly, interesting, and easy to converse with. But on another level, she wasn't."

"What do you mean?" said Goldfarb.

"It's hard to explain, and I know this probably sounds stupid, but wherever she was, she was never really there. I mean, she'd look you in the eye when she spoke to you, and she always paid attention to what you were saying and all that. But where she really was, all the time, was way down inside her head, going wherever that mind of hers would take her. And it never ended, at least as far as I could tell. Wherever she was in the conscious world was one thing, but she was always in that other world, too. I think that was the reason it was so hard for me to keep my eyes off her: I wanted to know where she was, because wherever it was, it was beautiful; I could see it on her face, and I wanted to be there too."

* * * * * *

We were on the way back to my office, driving in silence, I think both of us trying to fathom the meaning behind Richie's last words, when Detective Goldfarb's phone rang. He had the phone linked to the car's Wi-Fi system, so I could hear the voice on the other end of the line. It was a voice I'd known most of my life.

"Goldfarb?"

"Yes, Chief," said Goldfarb, sounding relaxed, but looking wary.

"Where are you?" said Chief of Police Eddie Shepherd.

"Matt Hunter and I are on the way back from talking to Richie Glazier at the Latitude about Ada Danforth."

"What the hell is Richie Glazier going to tell you about Ada Danforth?" said Eddie. Eddie Shepherd didn't have a whole lot of use for Richie Glazier for the same reason he didn't have a whole lot of use for me: old jealousies going back to our high school football playing days. He'd been the backup running back on offense, but Kenny Cooper, the guy he played behind, was probably the best high school running back the Hudson Valley had ever seen, and he was a horse who played every offensive down of every game. Eddie also played linebacker on defense, but David Chandler and I, when we weren't completing sixty-yard scoring touchdowns on offense, were the other two linebackers, so nobody ever noticed what Eddie was doing which, not to be uncharitable, wasn't much. He was a weak link on the best high school football team in Orange County history, and he was the only one who didn't seem to know it.

"Actually, quite a lot Chief."

"Yeah, well, we'll see about that," said Chief Shepherd. "Now, get me off the speaker, will you? We don't need Hunter listening in on official police business."

Eddie was obviously having one of his bad days, but I didn't take the bait. I made a lot of money from my work with the Devon Police Department, and besides, I knew he'd get over his snit. He never did have much of an attention span. From that point on, all I heard was the occasional "Yessir" and "Copy that, sir" from an obviously displeased Detective Steven Goldfarb.

"Damn," he said when he finally got off the phone.

"What was that all about?" I said.

"There was a burglary at the Shell station on Route 32, and he wants me to go over there and look into it."

"He knows you're working on a murder, and, by the way, you've been up all night, right?"

"Ah," said Goldfarb, "I'll deal with it. Everybody else is stretched just as thin as I am, so I can't complain. And anyway, we've got you working the Ada Danforth case. You're really going to have to step up here, Matt."

"Fine with me," I said. "I'll make sure I keep you up to speed while you're dealing with your other stuff."

"Thanks, man," he said as he pulled up in front of my office. I opened the door and was getting out of the car when he said, "And, hey, I want to hear all about what's in the envelope, okay?"

"As soon as I know what's in it, you'll know too."

I was bone tired as I climbed the steps to my office, but, as my mother used to tell me, in this life there is precious little rest for the weary, and none for the wicked.

*   *   *   *   *   *

When I got back to my office, the first thing I noticed was that the envelope wasn't on my desk where I was sure I'd left it. I shuffled through my inbox, but it wasn't there, and I was starting to panic when I finally found it in the drawer where I'd been keeping it all along. I could have sworn that I'd left it on my desktop, but it had been a long day, and I figured I just must have forgotten putting it back in the drawer before I'd left for the Latitude. I put it all out of my mind as I sat down and picked up the envelope. The tape I'd put on it with my writing was intact. I checked it closely to make sure that there was no indication that anyone had even attempted to tamper with it. I placed the photo of Ada that was clipped to the envelope's cover on my desk and stared at it for a minute, then I carefully removed the tape and opened it up.

*   *   *   *   *   *

CHAPTER SIX

"I DON'T KNOW WHAT YOU WANT ME TO SAY," said Doreen, looking puzzled.

We were sitting at the kitchen table, each of us with a copy of the document sitting in front of us. Before I'd left the office I'd made two copies, one for Doreen, and one for Steve Goldfarb, who was going to arrive shortly. He was probably out on his feet with fatigue, but his tired voice had grown immediately alert as soon as I'd told him about the envelope, and he said he'd be over as soon as he could. Doreen's glass of red wine sat in front of her, untouched. The martini sitting in front of me was half finished, as was the bowl of dry roasted peanuts that sat between us. Doreen had, I think, eaten one.

"I guess I was hoping that you'd tell me that there was a rational explanation for this," I said.

"Well, you know what Dante said," she replied.

"Abandon hope?"

"I don't know what to tell you, Matt."

Before we had a chance to say anything else there was a loud knock on the front door. Doreen jumped up to get it before I had a chance, and when she returned it was with an exhausted looking Steve Goldfarb.

"Can I get you anything, Steve," said Doreen, "a beer?"

"Not unless you want me to spend the night sleeping on your kitchen floor," said Goldfarb, "but I could use a cup of coffee if you have any in the pot."

There was always a pot of coffee on in Doreen's kitchen. I got up and poured him a cup, not bothering to ask if he wanted anything in it; he always drank it black. He was already perusing his copy of Ada's document when I put the cup down in front of him.

"*What?*" he said when he was finished. "What is this, some kind of joke?"

I stared back down at the document, and I couldn't blame Goldfarb for his reaction. I'd already read it at least a half-dozen times, but I read it once again:

Dear Mr. Hunter,

I have come to you at the recommendation of Mr. Richard Glazier, a man whom I both respect and trust. I will get right to the point.

I am going to be murdered on December fourth of this year. The cause of death will be blunt force trauma to the back of my head. You will find me slumped to the floor, wedged between my chair and desk, my arms folded over my chest. The headline of that day's Times Herald-Record is: "County Strapped For Snow Removal Funds." I did not have a "vision," Mr. Hunter. I have been there.

I know who murdered me, but I don't think a letter from a dead person will help you close your case, so I think for your own legal purposes, and for my own personal reasons, I will leave you to find that out for yourself.

I know that you possess no knowledge of quantum mechanics. But what you do possess, I have learned, is that rare ability to view the world through the lens of an alternate reality, and accept it for what it is. That is a rare gift, Mr. Hunter, a gift that I believe will be necessary not simply to solve my murder, but to understand it. And that is what I want more than anything, Mr. Hunter. I want to be understood. I will help when I can.

I wish you all the best.

Your new friend,
Ada Danforth
P.S. Yes, you left the file on your desk.

"What do you think?" I said to Goldfarb.

"I think she was a kook, is what I think," he replied, looking almost angry. "I don't blame you for not showing this to me right away; it's just complete nonsense."

"The problem is," said Doreen, "that she may have been a kook, but she was a brilliant one."

"So, you agree with Steve?"

"Of course I do. What else are we supposed to think?"

"Then how do you explain the letter?" I said. "She left that envelope with me four months ago, and it's been sitting in my desk drawer ever since, and it hasn't been tampered with. How did she know that she was going to be murdered, and how," I said, walking over to the stack of newspapers that we kept by the back door for recycling, "do you explain this?" I held up the front page of yesterday's newspaper, with its headline: "COUNTY STRAPPED FOR SNOW REMOVAL FUNDS."

"It's just a stunt," said Goldfarb, sounding disgusted. "Look, Matt, she clearly wanted to stage her own death. Why? How do *I* know? It's not my business to explain why crazy people do crazy things."

"But she's dead, Steve! How could she have planted the letter?"

"Look, for all I know, she handed you an empty envelope four months ago, and then today while we were out, she had planned for someone to sneak in to your office and plant this letter with all of this information in it."

"But I took precautions against that, and I don't think the envelope's been tampered with. And what if I'd opened it? What if I'd opened it the minute she left my office back in July?"

"She had you figured out, I guess. She knew you wouldn't open it because you said you wouldn't."

"She never even met me before, Steve!"

"You came highly recommended from Richie Glazier; that's all she needed to know."

"Okay, but how did she know I'd be out of my office for hours today?"

"Because you're a private investigator, Matt. You spend most of your days out of your office. On top of that, if she did plan her own death and plant this letter in order to leave the world thinking she'd made some profound discovery, she'd have known that you'd probably be out investigating her death. She wouldn't be the first person in this world to die in order to call attention to herself. Hell, that describes about half of the suicides I've investigated. So, it all doesn't sound that improbable to me. Are you actually telling me that you're buying into this con game?"

"I'm not buying into anything," I said, knowing that I probably was. "I'm just trying to keep my mind open, that's all. And I guess I would have thought that you'd be willing to do that, too."

"Because of the Peter Lucky thing, right?"

"Well, yeah."

"Look," said Goldfarb, "I'm never going to understand what happened there, and I understand what you're saying, but that doesn't mean I'm going to believe every huckster that comes rolling into town with a tale to tell."

"Do you really think that's what Ada Danforth was – a huckster?"

"Until something comes along to change my mind, that's what I have to think. I think we have to pursue this investigation as if that piece of paper – whatever it is – doesn't exist. I think we both have to do that, Matt."

"Just one last question," I said, looking at both of them. "Did you read that postscript?"

"I meant to ask you that, Matt," said Doreen. "What's that all about?"

"Steve, do you remember what I did with the file when we left the office to go to the Latitude?"

"Yeah," said Goldfarb. "You left it on your desk, just like that postscript says."

"When I got back to my office the envelope wasn't on my desk anymore. It was back in the drawer, exactly where I'd been keeping it since July." That set them both back a step, but it only took Doreen a few seconds to respond.

"For all you know," she said, "Linda Morris came in to your office to deliver your mail while you were out and she straightened up while she was in there."

"Linda *never* straightens out my office. That's a rule we have."

"Then probably," said Goldfarb, "the person who snuck into your office to plant this fake letter moved it around while he or she was in there."

"What, and then sat down at my desk, at my laptop, which is password protected, typed out this letter, and then printed it off on the only printer in the office, which is behind Linda's desk?"

"No," replied Goldfarb. "The person who did all this already had a duplicate document and a duplicate envelope with him, or her. All they had to do was copy what you did with the tape and your name. Face it,

Matt, what you laughingly call your handwriting isn't exactly difficult to mimic."

"But that doesn't explain the postscript, does it? And you'll still have to explain to me how this mysterious someone got in and out of the office. Linda is *never* out of the office if both Harvey and I are out. That is an ironclad rule. We don't have security cameras in the office because we want to protect our clients' privacy, so Linda never leaves the office empty. If we're out of the office during lunch, Linda either plans to bring her lunch in, or she orders something from Sally's for delivery. And I'm telling you, that envelope had *not* been tampered with."

"Look," said Steve, "I'm too tired to sit here and try to figure out the answers to all these questions. All I'm saying is that I'm a firm believer in Occam's Razor, and the simplest conclusion to draw from all this is *not* that someone travelled through time to witness her own murder and then left you a letter to tell you all about it. So, even though I can't figure out all of these things you're bringing up, I think the only logical conclusion to draw is that someone, for some reason, is messing with us – probably Ada's murderer, or even Ada herself. They probably figure that because of her reputation, this letter will pull us off the real trail long enough for the scent to go cold, and they'll walk away laughing. So, for now, we have to go about the business of solving Ada Danforth's murder without getting sidetracked by all the misdirection that's getting thrown our way."

"Matt?" said Doreen.

"What do you think Doreen?" I said. "You're the only one here who's not sleep deprived."

"I think Steve is right, Matt. And I also think that both of you are beyond exhausted, and you need a decent night's sleep before you'll be able to make any sense of this."

"I can't argue with either of you," I said, "at least not right now." I turned to look at Detective Goldfarb. "Don't worry, Steve; I'm not going to let myself get sidetracked by any of this. I'm going to conduct the investigation by the book."

"I know you will, Matt," said Goldfarb. "And now I've got to get myself home while I can still drive. Oh, and Matt?"

"Yeah, Steve."

"You know that altercation I told you about that Kevin Waldron was mixed up in out in Washingtonville?"

"Sure."

"I looked it up. It happened on August sixteenth, last year."

"Right after the incident at the Latitude."

"That's right. And that," said Goldfarb as he turned to leave, "is what we call a clue."

*   *   *   *   *   *

"Matt? Matt?"

I felt a light tapping on my shoulder. I hadn't realized I'd fallen asleep. Doreen and I had eaten a quick bowl of soup for supper, and then I'd grabbed a cup of coffee and sat down in the living room to drink it while Doreen had gone into her office to get some town correspondence out.

"You were talking in your sleep, Matt," said Doreen. I felt her take the cup of coffee out of my hand.

"Cripes, that's embarrassing. What was I saying?"

"It was something about elves," said Doreen, grinning. "I think you ought to get to bed."

"Good idea," I said, struggling to get myself off the couch.

I had an appointment the next morning with one of Ada Danforth's colleagues at Orange County Community College, during which I hoped to learn more about her recent life, and maybe a little bit about quantum physics. I'm sure I'd have a lot to think about after that.

But now wasn't a good time to be thinking about anything. It certainly wasn't a good time to be thinking about elves.

*   *   *   *   *   *

CHAPTER SEVEN

"I WOULDN'T REALLY CALL HER A COLLEAGUE, Mr. ah, Hunter," said the small, modest looking man sitting across from me as he stared at the business card I'd just given him. He was bald, with only a fringe of closely clipped gray hair forming a halo around his head, and he was clean-shaven. He was slender, but didn't seem fragile in any way. He looked like a man who lived a disciplined life and took good care of himself. I guessed him to be about sixty, but I could have been wrong by ten years either way.

Dr. Paul Janssen was the chairman of what was called the "STEM" department at Orange County Community College. "STEM," he had explained to me, stood for "Science, Technology, Engineering, and Mathematics." As a two-year school, "OCCC," said Dr. Janssen, pronouncing it "Ock," was too small and too limited in its academic scope to have separate departments for Physics, Chemistry, Mathematics, and the like. They offered their students introductory courses in the basic sciences, and only a few of them would move into engineering or scientific programs at major universities. It was basic training, Janssen explained, to qualify them for jobs as technical assistants, engineering aids, and computer technologists at major tech companies. It sounded like the kind of practical education that so many kids needed and so few ever got, I thought; but I hadn't come to Middletown, New York, to philosophize.

I had begun the visit with a quick look at Dr. Danforth's office, but only to get an impression of it. The Devon police had already conducted a thorough search and found it at least as sterile as her home. There wasn't even a laptop in it.

"Do you mean you weren't friendly with her?" I asked.

"Oh, no, not at all," said Janssen quickly.

"Then what?" I said.

"Let me be frank with you, Mr. Hunter," said Janssen, looking at me with an expression bordering on amusement. "Ada Danforth didn't belong here. I do."

"I'm not sure I'm following, Professor Janssen."

"Dr. Danforth and I both have Ph.D.'s in physics, and we both got them from Cornell, but that is where the similarity ends. By the time I finished my education at Cornell, I knew that I would never be one of the elite in my profession, one of those who would go on to do all of the ground-breaking research in my field."

"Why is that?"

"Because I simply didn't have the talent, that's why. It's like professional baseball, Mr. Hunter. Only a tiny percentage of the kids coming out of high school every year have the raw talent to have a chance of becoming a professional ballplayer someday. But even though it's a tiny percentage, that's a lot of young kids, thousands of them, coming out of high school in this country and from all over the world, and they get drafted by a major league ball club and assigned to the Rookie League, or maybe Class A. Most of them never get any further than that. But some of them move up to Double-A, and maybe even Triple-A. But almost none of them ever make it to the Major League level. Think of it, Mr. Hunter, at any given time there are only eight hundred some odd young men playing major league baseball. And to be frank, only about half of them really belong there; the other half spend their careers bouncing between the major leagues and Triple-A, mostly being called up because other players are injured or slumping. And at any given time, of those eight hundred, only a handful will ever go to Cooperstown and get inducted into the Hall of Fame."

"So, you're saying?"

"What I'm saying is I'm Double-A, Mr. Hunter. I was one of the most gifted kids in my high school class, and I excelled in college, but I belong where I am. I'm proud of the work I do here, and I'm good at it, but the major leaguers left the people like me behind a long time ago."

"And Ada Danforth was a major leaguer, is that what you're saying?"

"I'm saying," said Janssen, "that Ada Danforth was a Hall of Famer from the day she walked onto the field. She was a rarity among rarities. She towered over even the most elite minds in our field. So, was I her colleague? Technically, yes, and it's a credit to Dr. Danforth that she always referred to me that way, but I would have been too embarrassed to refer to myself in that manner."

"I guess I have to ask," I said, "how did she fit in here?"

"She fit in beautifully," said Janssen, with real warmth in his voice. "She was an excellent instructor, and the kids loved her, even though most of them had no idea who she was. She had a gift for explaining complex concepts in terms that the kids here could understand. And she got along with the rest of the faculty wonderfully. She never held herself aloof, and she never tried to assert any kind of academic superiority. And trust me, asserting academic superiority in the collegiate world is a blood sport."

"Did it ever seem to you that she was frustrated or angry at the way things turned out? I mean, like you said, she'd been at the Fermi Labs; she'd been at the top of her field, and all of a sudden she finds herself at, you know –. I'm sorry, Dr. Janssen, that didn't come out right."

"Don't apologize, Mr. Hunter; you are absolutely right. It's a long way from the Fermi Labs to Orange County Community College. But no, to answer your question, she never displayed any frustration or resentment at all. I think she derived great satisfaction from working with the young students here."

"But what about her research work? I mean, from what I've been able to learn, she was on the verge of being awarded a Nobel Prize. She must have been at least a little angry to be separated from a place like the Fermi Labs, with all of the facilities and equipment she must have needed to pursue her research."

Paul Janssen folded his hands on top of his desk and leaned toward me.

"Do you know who Sir Isaac Newton is, Mr. Hunter?"

"I've heard of him," I said, "but I don't really know who he was or what he did. I didn't even take physics in high school, I'm embarrassed to say."

"I didn't ask you the question to embarrass you," replied Janssen, "and I apologize if that is what I did. I only meant to draw a comparison between Ada Danforth and one of the few people in scientific history whom I would consider her peer."

"But he lived a long time ago, right?" I said, determined to show that I at least knew something.

"Yes," said Janssen, "he lived in England in the 17th century. He went to Cambridge University, but while he was still an undergraduate the university had to close temporarily because of an outbreak of the plague. So, young Isaac Newton went to an isolated cottage in the English countryside, alone. He had no labs, very little equipment, and no colleagues. He didn't leave that cottage for two years. He just lived there, alone with his thoughts. But by the time he emerged, he had created modern physics and optics; he had explained the physical world to the rest of us; and just for fun he had invented calculus so that his new science had a mathematical language to express itself. It is arguably the single greatest intellectual accomplishment in human history. And to this day, despite all of the profound advances we have made in our scientific knowledge, when young students embark on their engineering and scientific careers, they start by learning Newtonian physics, and they learn calculus before they learn anything else."

"And you're saying that Dr. Danforth was like Isaac Newton?"

"What I'm saying, Mr. Hunter, is that Dr. Ada Danforth didn't need the Fermi Labs for her research. She carried the Fermi Labs around with her in her head. She didn't need pieces of equipment, and she certainly didn't need any colleagues, especially that gaggle of jealous, petty, intellectual Lilliputians who tried to destroy her."

"Are you saying, Dr. Janssen, that Dr. Danforth was continuing to pursue her research? Here?"

"No, not here," said Janssen, tapping his index finger on his desk. "Here," he said, using the same finger to tap his head.

"Did she ever publish any new findings? Did she ever share her research with anyone?"

"No, she didn't," said Janssen. "She was finished with the academic world, and they were finished with her; and that wasn't going to change."

"Did she ever share anything with *you*, Professor Janssen?"

Paul Janssen hesitated, his intelligent eyes quietly regarding me.

"Not really," he finally said. "But I guess you could say that in her own way, to the extent that she could penetrate my shallow mind, she did. Yes."

"I think I'd like to hear about that."

* * * * * *

It was getting on toward lunchtime, and Professor Janssen suggested that we walk over to the student canteen for a bite to eat.

"I'm not picky," I said, getting up and putting on my jacket. It had turned back into December overnight.

"You really don't have to be," he replied. "The food there is really quite good. Young people these days are very demanding eaters, and the staff works very hard to serve healthy food that they will enjoy."

"I'm sure they do," I said. Brats, I thought.

What I really wanted was one of Sally's deli sandwiches, or a small pepperoni and anchovy pizza from my brother-in law, Anthony Fornaio. What I wound up with was some kind of an organic, vegan, non-GMO, gluten free salad, with a tasty vinaigrette dressing made from olive oil hand pressed, I was sure, by Greek virgins, and a champagne vinegar whose grapes had been crushed by the bare feet of young French – oh well, probably not. It was actually pretty good, and I also knew I'd get virtue points from Doreen, who monitored my day-to-day diet with suspicion. Virtue points from Doreen are always a good thing to have. Paul Janssen had gotten himself a gluten free, organic, rabbit food sandwich of some sort, which he bit into without a lot of enthusiasm. But the cafeteria was a bright, pleasant space, and crowded enough with students and all their attendant noises to give us a sense of privacy.

"So," I said between bites of salad, "maybe you should start at the beginning and tell me what quantum physics is."

"Oh, Mr. Hunter," replied Janssen, grinning, "you seem to have a sense of humor after all."

"What does that mean?"

"Never mind," he said. "That was my attempt at humor, so let's move on."

"Sounds like a good idea to me," I said. The last thing I wanted to hear was physics humor.

"Okay," said Janssen, taking a final bite of his sandwich and setting his plate aside. "As I told you, Isaac Newton explained the physical world around us, the actual world we live in, so well that we still use his formulas to work out problems in our day to day lives – everything from how to build a car or a house, or even how to put a man on the moon. But there have been discoveries over the centuries that have given us glimpses into unseen worlds: a larger world that exists contrary to our common sense, and a tiny, sub-atomic-sized world that Newton could not even have guessed at.

"For example, we still use Newton's formulas to measure gravitational forces, even though his formulas never really *explained* gravity, they just measured its effects. Then Albert Einstein came along and *explained* gravity. He explained that what we observe as an attraction between any two objects that have mass is really the phenomenon of those objects actually *bending space*, sending other objects around them into a free fall."

"I have no idea what you just said."

"Don't worry about it," replied Janssen, "because it has no practical everyday applications. As I said, we still use Newton's formulas to measure the force of gravity in the day-to-day world. I'm just trying to introduce you to Ada Danforth's world. This was just basic stuff to her."

The image of Ada Danforth - young, modest, unprepossessing - floated through my mind. Basic stuff. I was headed for trouble.

"Okay," was all I could think of to say. "Maybe we could just move on."

"Sure," said Janssen, clearly warming to his task. "What Einstein also pointed out to all of us – and this is really important to understanding Ada's work, Mr. Hunter – is that time is a lot more complicated than we thought it was."

"What do you mean?" I said. "You're not going to tell me that time machines really work, are you?"

I thought I was making a joke, but Janssen regarded me seriously for a few long seconds.

"Perhaps we should just keep going," he finally said.

"Sure," I replied, hoping that he didn't take my comment to mean that I wasn't taking him seriously. Once the class clown, always the class clown, I guessed.

"Okay," said Janssen. "We tend to think of time as something that moves in one direction, and always in a straight line. Most importantly, we make the assumption, simply because we have to, that time is the same for all of us. But Einstein saw things differently. He discovered that time is relative, that as we move in relation to one another, the way we observe time also changes."

"How did he do that?" I said.

"He did it by demonstrating to us that we all observe light traveling at the same speed, even when we are moving in relation to one another."

"That doesn't make sense."

"I know, right?" said Janssen, grinning. "But it's true. So, for example, if I'm standing still, shining a flashlight, and you drive by me in your car going seventy miles an hour, we will both observe that beam of light travelling at the exact same velocity: the speed of light, 186,000 miles per second."

"That's impossible," I said.

"It's only impossible if you cling to your familiar concept of time. The speed of light can only be observed as a constant if we can get our heads wrapped around the notion that time is different for all of us when we move in relation to one another."

"But time *is* the same for all of us," I said, tapping the watch on my wrist. "We can measure it."

"Yes, we can, and no, it isn't. Of course, at the speeds at which we travel here on Earth in our daily lives the differences are miniscule, and you can't really observe them, so the world makes sense to us with our traditional concept of time. But at higher velocities, the differences become noticeable. For example, when the astronauts were travelling to the moon, they were travelling at speeds of tens of thousands of miles per hour. And when they looked at their on-board clocks – highly accurate atomic clocks that had been synchronized with the same types of clocks back on Earth - the two sets of clocks were moving at different rates relative to one another. The differences were ever so slight, but they were there, and they matched precisely Einstein's predictions."

"I never heard any of this," I said.

"Well," said Janssen, "the lunar program ended before you were born, and, sadly, Americans just aren't all that fascinated with science anymore."

"Everybody just wants to be left alone to play games on their smartphones."

"You said it, not me."

"So," I said, hoping that this conversation would end before my head exploded, "is that what Ada Danforth was working on?"

"Oh, no."

"Oh, no."

"Don't worry," said Janssen, chuckling, "I'm going to keep the rest of this brief, because I really don't understand it that well myself."

"Great," I said.

"So, now, we're getting close to Ada's work."

"Do you think we could get a cup of coffee before you start up again?" The only reason I wasn't getting sleepy at this point was that I was still hungry after chowing down my salad.

"That," said Janssen, "is a great idea."

We went over to a dispenser and poured our cups of coffee. Just as we were about to return to our table a woman approached Professor Janssen. I guessed that the woman was probably a few years younger than he was. She was slender to the point of gauntness. She wore no makeup, and her hair, which she kept in a tight bun, was streaked with silver. She was a good-looking woman, though, even though the lab coat she was wearing lent her a severe aspect. She was clearly Asian, although of which specific ethnicity I couldn't tell.

"Hello, Justine," said Janssen, in a tone that, though it didn't sound unfriendly, seemed guarded.

"Hello, Paul," the woman replied. Her voice was pleasantly alto.

"Justine," said Janssen, "I'd like to introduce you to Mr. Matthew Hunter."

"Pleased to meet you, Mr. Hunter," she said, not sounding really pleased. She spoke with a flat, midwestern accent, but it wasn't heavy.

"Matt, this is Dr. Justine Tan. She teaches biology and ecology here at OCCC."

"Pleased to meet you," I said, reaching out to shake her hand, but she didn't reach out with hers, and it made for an awkward moment. She ignored me and turned to Janssen.

"Look, Paul," she said, "I just wanted to give you my condolences, that's all."

"Thank you," said Janssen, sounding like this was a topic he didn't want to discuss.

"Dr. Danforth was a fine woman and a brilliant scientist."

"Yes, she was."

"Well, then," said Dr. Tan, "that was all I wanted to say, and I can see you have other things to do right now, so I'll leave you be. Nice to meet you Mr. —"

"Hunter."

"Yes, Hunter," she said, and with that, she turned and walked away. Janssen looked after her for a brief second, and then turned to head back to our table. I followed.

"Where were we?" said Janssen, clearly not wanting to elaborate on Professor Tan. There was something odd about their exchange, or maybe it was their body language, but I couldn't put my finger on it, so I let it drop. I had too much else to think about for the moment.

"I think we were getting to the part where you were going to tell me all about quantum physics."

"Well," replied Janssen after taking a sip of his coffee. I'm certainly not going to do that, but I'll try to explain to you what Ada – Dr. Danforth – was studying."

"The simpler you can keep it, the better, Professor Janssen," I said.

"Okay," he said, taking a sip of his coffee and putting the cup aside. "As I said, Newton's physics help us understand the larger world around us. Quantum physics, on the other hand, helps us understand the world, the universe, at the atomic level and the sub-atomic level; and at that level things stop making intuitive sense to us very rapidly."

"In what way?"

"Well, let's get to the heart of the matter, the area where Ada was so deeply involved: Subatomic particles, like electrons, and wavelike particles, like photons, the building blocks of light, have been observed existing in two places at the same time. That's not just theory, Mr. Hunter; there is verifiable, repeatable experimental evidence of that phenomenon. And it is even being put into practical use by companies like IBM and Microsoft, who are developing what they are calling quantum computers based on these theories."

"And what would a quantum computer do?" I asked, wondering if I really wanted to know.

"Well, I think you probably know that all the bits of information that a traditional computer uses are in binary code, that means every bit has to be either a zero or a one. And all computer programs are just an endless series of zeroes and ones."

"Yes, I've heard of that."

"Well, in quantum computers, bits of information can be zeroes, ones, or zeroes and ones *at the same time*. That will increase computing speeds and power exponentially, some say scarily."

"Okay," I said. "I think you've told me all I want to know about quantum computing."

"I understand, but try to stay with me a little longer. Think about this: How is it even possible that the same tiny particle can be in two places at once, or that the same bit of information be two things at the same time?"

"Professor, I have no idea."

"You're in good company, Matt. But that doesn't keep people from guessing, and some of the guessing is pretty fascinating, and tends to blur the line between science and philosophy."

"For example?"

"For example, some people theorize that in order for a particle to exist in two places at the same time, there must be two separate universes where it can exist; and further, if there can be more than one universe, there could be multiple universes, even an infinite number, what some scientists are calling the 'multiverse.' In fact, if you're a believer in free will, some people theorize that there is a unique universe for each choice we make."

"What do you mean, 'if you're a believer in free will'? It seems pretty obvious to me that I can make my own choices. Like this —" I picked up my empty coffee cup and moved it to the other side of the table. "See? I just decided to do that."

Janssen grinned. "Now you're warming up to the subject, Matt. But let's look at it another way. There are some people who theorize that all time exists – just as all space exists - the past, the present, and the future. It's like a mountain range: it's all there, but we can only see it through a fixed telescope that allows us to see just the present and what has already happened. Time doesn't allow us to rotate the telescope to see what is yet to come."

"So that means…," but I didn't know how to complete the thought.

"So that means," said Janssen, who apparently did, "that when you moved your coffee cup, it is only because that is what you always did at that moment, only you couldn't have known that until the moment revealed itself. You never had any choice in the matter; you are just a witness to events that have already been decided."

"Decided by who?" I said.

"Who knows?" said Janssen.

"But on the other hand," I said, suddenly feeling smart, "if I actually have free will, I create a new future, a new universe, every time I make a choice."

"Yes, Matt," said Janssen, his serious eyes brightening, his face flushing. "There is now a universe where you did move the cup, and a universe where you didn't."

"And there's a universe where I did meet my wife, and there's another universe where I didn't."

"Yes, Matt! And the whole future changes every time you make a decision. And there's a universe where Hitler died in World War I before he ever had the chance to perpetrate the Holocaust, and there's a universe where Lee Harvey Oswald missed."

"And there's a universe where Elvis is still alive."

Janssen laughed out loud at that, a sound I never thought I'd hear. "Now you've got it!" he said, but then his expression turned serious again. "But now you have to understand the implications of all this."

"I was afraid you were going to say that."

"Think of it, Matt. Let's go back to the first supposition that all time exists, and our actions only reveal the future as it has always been."

"Okay."

"Now think about this: What is the foundation of all Western religion, and by inference, all Western civilization?"

"Please don't make me try to answer that, professor."

"It is," he said, barely skipping a beat, "the existence of sin and redemption. And how can sin exist, Matt, without free will? We believe that we are creatures capable of choice, and that we must live with the consequences of those choices. It is the fundamental assumption that orders our world. All our laws, all civil society, hangs on that one assumption. The religious people among us believe that only God can forgive us for our choices; and even most non-religious people believe that we must accept responsibility for our behavior and are responsible for atoning for our bad behavior. That's why we have prisons, right? What happens to that if there's no such thing as free will?"

"Right, I guess. So, is this where Dr. Danforth got herself into so much hot water?"

"Not really. What I'm telling you is what armies of armchair philosophers and young undergraduates argue over every day in cafés and student lounges the world over, with a suspiciously heavy concentration, of course, on the Left Bank of Paris."

"Then what *did* she get into trouble about? Was it really all about that termite comment?"

"I know it sounds petty, but yes. Elite physicists do not appreciate being equated with termites. They have enormous egos, and they guard them jealously. Those people who ostracized her don't think of themselves as merely physicists; they see themselves as the elite, the new oracles of our time – the new priesthood if you will – the keepers and disseminators of all knowledge. They need to know that average people will believe whatever they tell them, all the time. If not, if average people start to cotton to the fact that these folks are just as fallible, prone to error – and as fundamentally ignorant – as everyone else, their image, most importantly their *self-image*, will be destroyed. They weren't just skeptical of her ideas, they were *angry* about them, and at her."

"Yes," I said, "because she wasn't just questioning them; she was defrocking them."

"That's as good a way of putting it as any," said Janssen.

I was done. My head felt like a jug that was filled to the brim, and that would start to spill out its contents if someone tried to add just one more drop.

"Dr. Janssen," I said, feeling almost unsteady as I stood to leave, "I can't thank you enough."

"I'm always here if you want to talk about all this any further," he replied, but with the look of a man who knew he'd just bested another.

"Sure," was all I could think of to say as we shook hands and parted.

I guess I meant that, but I also knew that he had just handed me an entire population of fresh suspects in Ada Danforth's murder, all of whom could talk, and think, rings around me, just as Dr. Paul Janssen just had.

* * * * * *

It was only mid-afternoon by the time I left the OCCC campus, but I was starving, so I swung by my favorite health food emporium, McDonald's, to pick up a Filet O' Fish sandwich and some fries. It wouldn't earn me any virtue points from Doreen, but I figured I could talk up the salad.

I'd paid for my order and was turning around to head for the dining area when I spotted my sister Lacey sitting at a table by a window, her long blond hair reflecting the afternoon sun. Judging by the pile of empty containers and wrappers in front of her, she had just polished off her second Big Mac and was contentedly munching on her second large container of fries, all washed down by a quart-sized plastic cup of Coke. It appeared that she still had an apple pie and a cup of coffee awaiting the firing squad after that. I looked down at my tray. I figured I'd be able to protect my Filet O' Fish simply by physically hanging on to it, but I feared the fries were lost. But for all that, and for all the pizza pies her adoring husband, Anthony Fornaio, made for her in the little hideaway pizzeria he still maintained, tucked behind the trendy northern Italian trattoria that had earned him both a Michelin star and a fortune, Lacey remained as skinny as a rail. She had overcome a lot in her life, including years of drug abuse, homelessness, and barely avoiding jail time as a legendary computer hacker. But she had turned her life around with the help of Anthony and Anthony's uncle, Tommassino Fornaio, the mobster who controlled all underworld activity in New York north of the five boroughs of New York City. Nobody knew what the connection between them was, but it was profound, and Lacey loved him like a father.

"Hey, Lace," I said walking over to her table. "Does Anthony know you're here eating Big Macs instead of enjoying one of his pizzas?"

"Who says I didn't enjoy one of his pizzas?" she said, deadpan.

"I should've known," I said. I sat down and began to unwrap my sandwich.

"So, how's the investigation going," said Lacey. It wasn't a question as much as it was a demand for information.

I was tempted to say, "What investigation?" but it would have been pointless. Lacey was the best-connected person I had ever known.

"It's going," was all I said.

"You have a good chat with Richie?"

"Yeah, I did," I said, determined not to react.

"And how was Professor Janssen today?"

"Do you know Dr. Janssen?" I asked, trying not to sound incredulous. Jesus, where did she get this stuff?

"Of course I do. I teach a course in basic network security at OCCC, and I've given some advanced training to faculty members and staff. And don't say it."

"My lips are sealed."

"And I guess you also met Justine Tan."

"Who? Oh! Dr. Tan, the biology professor. Yes, I did."

"What did you think?"

"I guess I didn't think much. All I did was say hello to her. I guess the only impression I had was that she seemed kind of cold, and that maybe there was something personal going on between her and Dr. Janssen, or at least there had been at one point."

"Gee, you should be a private eye."

"What have you heard?"

"I heard," said Lacey, taking a bite of her apple pie, "that she and Janssen had once been considered an item, but now maybe not so much. I also heard that maybe Dr. Tan blames Ada Danforth for that. But you hear a lot of things on a college campus. You'd have to ask one of them."

"Thanks," I said, savoring the last bite of my sandwich. "I guess that means I'm going to be making another visit to Middletown."

"You probably are. But that's not what I came here to tell you."

"Cut it out, Lacey. I didn't even know I was coming here until a couple of minutes before I pulled into the parking lot."

"Matt, you are like the swallows returning to Capistrano. You are the most predictable man on Earth."

What was I supposed to say? Doreen told me the same thing all the time.

"Okay, okay," I said. "What did you come here to tell me?"

"You know that phone call that tipped the police that there had been a murder?"

"Yeah."

"It came in at 10:32 PM, right?"

"Yeah."

"And the M.E. said the time of death was about 10, right?"

"Yes, Lacey, that's right. And Steve Goldfarb forwarded me an email from Dr. Heath this morning. She's refined her estimate, and she's now saying that the murder was committed between 10 and 10:15, but not later than 10:15."

"Interesting," said Lacey, looking uncharacteristically mystified.

"Why is that interesting?" I said.

"Because," said Lacey, "the police department forwarded me the tape of the 911 call to see if I could get anything out of it."

"It wasn't a very good recording, I guess."

"No, it wasn't, but it was good enough, as long as you have the right equipment."

"And you've got the right equipment."

"Sure I do."

"Was it good enough to make a voice ID?"

"Yep."

"Holy crap, Lacey! Why were you holding out on me? That was the voice of the murderer! What, did you get a match off of old recordings of police interrogations?"

"Matt, the voice on the 911 phone call was not the voice of any murderer."

"How do you know? Who was it?"

"The voice on the 911 call belonged to Ada Danforth."

"Lacey, that's impossible."

"Maybe, maybe not. Maybe Dr. Heath got the time of death wrong. It only has to be a few minutes off for all of this to make sense."

"If it was, it'll be the first time in my experience, but I'll check back with her. Where did you get a recording of her voice to match it to, anyway?"

"I got lucky. I figured that there was a good chance that whoever murdered Dr. Danforth may have been connected with OCCC, so I got samples of a bunch of faculty members' voices from tapes of lectures and speeches, and stuff like that. It was easy."

"Okay," I said, "but I still say that it's impossible for the voice to have been Ada's."

"Don't look at me," said Lacey, a glint of humor in her eyes. "I'm just telling you the facts. You're the ace detective around here, not me. You figure it out. You want to pass me those fries? They're not getting any younger, you know."

* * * * * *

CHAPTER EIGHT

"**D**ON'T WORRY, STEVE," said Doreen, "it's kosher as long as you don't put any sour cream or grated cheese on it."

Doreen loved cooking for a crowd, and she had whipped up a huge pot of *chili con carne* and a magnificent bowl of salsa when I'd given her a heads up that we'd probably have a lot of people at the house that night. Doreen had kept the enormous house we lived in as a part of her divorce settlement from her first husband, my former best friend and teammate, David Chandler, and for good reason: she'd paid for it. David had actually believed that his mediocre salary as a junior vice president at a local bank had been enough to fund the lifestyle that he, Doreen, and their two kids had enjoyed. But the truth was that Doreen had quietly made a fortune developing voice recognition software while she, to all appearances, had been a quiet, stay-at-home wife.

The oversized, square-shaped kitchen was equipped with professional quality appliances and cookware, with custom cabinetry and granite countertops surrounding the perimeter. In its center was a round dining table made of solid cherry, expandable to seat fifteen people comfortably. At the far end of the room was a small seating nook furnished with a loveseat, a couple of upholstered chairs and a low coffee table. A small television sat across from the furniture. It was the room Doreen loved best, and it was where we lived our daily lives when the weather was too cold to sit out in the backyard, next to the half-size Olympic swimming pool. The pool yard also boasted a cabana with a changing room, a shower, and a fully equipped outdoor kitchen. Doreen had done really, really well.

"I'll take your word for that," said Steve, as he scooped a generous dollop of the salsa onto a Tostito chip and chased it with a heaping spoonful of the chili.

"You outdid yourself, Doreen," said Richie Glazier, as he polished off what had been a heaping bowl of the chili just a few minutes earlier while Doreen looked on, beaming. Richie was a lot of man to feed, but she always proved herself up to the task. Keeping Richie well-nourished was one of her personal missions.

Of course, Lacey was there, scarfing down the chili as if she hadn't eaten in a week.

Beth Gardner sat at the table, looking tiny and very young out of her uniform. She had let her dark hair down, and it was longer than I had assumed it was. Her chocolate-colored eyes were large and luminous, and I couldn't help imagining that she'd had to fend off more than her share of young men in her brief life. Goldfarb obviously thought highly of the rookie officer, and he wanted her immersed in the murder investigation. I couldn't argue with him, and I could use all the help I could get. Beth looked at Doreen with awe as she nibbled at her meal. She hadn't even been born yet when Doreen had been homecoming queen, prom queen, class president, and class valedictorian all in the same year. But Doreen had become a legend in our little town, and she was acutely aware of the fact that young women knew of her prodigious personal and professional accomplishments and looked up to her as a model of what they, too, could accomplish with their lives, and she took her role seriously. I'd noticed Beth talking earnestly to her and watching her every move as she'd been preparing the meal. Good. She couldn't have a better mentor.

Detective Goldfarb had made sure that his boss, Chief Eddie Shepherd, knew of the meeting and that he would be welcome, but he hadn't shown, which was a disappointment to me. Eddie and I needed all the chances we could scare up to maintain our fragile relationship, and I thought this would have been a good opportunity to work together professionally, and perhaps to socialize. Besides, I knew that Eddie had been completely intimidated by Doreen since we were all kids, and he would have been on his best behavior. But we had plenty to do, so I didn't dwell on it.

I gave them all a complete rundown of my meeting with Professor Janssen. I didn't get a lot of feedback, mostly, I think, because they were just as baffled as I was, and they all had to hear it second-hand from me, which made it twice as confusing. I also thought that although all of us thought at that point that it was all really interesting from a Carl Sagan "Cosmos" perspective, no one, including me, could see how it all could help us solve the crime.

"Except," said Goldfarb, "that jealous scientists – perhaps dozens of them – are now possible suspects."

"I can't think of it like that, Steve," I said. "It'll just paralyze me; it'll paralyze the entire investigation."

"I can't argue with you," said Steve, "but keep it in mind. If any scientists pop up on your radar screen during the investigation, give them a good, hard look."

"Sure thing."

"By the way," said Goldfarb, "did you have a chance to get back to Dr. Heath on her time of death estimate?"

"Yeah, I did," I said. "She's standing by her estimate. Remember, she got to the crime scene while the body was still warm, so she considers her estimate to be extremely precise. She said there's simply no way Dr. Danforth could have died after 10.30 PM, even by just a couple of minutes."

"We'll figure it out somehow," said Goldfarb, turning to my sister. "Which brings us back to the tape. Lacey, did you have a chance to take a second listen to it?"

"I didn't have to," said Lacey, putting down her spoon, "but I did."

"Just to humor me?" said Goldfarb.

"You said it," said Lacey.

"And you didn't find any irregularities?" I asked.

Everybody had been positive, except for me – I was only pretty sure – that with a closer inspection Lacey would find evidence of voice splicing, that the recording had actually been composed of words and syllables taken from older recordings of Ada Danforth speaking, and recombined to make it sound like the mysterious message that we had all heard.

"No, I didn't," said Lacey, suddenly serious, "and I looked damn hard."

"Maybe whoever did it just did a perfect job," said Beth Gardner.

"There's no such thing as 'perfect' when you do something like that," said Lacey. "Not even I could have done it that perfectly, and I'm the best there is. I don't care who you are, or what kind of equipment you have; you're always going to leave a footprint behind."

"Then how do you explain it?" said Richie Glazier.

"I don't," answered Lacey, looking genuinely baffled and uncharacteristically humbled. "I don't know. There's a first time for everything, I guess, and maybe someone *did* do a splicing job that I can't detect. There's no other rational explanation."

"The only thing I can think of," said Doreen, "is that Ada was involved in this whole setup from the beginning, and she made the tape herself for someone else to play over the 911 line when the time came."

"All due respect," said Richie, "I just can't buy that, Doreen. People don't usually fool me. I got to know Ada pretty well over the years, and I just can't see her doing something like that."

"You can't see her playing a hoax," said Goldfarb, "or you just can't see her deliberately planning to have her own life taken?"

"The whole thing," said Richie. "I mean, despite everything that happened to her, Ada Danforth was a happy woman. I run a drinking establishment, and I've seen my share of people come in to the Latitude at the end of their ropes. I know how to recognize the patterns, and Ada just wasn't like that. And besides, let's say she was. She was just an honest, forthright woman, and she wouldn't have gotten herself mixed up in this kind of a hoax, not for any reason."

"Do you think she could have been threatened or bullied into it?" I said.

"No, and no," said Richie.

"But how can you know that?" said Lacey.

"Because Ada and I are both people of faith, and we talked about it openly with each other. She was at peace with her own mortality, and she wouldn't have been manipulated into a scheme like that just out of fear for her own life."

"Okay, then, Richie," said Goldfarb, "what's your explanation?"

"I'm with Lacey; I don't have one," said Richie. "But there's a lot of things in this world that I can't explain, and this of just one more."

"You're not saying all this quantum stuff might be true, are you?" said Goldfarb.

"No, I'm not. But what I know about quantum physics could fit through the eye of a needle, so my opinion doesn't count."

"Okay," said Goldfarb. "Look, we can't let ourselves get distracted by this stuff, because that's probably what somebody out there wants. We just need to put it all out of our minds and get on with the investigation. I hear you about Dr. Heath's estimate, Matt, but for now I'm just going to assume that the TOD was a little bit off, okay?"

"Fine for now," I said. I wasn't ready to capitulate, but I didn't want us getting mired in an argument about it, either. "Have you gotten anything back from the crime scene investigation, Steve?"

"We're still waiting on some stuff," said Steve, "mostly analysis of the material that we vacuumed up off the floor, stuff like that, but I'm not hopeful. I've never seen a crime scene so clean in my life. If I had to draw any conclusions based on the evidence I've seen so far, I'd say that the only person ever to be in that home was Ada herself."

"I guess we shouldn't be surprised," I said.

"Why do you say that?" said Steve.

"Because I think whoever did this was highly intelligent and capable of planning and executing a nearly perfect crime."

"I thought there was no such thing as a perfect crime," said Richie. "At least that's what all the crime shows say."

"Well, they'd be wrong," I said. "Judging by the number of cold case files we had at the NYPD, perfect crimes are committed all the time."

"Well, I'm not about to let this become one of them," said Steve.

"Don't get me wrong, Steve, neither am I," I said. "But if the physical evidence isn't going to help us, that means we really have to focus on developing a list of suspects, and that means starting with family, friends, and colleagues. I'm going to visit Ada's parents tomorrow. I don't know what I'm going to get out of them, but it can't hurt."

"You're right," said Goldfarb. "And I don't want them thinking that no one is doing anything about their daughter's murder, or that we don't care about the family."

"Don't they also have a son?" asked Doreen. "Does anyone know anything about him? Is he still in the area?"

"Yeah, he's still in the area," said Beth. "His name is Joseph. He's about five years younger than Ada, about thirty or so."

"What does he do?" I said.

"He's an electrician, I think," said Beth. "I heard somewhere that he dropped out of high school when he was sixteen and went to trade school."

"Married?" asked Goldfarb. "Family?"

"I don't know," said Beth.

"Look," I said, "why don't you do a little homework and find out where he works and lives, and dig up anything you can find about his family situation. Then we can circle back after I've had a chance to talk to the parents."

"Sure thing," said Beth. "And, sir?" she said, addressing Steve, but she was shifting her gaze between the two of us."

"Yes, Beth?" said Steve.

"We need to do a follow-up interview with Jeremy Carter. I think, despite all this other stuff, he still has to be a suspect, maybe even our prime suspect. I mean, he clearly had a lot of emotions wrapped up in Ada, and he's got a really bad temper."

"You're right, Beth," I said. "I was planning to follow up with him as soon as I met with Ada's parents."

"I can do it tomorrow," said Beth, looking directly at me.

"Beth," I replied, "even Richie had trouble handling that guy, and he obviously doesn't know how to stop once he gets started."

"I'm either a cop or I'm not," said Beth, once again turning her gaze to Goldfarb. "I've been trained to handle people like that, and I'm confident that I can; and I really want a shot at the guy."

Doreen fixed Goldfarb with a stare that made the big man quail, and then she gave me the same look. Lacey gave Beth a nod, and then she gave me and Goldfarb another look just like Doreen's. In the end it was Steve's call, so I kept my mouth shut.

"You're right, Beth," he said, without hesitation, which was the only way he could have said it. "Go ahead. But I also don't want you to forget Joseph Danforth, okay? You're going to have a busy day tomorrow."

"Thank you sir," said Beth, a proud smile lighting up her face. "I'll get it done."

"Okay, then," said Goldfarb, knowing that dwelling on the subject would be condescending, "let's wrap this up. Tomorrow's going to be another long day." He reached for his jacket and started to head for the door before he realized that no one was following him.

"What?" said Goldfarb. "Did I forget something?"

"No, no," said Richie. "I was just going to stay and have a little more of that chili, if that's okay with you, Doreen."

"Fine with me," said Doreen.

"C'mon, Steve," I said, "I've got a six-pack chilling in the fridge, and we can open a bottle of wine, or maybe two. 'All work and no play makes Jack a dull boy,' right?"

"Doreen," said Goldfarb, "you okay with this?"

"What else am I going to do with all this food?" said Doreen. I cast a suspicious glance in Lacey's direction, but she just gave me an innocent stare back. "Come on everybody, let's eat. And Matt, get after that beer and wine."

*   *   *   *   *   *

"Thanks honey," I said, as I climbed into bed. It was close to midnight, but the evening had been a break from the intensity of the investigation that everyone had needed. "I think everybody really appreciated that."

"It was fun," she said, "and I'm glad that I was able to help."

I lay down under the covers and reached for her.

"You're naked," I said, my entire body suddenly at attention.

"Sorry," she said, with a wicked smile, "I seem to have misplaced my elf outfit."

"Well then, why don't you do me a favor?" I said, as I drew her into my arms.

"What would that be?"

"Don't look too hard for it, okay?"

"Gotcha," she said, as she led me to that heavenly place where only she could take me.

CHAPTER NINE

HE DOORMAT BENEATH THE FRONT DOOR ANNOUNCED, "WE'RE RETIRED!", with images of champagne glasses and bottles meant to offer, I guessed, a festive air to the announcement. The house itself was small and unremarkable, located on one of the few streets in Devon-on-Hudson that I had never before visited.

The man who greeted me at the front door, presumably Ada Danforth's grieving father, Vincent, was wearing a floppy straw beach hat, a loud tropical shirt, and Bermuda shorts. I was wearing a coat, a flannel shirt, and khaki trousers because it was December, and it was cold.

"Welcome aboard, mate!" said the man, a toothy grin splitting his puffy face. He sported a sagging pot-belly, and the legs protruding from the shorts were pale, thin, and inked with a network of blue veins.

The woman standing behind him, presumably Ada's grieving mother, Barbara, was wearing a brightly patterned one-piece, fairly aggressively cut bathing suit underneath a sheer white blouse. I tried not to stare, but she seemed to give me a shy smile when I failed.

They both held drinks in their hands. It was ten o'clock in the morning. I'd called ahead. They'd known I was coming.

Vincent Danforth wasn't kidding about the "Welcome aboard!" part. I stepped into a living room furnished with deck chairs and small, umbrella-equipped tables. There were beach towels stacked in one corner, and a placard above the hearth that announced it to be the "LIDO DECK." The walls were festooned with large, bright posters of tropical islands and cruise ships. An enormous flat screen TV swallowed up one wall. Various other signs in the room pointed down a hallway and through an entryway to the

"GALLEY," the "HEAD" and the "STATEROOMS." The thermostat had to be set at somewhere between 75 and 80, and I could already feel the sweat starting to flow. I took off my jacket, but it didn't help.

"Yep," continued Vincent, "Barb and I went on a Caribbean cruise to celebrate our retirements two years ago, and we had the time of our lives. So, when we got home, we just said to ourselves, 'Hell, just because we're off the ship, doesn't mean the cruise has to end. After all, we're retired!'"

"It was very liberating," said Barb, giving me another shy smile.

"That's great," I said. I guess you could argue that it was.

"You were one of those football players, right?" said Vince.

"Yes, I guess I was."

"I knew I recognized you," he said, pointing at his head. "You still have to get up pretty early in the morning to get anything past ol' Vince! Isn't that right, Barb?"

"That's right," said Barb, smiling cheerfully, but perhaps not sincerely.

"You can watch all the sports you want from the Lido Deck!" said Vince.

"That's great," I said.

"Can we get you anything?" said Vincent, holding up his glass.

"No, thanks," I said. "I'm fine for now."

"Okay," he said, "but don't forget, the bar is always open on the Lido Deck!"

"Good to know," I said.

"Please, take a seat," said Barbara, gesturing to one of the deck chairs. I did, as did Vincent and Barbara. The chair was surprisingly comfortable.

"I suppose you've come to talk about Ada," said Barbara after an uncomfortable silence. She was an attractive woman. I knew that she and Vince were both about sixty, but unlike her husband, Barbara Danforth had clearly made an effort to take care of herself. She was slender, seemed to have good muscle tone in her legs and arms, and her skin, generously on display, was still youthfully smooth. Her hair was unapologetically silver, but professionally cut and styled.

"Yes, Mrs. Danforth, I have," I said.

"Please!" said Vincent. "It's 'Vince' and 'Barb'! First names only on the Lido Deck!"

"Then please, just call me Matt," I said. When in Rome.

"Sure I can't get you that drink, Matt?" said Vince, rising from his chair and heading over to a copiously stocked wet bar, where he sloshed a couple of fingers of Jack Daniels and an ice cube into his glass. I noticed that Barb didn't make any move to refill her own glass, and she hadn't taken a sip from it since I'd walked in the door.

"Really, I'm fine," I said, hoping it would take this time. Vince returned from the bar and plopped himself down heavily on his deck chair. I hoped that the Lido Deck had plenty of spares. Barbara, sitting beside him, placed her drink on a side table, and looked at me, clearly waiting for me to speak.

"First of all," I said, "I'd like to offer you my personal condolences on the loss of your daughter, and also on behalf of the entire Devon Police Department and from the mayor, who is my wife."

"Thank you," said Barbara, keeping her gaze on me while Vincent stared at one of the posters on the wall. Not exactly a touching display of grief, but I wasn't there to judge, so I moved ahead.

"It would be extremely helpful if you could tell me anything that might help us find your daughter's killer. Did she seem different to you recently? Did you notice her in the company of anyone you hadn't seen before, or who may have seemed suspicious to you?"

"I'm afraid we won't be of much help," said Barb. "We haven't been in touch with Ada for a very long time."

"But she's been living just a short drive from here for almost fifteen years. You must have seen her at least off and on."

Barbara just stared at me while Vince ignored me.

"Not to pry, but did something happen between you that caused you to become estranged?"

"Estranged," said Vince, keeping his eyes on the poster. "Huh. Would've had to be un-estranged first."

Barbara turned to her husband and glared at him, then turned her eyes back to me.

"It was nothing like that, Mr. Hunter. But you have to understand that we were never all that close to Ada."

"Well," I said, "I know that she left home at a very early age."

"Yes, she did," said Barbara, "but that really wasn't it."

"Always off in space, that one," said Vincent.

"Sir?" I said.

"Don't sir me!" said Vince, turning to look at me, his face reddening. "I told you, this is the Lido Deck!"

"Sorry, Vince," I said, noticing that his glass was already in drydock. I'd have to be careful not to make him surly. His gaze returned to the poster.

"You have to understand," said Barb. "Ada was a, uh, unique child from a very early age. For a while we thought she was autistic, but her teachers told us she was always attentive in class and socialized well with the other kids, except when she, you know, drifted off."

Richie Glazer's words came back to me. "What do you mean, 'drifted off'?"

"It's so difficult to explain," said Barb, clasping her hands together. "It wasn't like she was daydreaming; it's like she just wasn't there. I mean, her body was there, but she wasn't."

"Do you remember when you first noticed that?"

"Oh, by the time she was ten, I'd say. She could read and write and speak like an adult by her third birthday, but it was about her tenth birthday when we felt like we'd lost her. We tried our best, Matt."

"Did our bit," mumbled Vince. "Fought the good fight."

"And then she went away to school," said Barb. "For all those years. And then to Chicago. And then she was suddenly back here, and we really couldn't understand why. We tried to stay in touch with her. We went to Mass together, had her over to Sunday dinner, things like that, but that didn't last long. It was just the same as it was when she was a child. Maybe it was the wrong thing to do. Maybe we were bad parents; I don't know. But I don't think we've seen her three times in the past ten years."

"Fought the good fight. Did our bit," said Vince, getting up to refloat his ice cube.

"And then we had Joseph to consider, of course," said Barb, scowling at Vince's back, but saying nothing.

"Joseph?" I said.

"Joseph, our son," said Barb.

"Are you still close with him?"

"I wouldn't say close, but he stops by periodically."

"Were he and Ada ever close, do you know?"

"You'd have to ask him," said Barb, "but I don't think so. He was only seven when Ada left home, and he was still in high school when she came back. I know they were brother and sister, but they couldn't have had much in common."

"Wasn't the boy's fault," said Vince, plopping back into his seat so hard that some of his drink sloshed out of the glass and onto his shorts, but if he noticed he didn't show it.

"Do you know of anyone she was close with here in this area? Any childhood friends?" I felt foolish just asking, but I felt as though I had to. Barb stared at me incredulously, while Vince suddenly looked like he'd had enough.

"Well, Barb, Matt," said Vince, rising unsteadily from his chair, "I'm going to head back to the stateroom. I feel a nap coming on. Too much of this tropical sun, I guess!" He walked unsteadily down the hallway, drink in hand, as if his sea-legs had suddenly deserted him.

Barb's eyes followed him down the hallway. I heard a door open and close, and then a toilet flush.

"He won't be back," said Barb, picking up her glass and rising from her chair. She came over to me and stood uncomfortably close. "I'm going to bring this glass back to the kitchen," she said. "Is there anything I can get you while I'm there? Coffee, perhaps?"

"No thanks, Barb," I said, looking up at her from an awkward angle. "I probably ought to get going." I'd only been there a short while, but I was getting nowhere, and there was no reason to think that things were going to change.

"Oh, please, stay just a little longer," she said. "I'll be right back."

I heard rustling and rinsing in the kitchen. I decided that perhaps I should stay long enough to see if she had anything else to offer me now that Vince was out of the way.

As it turned out, she did.

When she came back into the room, she was still wearing the sheer blouse, but the bathing suit was gone. The male animal inside me was suddenly alert and on the prowl. Age be damned; Barbara Danforth still had what it took. My eyes widened and I suddenly felt warm.

"You still play team sports?" she said, the smile back on her face, the smile that was no longer shy. She knew what she was doing to me, and she was going to press her advantage.

"Barb…Mrs. Danforth." I wanted to stand up, but at that moment it would have sent the wrong message. "I hope I didn't do anything to make you think that I was, you know…Mrs. Danforth, I'm a married man."

She walked over to me and stood so close that we were practically touching. I found myself staring directly at her breasts - her generous, still youthfully firm breasts - further complicating matters. "And I'm a married woman," she said. She touched the back of my neck with her hand, sending a jolt of electricity through my entire body. My male animal growled and paced, ready to pounce. "Your point?" she said.

I had to stand up now, no matter how embarrassing it would be. She didn't back away, and we were almost touching. She looked down, and then back up. Her smiling lips parted. Her hand reached for my groin, which by then was a target that was pretty hard to miss.

"Dammit, Barbara!" I said, backing away and holding her by the shoulders at arms distance. "Listen to me! This is not how I behave! I'm not going to judge you, and I'm not going to judge your marriage, but please, respect how I feel."

She was too proud to keep trying, and that's what saved me. The seductive smile fled her face, but it was replaced not by shame or anger, only resignation. She turned, giving me an excellent view of the rest of what I'd be missing, went back to her chair, and sat down. She sat with a straight back and looked directly at me. She made no attempt to cover herself up.

"I'm not going to apologize for my behavior."

"I don't expect you to," I said.

"You know," she said to me, her resigned expression turning contemplative, "in his own sad way, Vince is right. We fought the good fight, all our lives. We were good parents, Matt. We loved our children. We worked hard, we were active in our church and in our community. But nothing worked. Ada was who she was, and poor Joseph is a troubled young man, and who can blame him? So we finally gave up, and we decided to make a clean break. We retired from our jobs, we stopped going to church, and we booked a month-long cruise in the Caribbean, first class all the way."

"I don't think anyone would criticize you for that," I said, but I don't think she heard me.

"But before we left, Vince was diagnosed with early-stage prostate cancer. The surgeon said it would be a low-risk surgery because the cancer had been discovered so early, and that he'd be good to go long before we ever boarded the cruise liner. But the surgery was botched, and now Vince is completely and permanently...non-functional. He'd never been much of a lover in the first place, but I'd been a faithful wife, Matt. I want you to understand that. I want you to believe that."

"I do, Barbara, I do," I said. I didn't want to hear this, any of it, but I wasn't going to make her stop. Barbara Danforth had been a good Catholic all her life, and now she was in the Confessional, and she was going to confess.

"Vince had never been much of a drinker, and he'd always looked after his appearance, but by the time we boarded the cruise ship he was, well, you've seen him. He'd drink all day, and then he'd be passed out by dinnertime. He gained thirty pounds. And there I was, Matt I was lonely, awfully lonely, but it was more than that. I was still young, at least that was how I felt, and I simply couldn't imagine living the rest of my life without physical affection, physical intimacy.

"After the first week on the cruise, one of the young members of the cast of entertainers the cruise company had hired started paying attention to me. He'd obviously noticed Vince's behavior, and he saw me sitting alone night after night. He was very sweet and attentive, and very, very attractive. I don't think I have to tell you what happened after that. Ever since then, if an opportunity comes along..."

"Like today."

"Yes, Matt, like today. I guess by now you can fill in the details."

Yes, I could. I'd been in a barren marriage for years before I'd finally gotten divorced, and before Doreen had miraculously re-entered my life. I had no idea what my life would have been if Doreen hadn't saved me, but I looked at people like Barbara Danforth, and who knows? I was no one to judge, I knew that.

"Does Vince know?"

"Oh, of course he does. But he doesn't say anything, God bless him, and neither do I. I do my best to care for him and look after him, and to love him as best I can, but I'm afraid he's lost, and I worry. So I humor him with the permanent cruise game we play and hope for the best."

"He must be angry," I said. "Not at you, I didn't mean that, but just at the way his life has turned out. I guess anybody would be."

Barbara Danforth was not a stupid woman, not by a long shot, and she knew exactly what I was getting at.

"Somewhere deep down inside, I'm sure he is," she said. Tears began to well in her eyes. "But if you think he might have directed his anger at Ada, you're wrong. Despite the things he says, Vincent loved Ada deeply. He is a dear, sweet, harmless man who I don't deserve."

"Don't say that, Barbara."

"You're very kind," she said. She stood up. "But now, I'm going to dress myself in something other than that ridiculous bathing suit and make myself a drink." My male animal blinked his eyes open at the sight of her, and she couldn't help but notice. "You're welcome to join me if you want."

Her expression was impenetrable, but the loneliness emanated from her eyes like the beacon from a distant lighthouse, offering shelter from the storm in return for nothing more than acknowledgment of its existence. I wanted to stay, if for no other reason than to keep her loneliness at bay for just a few minutes longer. But I knew I couldn't, and she knew it, too.

"I think I have to go now, Barbara."

"Yes, I guess you do."

She walked toward me. She had bared more to me than her body, and we were both oblivious to her nakedness. She put her arms around me, and I put my arms around her.

"Find my daughter's killer, Matt."

"I will, Barbara. I promise."

When I got back to my car I turned back and looked at the small house, imagining Barbara, and Vince, inside it. I remember someone once said that hell comes in little boxes.

Whoever said that was right.

* * * * * *

"Jesus," said Doreen, panting, her hair damp with sweat at her temples, her nipples still hard. "Maybe you ought to get propositioned by strange women more often."

"Maybe," I said, feeling my male animal finally settling himself in for a nap.

I'd come straight home from the Danforths' and found Doreen working in her home office. I sat down and told her everything – everything – that had happened, not knowing how she would respond. I only knew I had to tell her. I don't think she actually said anything to me before taking me by the hand and leading me to the bedroom. I don't remember getting undressed.

It would be difficult to call what we did "making love." It was animal, it was primitive, and it was something, for reasons that Doreen understood but that I hadn't yet fathomed, I desperately needed.

I pulled Doreen close to me, and before I knew it, I felt myself dozing off. But before I did, I heard my wife whisper in my ear, "You have nothing to be afraid of, Matt. Don't ever forget that. You have nothing to be afraid of."

* * * * * *

CHAPTER TEN

I T WAS MID-AFTERNOON when I got a call from Officer Gardner telling me that she'd been able to get in touch with Joseph Danforth, and that he'd agreed to meet with us at five o'clock at a nearby pub. I suggested that she swing by the house and pick me up in her patrol car. That way we could catch up on what she'd found out about Ada Danforth's brother on the way to the pub.

"Have you talked to Jeremy Carter yet?" I asked.

"Yeah, I did," said Beth. "Don't worry, no bumps and bruises, but we can talk about that later, okay?"

"Sure."

Before we hung up I gave her an update on my visit to the Danforths. She told me that Steve Goldfarb was in his office, and that she'd pass along the information to him, which saved me a phone call. I left out the detail about my encounter with Barbara Danforth, not because I was trying to hide anything, but because it was something I just didn't want to discuss over the phone.

As it turned out, Beth had uncovered an impressive amount of information about Joseph Danforth in the little time she'd been given, and I told her so.

"Well," she said, "I had some help."

"Lacey, right?"

"Yeah. That is one cool woman."

"She's something else, alright," I said. It was fun watching the young officer rapidly developing a support network that would stand her in good stead during a long career.

Joseph Danforth was, in fact, an electrician, she told me, but there was a lot more to it than that. His early academic records indicated that he was a highly intelligent young man - nothing approaching his sister, but he was clearly university bound. His teachers noted his early interest in any form of electronic machinery, and began to encourage him to think about pursuing a career in electrical engineering.

But instead, young Joseph, or Joe, as he was apparently known to everyone, with no explanation to either his teachers or his family, suddenly dropped out of school on his sixteenth birthday and began an apprenticeship program in order to become a licensed electrician. It had apparently worked out well for him, and all the indications were that he was successful and prosperous.

I asked about his family status, but Beth said that he had none other than his parents and his sister. He had never married; he had no children, and he apparently never even dated.

We pulled up in front of the pub, a place called McAfee's in south Newburg, just before five and, because we could, parked illegally in front of an alleyway instead of a block and a half up the street at the first available legal parking space, which was metered.

The evening was cold, and the pub felt pleasantly warm as our eyes adjusted to the dim light. We didn't see anyone who fit the bill for Joe Danforth, so we grabbed a table for four in a quiet corner. A waiter came to the table, and we both ordered coffee, Beth because she was on duty, and driving, and me to keep her company.

The coffees had just arrived when a tall, sandy-haired young man walked in. He was wearing a down fleece, stained jeans, and heavy work boots. A hardhat dangled from his left hand. He gave the waiter a nod and walked straight over to our table as soon as he spied us. I think Beth's uniform was the giveaway.

"You must be Officer Gardner," he said, a friendly smile on his face. "I'm Joe Danforth. Pleased to meet you." He smelled of strong tobacco, and I spotted a pack of unfiltered Camels in his shirt pocket when he unzipped his fleece.

"Pleased to meet you, too," said Beth.

"And you," he said turning to me, "must be Matt Hunter. Believe it or not, Mr. Hunter, when I was six years old my Dad took me to a

Devon Central High School football game, and we watched you and your teammates tear Washingtonville High to pieces. I still remember it. You ran a post pattern and caught a fifty-yard touchdown pass from David Chandler that he threw from his own forty. You guys really put our little town on the map, didn't you?"

He could have been telling the truth, or he could have just been being polite. I'd caught too many fifty-yard touchdown passes from David Chandler to remember any one in particular.

"Yeah, I guess we did," I said, just as the waiter came over and placed a pint stein of beer and a brimming shot of whiskey in front of Danforth.

"Cheers," he said as he drained a quarter of his beer in one gulp. Then he put his mug back on the table and dropped the whiskey, glass and all, into the mug. A classic boilermaker. A man who didn't drink Michelob Ultra and vape. I could learn to like this guy. I was jealous, and it probably showed. "A great way to call an end to the day," he said, smiling at me.

"Thanks for agreeing to see us, Mr. Danforth," said Beth.

"No problem," he said, "and call me Joe. Mr. Danforth is my father. Anyway, I was working on a site right across the street today." He pointed out the window to the metal framework that would become what appeared to be a very tall building.

"Looks impressive," I said.

"It's going to be a twelve-story data center for Amazon, and the electrical specs are mind-boggling."

"How long have you been working on it?" said Beth.

"Oh, I've only been working here for a couple of days. I'm what you call an 'electricians' electrician.' I get called in when the electrical contractors on a construction site run into a problem that they can't figure out."

"That must be challenging work," said Beth.

"It keeps me from getting bored," said Danforth, "and it feeds the bulldog. I bill out at a thousand dollars a day, and I work six days a week when I want."

So much for engineering school, I thought.

"But you're not here to talk about the fine points of circuit breakers," he said. "You're here to talk about my sister."

"Yes, we are," said Beth. "But first of all, we would like to offer you our deepest condolences."

All we got back was a blank stare. It reminded me of the reaction I'd gotten from her parents.

"Let me get one thing out of the way, Joe," I said. "Where were you on the night your sister was murdered?"

"I don't know for sure," he replied, looking me straight in the eye. "I work long hours, and every day seems to run into the next, you know? All I know is, I'm single, and I usually just find a friendly looking place for a couple of beers and a meal and come home. Maybe if I checked my calendar I could tell you where I was working that day, and maybe where I went afterwards."

"Why don't you do that," I said.

"Sure."

I decided to move on.

"Your parents told me when I visited them that you and Ada weren't that close..."

"You saw my parents? When?" said Joe, his blank stare replaced with a hint of suspicion clouding his eyes.

"Today. Why?"

Joe took a hit off his boilermaker before he answered. "No reason. But look, my folks were right: Ada and I weren't close. As a matter of fact, we barely knew each other, so I really don't know how I can help you."

"Then why did you agree to see us?" said Beth.

"I was just trying to be cooperative, okay? I didn't want you to think I didn't care or anything."

"But you don't," I said.

Joe Danforth stared at me long and hard. He took another sip of his drink, a bigger one this time. For a second I thought he was going to get up and leave, but then he seemed to sag a little, like he was giving in to something against his will.

"So, you've seen my parents."

"Yes, I have."

"God, that's embarrassing."

"It's all right, Joe. We had a good talk."

"No you didn't. Dad was drunk and Mom tried to seduce you. You don't think I know? You think somehow you were special?" Beth gave me a funny look. I knew I'd have to come clean with both her and Goldfarb about what happened between me and Barbara, but now wasn't the time, and Beth quietly let it pass after she saw the look on my face.

"Don't judge your parents, Joe," I said.

"You're missing my point! I'm not judging them!" he said so loud that the bartender looked over.

"You blame your sister," I said, quietly.

"Yes, I do," Joe said, pushing his beer mug off to one side. "My parents were good, decent people. Do you think what you saw today is what they wanted to be at this point in their lives? Do you think that's what they deserved? But there she was, weird Ada, spooking everybody. After a while nobody could take it anymore. I quit school and left home as soon as I could because I didn't want to be around when she stopped by on vacations, and I didn't want to have to look at what she was doing to my parents even when she wasn't there. It was the smartest thing I ever did. I got away. My parents weren't so lucky, and now look at them."

"What do you mean about Ada spooking everybody?" I said.

Joe stared into his Boilermaker for what seemed like a long time before finally looking up. "Let me tell you a story," he said. He looked back at his beer mug, but he didn't reach for it. "Ada came home from Cornell for a semester break one time. I guess it was when I was in middle school. She'd only been back for a few days, but she'd already weirded everybody out. We'd all just finished dinner and it was still early, but I decided to go upstairs to my room because I couldn't stand to watch her just sitting there like that. I knew it was driving Mom and Dad crazy too, but they didn't say anything. I was walking down the hallway to my room, and I had to walk by Ada's room to get there. Her door was open, so I looked in, and there was Ada, sitting on her bed. But that was impossible, right? I'd just left her downstairs, and there was no other way to get upstairs. But there she was, sitting there."

"What did you do?" said Beth, looking suddenly pale.

"I didn't do anything. I went to my room and started working on a little robotic device I was trying to build, and I tried to put everything out of my mind."

"And that was it?" I said.

"No, it wasn't," said Joe. He was beginning to perspire just from reliving the memory. "I wish it had been, because then I would've been able to convince myself that it hadn't really happened. But Ada wasn't going to let that happen. Oh, no."

"What did she do?" said Beth.

"She came upstairs, and I heard her coming down the hallway, towards my room. I hadn't closed my door, but all of a sudden wished I had, and then I saw her standing in the doorway, just staring at me. 'What?' I said. And then she said, 'Joe, you need to understand that things are not always as they appear to be. It's okay.' And then she just walked away."

"That was it?" I said. "Nothing else?"

"Nothing else," said Joe, "and I guess that's all I've got to say. If I talk about this anymore, it's going to put me in a place I don't want to be. Good luck with your investigation." He drained the rest of his boilermaker in one huge gulp. Then he got up and walked away. He was reaching for his Camels before he got to the door.

And now, I thought, we have three more suspects. Or maybe only two. I didn't think that Ada's father, despite his obvious anger, could have roused himself to act, or to be as meticulous as he would have had to be. So there were two. Two more. Mother and brother.

*   *   *   *   *   *

"Sometimes I wish I could just be out writing up traffic tickets with all the other rookies," said Officer Gardner, more to Doreen than to me.

She had clearly been upset by our visit with Joe Danforth, and she'd said as much on the drive back to town. She hadn't shared much of her personal life with me, but she'd told me enough for me to know that she was single and lived alone in a small apartment in the same complex where I'd lived when I'd first moved back to town. Her mother had died when she was young, and her father had remarried and moved to Florida as soon as Beth had gone off to college. She'd been on her own ever since. I knew lonely, and I knew the last thing she needed right now was to return to an empty apartment. So I'd suggested that maybe she'd like to stop by our house for a bite to eat. She'd accepted immediately, and we swung by the police station just long enough for her to change out of her uniform and pick up her own car. I breathed a sigh of relief that both Chief Shepherd and Detective Goldfarb were gone for the day.

She'd made a beeline for the kitchen as soon as we walked into the house and attached herself to Doreen while she prepared chicken cutlets á *la Doreen* and a simple pasta dish. I'd poured them each a small glass of white wine and made myself a martini and sat down at the table with a bowl of peanuts as a way of doing my bit.

"That story Joe Danforth told you must have really upset you," said Doreen, as she gently coached Beth in the art of sautéing a cutlet.

"Yeah, it did," said Beth, sounding awfully young, "but it was more than that. It was, you know, the whole thing."

"Tell me," said Doreen.

"I mean, I grew up in such a nice family, at least while my mom was alive, and now I'm working on a murder case where three of the prime suspects are the victim's parents and her brother. And yes, I was freaked out by that story."

"The fact that you grew up in a nice family is what's going to get you through this," said Doreen. "Just keep your eyes on what you're doing, and don't get distracted by the other stuff, okay?"

"Okay," said Beth.

"Now, let's check on that pasta..."

We'd gotten about two bites into dinner when I saw Beth's head drop, and tears start dripping onto her plate. Doreen nudged her chair closer to her and silently put her arms around her.

She finally looked up after a few minutes. Her skin was blotchy and her eyes were bloodshot. She blew her nose and wiped it with her napkin. Luckily, Doreen had held back on the good linen.

"Some cop, huh, Mr. Hunter?"

"Beth," I said, "I don't know a single cop who hasn't cried on the job, and that includes me. You're doing a fine job, and don't you ever forget it."

She nodded her head. "Okay, Mr. Hunter," she said. She picked her fork up and took a bite of cutlet.

She'd be fine.

* * * * * *

CHAPTER ELEVEN

L UCKILY, I had put on my commemorative 1986 New York Mets World Series Championship bathrobe before I went stumbling down the stairs at 6 AM hoping that God had somehow prepared a hot pot of coffee for me.

God hadn't, but it turned out that Beth had.

When I'd gone up to bed the night before, I'd left Doreen and Beth chatting in the seating nook of the kitchen. It was clearly a conversation between the two of them, so I'd butted out, saying that I was going upstairs to read. In general, I'm not exactly a poster boy for literacy campaigns, but at night I'm hopeless. I don't think I've ever remained conscious for more than fifteen minutes on the sporadic occasions that I have attempted to read in bed before turning out the light, and last night had been no exception. But I had gone to sleep with the vague assumption that at some point in the evening Beth would go home. That, as Doreen would say, is what I get for thinking.

It was still pitch dark outside, and cold, and the warm lighting in the kitchen made it feel like a snug cocoon.

Beth was curled up on the loveseat of the sitting nook in the kitchen wearing one of Doreen's bathrobes, both hands wrapped protectively around a large mug of coffee, looking like she shared the feeling.

"Oh, Mr. Hunter!" she said, jumping up, almost spilling her coffee in the process. "I'm so sorry. I got up early so that I'd be out the door before I bothered you."

"And then you found out just how nice this room is on a dark morning, right?" Beth reddened at that. "Look, sit back down and enjoy your coffee.

No need to rush on my account. And thanks for the coffee," I said, as I poured myself a mug. I went over to the sitting nook and sat in one of the chairs facing her. "Wait till it's summertime and you can bring your coffee out to the deck and sit by the pool." The expression on her face made it clear that she'd already thought about that.

"Well isn't this cozy?" said Doreen as she walked into the kitchen, wearing her own robe. She grabbed a cup of coffee and came over to sit with us. "Sleep okay?" she said, looking at Beth.

"Great," said Beth. "Thanks so much."

"I'm glad you decided to stay," said Doreen.

"Look," I said, "I'm going to throw on some clothes and then make us some pancakes and sausages for breakfast. How does that sound?" It was literally the only thing I knew how to make for breakfast, my usual morning meal being either one of Doreen's concoctions or an Egg McMuffin from McDonald's. Before I'd married Doreen I'd eaten so often at Mickey D's that I should have been a shareholder.

"That's the best idea you've had all week," said Doreen.

"I can't argue with you," I said. "Beth, can you stay long enough for breakfast?"

"Sure," she said immediately. I didn't think she'd need a lot of convincing.

"Good," I said. "Let me warm up that cup of coffee for you. And then we have to talk about your visit with Jeremy Carter." I just hadn't had the heart to bring it up the night before.

It took me all of three minutes to run upstairs and throw on an old NYPD sweatshirt and a pair of khakis. I pulled some breakfast sausages that Sally made on the premises out of the freezer, laid them out on the built-in griddle on Doreen's massive stove, and got to work on the pancakes. They were done in no time, and pretty soon the room got quiet as we all dug in. I allowed a decent interval for us all to enjoy the food, and then I got back to business.

"So why don't you tell us about your visit with Jeremy Carter?"

"It was interesting in a couple of ways I didn't expect," said Beth. "First, did you know that he was fired from his teaching job day before yesterday?"

"No, I didn't," I replied.

"Yeah," said Beth. "It turns out that the school administration has had their eyes on him for a while because of a couple of other minor incidents he's been involved in, especially the troubles he's had at the Latitude. So earlier this semester he was told that he was on probation, and just this past week I guess he got into it with the football coach, who, as usual, is twice his size, so they fired him. I guess when the Principal called him in to give him the news, Carter went after him, too. Luckily, the wrestling coach was there and pulled Jeremy away before he hurt anybody, although I guess the coach got a black eye and a cracked rib in the process."

"So, how was he with you?" I asked.

"He was fine. We went to McDonald's and had a cup of coffee, and we had a polite conversation. The first thing he told me was that he'd lost his job, but he didn't seem all that upset about it. Then I asked him where he was and what he was doing on the night of the murder, and he gave me the usual credible but unprovable alibi: He'd come straight home from work, made himself a supper of leftover chicken and rice, washed the dishes, and spent the rest of the night watching TV. He even told me which shows he watched. I checked later and they were all on that night. He said he turned out his light around 11, which is when he always does. But, of course, he didn't see anyone, and no one saw him. I asked him if he felt any anger at Ada Danforth because of the failed relationship, and he said 'no.' He saved all his blame and anger for Kevin Waldron and Richie Glazier."

"What kind of car does he drive?" I asked.

"He drives a Volkswagen Passat, and I checked out the tires as we were leaving the restaurant. They're not brand-new, but new enough so that the car would have left clear tread marks if it had been parked in front of Ada's house."

"Okay," I said, "but we have confirmation that he has a dangerous, unpredictable temper, and he is more than capable of extreme violence."

"Yes, we do," said Beth. "But sir?"

"Yes?"

"Here's the problem. When I called the school later and asked the folks there about his previous violent altercations, they told me they were all with other men, usually big, strong men. I went out of my way to ask if he had ever behaved in a violent or threatening manner toward a woman, and they said no. The guidance counselor I spoke to has a graduate degree in psychology and she volunteers at the local women's shelter, and she said he just doesn't fit that profile."

"There's a first time for everything under the right conditions," I said. "I'm not a psychologist, but I am an ex-cop."

"She also went out of her way to say that, sir. But she said that, at least most of the time, men who behave violently or abusively toward women are cowards when it comes to altercations with other men."

"I have to admit that she's right about that," I said.

I was mopping up the last drop of maple syrup from my plate with my last bite of pancake when my phone rang. I was puzzled when I looked at the CallerID.

"Good morning, Dr. Heath," I said. "I didn't think the M.E.'s office was open this early." I listened to what she had to say for a few minutes, and then said, "You're sure?" She said she was. "Okay, then," I said. "Thanks." I disconnected the phone and looked up to see Doreen and Beth staring at me.

"Well?" said Doreen.

"Well," I said, "it appears that Ada Danforth gave birth at one time in her life, to what Dr. Heath believes was a full-term baby."

* * * * * *

I could feel the hairs in my nose freezing up as I walked from the parking lot at OCCC to the dining hall. The temperature had plunged overnight to close to zero, and even at nine o'clock when I left the house it was still in the single digits.

As soon as I'd told Doreen and Beth the news, Beth had jumped up, gotten herself dressed, and left the house looking pale. She planned to run back to her apartment, shower, and change, and then get to the police station to make sure that Detective Goldfarb and Chief Shepherd had gotten the medical examiner's news.

Doreen had volunteered to take care of the kitchen while I ran upstairs to take my own shower and ditch the khakis and the sweatshirt for a pair of wool slacks and a cotton dress shirt.

I'd spent the drive over to the campus trying to figure out the implications of the news we'd received, but at that point my brain was pumping a dry well. How could it be that Ada Danforth had gone through a full-term pregnancy and delivered the baby without anyone knowing of it? Or *had* someone known about it? I knew that Ada was estranged from her parents and brother, but wouldn't she have at least shared the news with them? Quite possibly not. She wouldn't have been the first young woman to hide a pregnancy from her family. I guessed that I shouldn't have been surprised that she hadn't had an abortion, because her devout Catholic faith would have mitigated against that course of action. Had the child been stillborn? Had she put it up for adoption? Was it being raised by his or her father? And what about her colleagues at OCCC? Could they have remained oblivious to a nine-month pregnancy? And what about Richie Glazier, one of the most perceptive human beings I knew, and a man with whom many people shared some of their innermost secrets? If she had told anyone her secret, my guess it would have been Richie. I thought of stopping by the Latitude on the way back from Middletown, but I didn't think anything would come of it, simply because I was positive the Richie would have told me if he had possessed that kind of information.

I had expected to meet with Paul Janssen privately, but when I walked into the welcome warmth of the cafeteria I found him sitting with Justine Tan, who was looking at me with a proprietary expression on her face, or at least that's what it seemed like to me.

I poured myself a cup of coffee I didn't need, walked over to the table, and sat down without waiting to be asked.

"Thank you for agreeing to see me on such short notice," I said, looking directly at Janssen. I could sense Justine Tan bristle at the snub, but I decided to ignore it.

"We are anxious to find out," said Dr. Tan, clearly deciding not to ignore anything, "what information you felt was so urgent that you had to come to see us immediately and in person to share with us."

It took me a second to overcome the pleasant urge to get into a petty little spat with Dr. Tan, but I knew I had more important things to do.

"Were either of you aware," I said, feeling expansive in my inclusiveness, "that Ada Danforth at one time in her life became pregnant, carried the baby to full term, and delivered it?"

"*What?*" said Dr. Tan, staring lethal daggers at Janssen.

"Oh, for God's sake, Justine, please!" said Janssen loudly and emphatically, but like all men, looking at least a little guilty in the face of a withering accusation, no matter how misdirected, from an angry woman.

"This is what I've been trying to tell you, Paul," said Dr. Tan, making a move to get up from the table, but I knew she wouldn't; she couldn't walk away from her own little triumph.

"I don't want to hear about it," I said. "I just want to know: Were either of you aware of Ada Danforth's pregnancy?"

"No!" said Janssen. "And I question the veracity of your statement. What rumor mill produced that tasty little tidbit for you?"

"I received the news directly from Dr. Patricia Heath of the medical examiner's office," I said. "And I accept it as a fact." That shut them both up for a second.

"Look," said Dr. Tan. "Ada Danforth was a petite woman, and sometimes women with her body type barely show their pregnancies."

"And she almost always wore a lab coat when she was on campus," added Janssen, "so I guess it's theoretically possible that she could have concealed a pregnancy. But I have to tell you, Mr. Hunter, I really doubt it. I was around Ada Danforth on almost a daily basis, and I have two children of my own from a previous marriage. I mean, I've been in close quarters with a pregnant woman in my life. I think I would have noticed something."

"How often did she take sabbaticals?" I asked.

"Never," said Janssen. "And she never took vacations, either, even though I urged her to do so." Dr. Tan shot him a look, but Janssen shot one right back and she looked away.

"Did she ever say why?" I said.

"She just said that the academic world was her life, and she wouldn't have a clue what to do with a vacation. She said the whole concept eluded her."

"Sure doesn't sound like someone who would carry on a surreptitious affair and have a secret child," I said.

"She could have been raped, you know," said Tan. "Sexual violence is a fact of life, even in the academic world."

"And she also could have had the baby before she ever arrived at OCCC," said Janssen. "Remember, she was already in her twenties when she started here."

"That," I said, "is a very good point. She was a teenager thrown into a world of much older men who possessed a great deal of power and prestige, both at Cornell and the Fermi Labs. She might as well have been walking around with a bullseye on her back."

"You have no idea how right you are," said Dr. Tan. I looked at her, but she was staring off in the distance beyond the windows of the cafeteria. She turned and looked at me, probably feeling my eyes on her, and the look in her eyes told me more than I wanted to know about Justine Tan.

"Have you checked the records at the local hospitals?" said Janssen.

"There hasn't been any time for that yet," I said, "and now that we've had this conversation, I don't know what good it would do. If she had the baby since she arrived here she clearly wanted to keep it secret, and she would have gone somewhere else to have the baby. And I'm convincing myself more by the minute that it's very probable that she had the baby before she ever got here in any event."

"Okay, then," said Dr. Tan, still clearly stricken by the memories that our conversation had dredged up. "Please excuse me, but I have to prepare for my next class." She stood up, gave Janssen and me each a nod, and left.

Janssen looked after her, and gave an almost imperceptible shake of his head. "I should probably get going myself," he said.

"Dr. Janssen," I said, "I have a couple more questions for you, if you don't mind."

He gave me a wary look, but said, "Sure."

"Remember how you were telling me that scientists have observed subatomic particles being in two places at the same time?" I felt like an imposter just saying "subatomic particle."

"Yes?"

"Is it possible that people could do the same thing?"

I could tell by the look on his face that Janssen wanted to know why I was asking such a question, but he didn't pursue it.

"Despite all of the philosophical fantasizing that I told you about in our previous discussion, the consensus scientific answer to that question is emphatically 'no.' The physical properties of small particles do not apply to larger objects."

"Is everybody sure about that?"

"Everybody is very sure about that. I guess I have to ask you, Mr. Hunter, why are you asking?"

Now it was my turn to hesitate, but not for long. I might not have the opportunity to have this discussion again. So I told him Joe Danforth's strange story about his sister seemingly being in two places in his parents' house at the same time. Janssen smiled before he replied.

"Mr. Hunter, I guarantee you that I could walk into the local grocery store and come out with three popular magazines that all contain similar stories."

"I'm sure you could," I said, "but most of those stories are pure fabrications. Joe Danforth was sitting across from me, and he was dead serious when he told me his story."

"I'm sure he was serious," said Janssen, "and I'm sure he was sincere, and I'm sure that he believed his story. But look, Matt, I don't have to tell you this, because you probably see it in your line of work almost every day: What people think they saw is quite often not what actually happened. Eyewitness testimony is, ironically, the least trustworthy evidence that police gather at crime scenes, right?"

He was right. More and more, with the advent of DNA evidence, people who have languished in jail, sometimes for decades, convicted of crimes based on eyewitness testimony, are being exonerated. In most cases, the eyewitnesses weren't lying; they remained utterly convinced of what they saw, but the DNA evidence said otherwise. It's a strange phenomenon, but it's true: Once people become convinced that they saw something - sometimes at the suggestion of an unscrupulous prosecutor, or sometimes just because their eyes played a trick on them - that memory becomes embedded in their minds as real, and they will never be convinced that it wasn't.

"Yes," I said, "you're right."

"Quantum physics is all about tiny particles, Matt. The things we observe at the subatomic level simply don't apply to the world in which we live our everyday lives."

"I understand," I said.

"But, Matt —"

"What?"

"I'm only going to say this because it might be relevant to your criminal investigation. But I just hesitate."

"Hesitate about what, Dr. Janssen?"

"Look, I don't want to say anything that would tarnish Ada Danforth's memory, that's all."

"Dr. Janssen, whatever it is you want to tell me, I guarantee you it won't go any further than necessary to investigate Ada's murder."

"Okay," said Janssen. He hesitated a few seconds longer, but I could tell by the look on his face that he'd decided to talk to me. "I just think you ought to know that I am pretty sure that what Ada Danforth was studying at the end of her life was precisely what you just brought up."

"What do you mean?"

"I can't be sure, Matt, because she never came out and told me anything directly, but she dropped enough crumbs to lead me to believe that she was about to turn the scientific world on its head by presenting evidence that the physics of small particles can also apply to the world of larger bodies."

"Are you telling me that Joe Danforth might be telling the truth?"

"I'm saying that if Ada Danforth were alive, she might be telling you that."

"And what about you, Dr. Janssen, what do *you* think?"

"I don't know, Matt. All I *do* know is that when I was with Ada Danforth, anything seemed possible. It was like I was being drawn by some mystical magnetic field into a place that I never wanted to leave."

"Were you in love with Ada, Dr. Janssen?"

Janssen picked up his empty coffee cup and stared into it for long seconds before he placed it back on the table. "God," he said, staring at the cup, "this is the same conversation that I can never escape with Justine." He looked up and his eyes met mine. "No, Matt, I was not in love with Ada Danforth. What I was in love with was the idea of her. I loved how I felt when I was around her. I loved having her fabulous mind take me to places that my own pathetic mind couldn't even begin to fathom. I loved the beauty that her mind showed me. But no, I was not 'in love' with Ada Danforth." He actually made air quotes.

"That's a pretty tough story to sell to a suspicious woman, isn't it?"

"You have no idea."

"Are you in love with Dr. Tan?" It was none of my business, but something told me that he might just want to say it out loud, even to a relative stranger like me.

"Yes," he replied, "yes I am. For all the good it does me."

"Don't give up," I said. "I didn't, and all I can tell you is that it was worth it." Matt Hunter, P.I., J.D., lovelorn advice columnist.

"Thanks," said Janssen, giving me a grim smile.

We both stood up from the table at the same time. I shook his hand. "I'll stay in touch," I said.

"I'd appreciate that," he replied.

Janssen headed back to his warm office while I left the cafeteria to make the cold walk back to my car, but I was too distracted to notice the chill.

*   *   *   *   *   *

It was getting close to lunchtime when I got back to town, so I went across the street to Sally's to pick up a sandwich before I went back to the office. The pancakes and sausage from breakfast were still sitting a little heavily on my stomach, so I stuck with a smoked turkey and Swiss on rye, mustard only, a Diet Coke, and no chips.

"I wish I had your discipline, Mr. Hunter," said Sally's daughter, Clara, as she handed me my order, giving me one of her fetching smiles. Clara had gotten married in the past year to a nice kid from Beacon who worked as a welder for a local construction company, and Clara was already obviously pregnant, even though I knew she wasn't due for another six months. "These days, everything looks good to me."

"You're eating for two now, Clara," I said, smiling back. "And you look wonderful. How are you feeling?"

"I feel terrific, thanks. I heard all these stories about morning sickness and everything, but I seem to have dodged all that, knock wood." She rapped her knuckles on the counter, even though it was Formica, and so did I. It's the thought that counts.

"Whad'ya think eh?" said Sally, looking up from a slicer where he'd been slicing up some mortadella, beaming. What I was thinking was that I should've gotten the mortadella.

"She's looking fabulous, granddad," I said.

"Yeah, she is," said Sally, his eyes moistening at the sound of the word. Sally was only a few years older than I was, and my two kids were already approaching their twenties. Yikes.

I said goodbye to both of them, and then ran back across the street to my office, thinking of Ada Danforth and her sadly mysterious pregnancy. I decided that all pregnancies should be like Clara's.

"Hello, stranger. What have you got there?" said Linda Morris, looking hungrily at the bag I held in my hand as I walked by her desk. Linda was prematurely gray and in her mid-fifties, but she didn't look it, and her cheerful personality was a welcome counterpoint to the dour moods that Harvey Golub and I too often brought to work with us in the morning.

"It's just turkey on rye," I said. "Sorry, Linda, I should have called ahead and asked you if you wanted anything."

"No big deal," she said. "I'll be wanting some fresh air in a little while anyway." I figured she was being polite, because no one wants fresh air when the weather outside was that cold, but I let it go.

"Anything going on?" I said.

"I just left a foot-deep stack of mail in your inbox, and you have eleven messages on your phone. Here," she said, handing me a piece of paper, "I made a list of them for you. I highlighted the ones that sounded important." I didn't know what I'd do without Linda. I saw Harvey Golub sitting in his office as I walked down the hall, but he was with a client, so I just gave him a quick wave before opening the door to my own office and walking in.

Linda hadn't been exaggerating. The pile in my inbox stared at me like a disappointed mother as I sat down behind my desk. I was going to have to put Ada Danforth out of my mind for at least a little while and attend to the rest of my business. I put the sandwich and the Coke on the credenza behind my desk and was pulling off my coat when I saw the single sheet of paper sitting on my desktop. I dropped my coat on the chair opposite my desk and picked it up. It didn't take me long to realize that lunch and the inbox were both going to have to wait. I picked up the sandwich and the drink and walked back down the hall to Linda's desk.

"Linda, did you put that sheet of paper on my desk?"

"What sheet of paper? Your desktop was clear when I dropped off your mail."

"When did you drop it off?"

"I told you, just a few minutes ago. Maybe twenty minutes."

"Okay," I said. "Look, could you go through my mail and sort out the urgent stuff, and call back the callers that you highlighted for me and tell them I'll get back to them as soon as possible?"

"Sure," said Linda. "What's up?"

"I'll have to explain that later," I said. I held up the sandwich bag and the drink. "You want this? I don't have time for it right now."

"Sure," said Linda.

"Good," I said, handing her the food.

I went back to my office, put my coat back on, and picked up the sheet of paper, the one that said simply, *"Find my child and you will find my killer."* I folded it, put it in my jacket pocket and headed back down the hallway. I said a quick goodbye to Linda and started down the stairs.

"What, no mayo?" I heard the voice behind me say. No good deed goes unpunished.

CHAPTER TWELVE

"**L**OOK," I said, "I'm not trying to convince you of anything, but I don't think you would have wanted me to keep this from you, right?" The three faces staring back at me were impassive, but one was angry, the other two just puzzled.

Chief Eddie Shepherd was the angry one, and Detective Steven Goldfarb and Officer Beth Gardner were the puzzled ones. We were sitting in Eddie's office at police headquarters, drinking sodas and eating snacks out of the vending machines in the lobby. I should have brought my sandwich.

Beth had already given Chief Eddie Shepherd and Detective Goldfarb a complete rundown on our discussion with Joe Danforth, the call from Dr. Heath, and her interview with Jeremy Carter by the time I got there, which made things easier, but not by much.

"He's got a point, Chief," said Goldfarb. "It's evidence, no matter where it came from, and evidence is something we don't have a lot of right now."

"But what good does it do us?" said Chief Shepherd. "For all we know, this is some prank to throw us off the real track, whatever that is."

"It might very well be," I said, "but that doesn't mean we shouldn't think it through."

"Okay, Perry," said Shepherd, "think it through for us."

"Actually," I said, "I'd be Paul Drake." I knew I was going to regret this, but I couldn't help myself. Eddie Shepherd and I had been doing this dance since we were playing Pee Wee football when we were ten.

"What the hell are you talking about?" said Eddie.

"Well, assuming you were referring to Perry Mason when you said 'Perry,' I'd be Paul Drake, since Perry Mason was a defense attorney and Paul Drake was his private investigator, you know, like me."

Eddie's face reddened, but he was never really good with a snappy retort, which left it up to me to clean up my own mess.

"Oh come on, Eddie, I was only kidding, you know that," I said. I was helped by the fact that he clearly didn't want to escalate an awkward situation in front of Beth.

"Okay, okay," he said, the angry flush on his face already beginning to fade. "Just get on with it, okay?"

"The Chief's right, Matt," said Goldfarb. "We don't have all day." It was a badly needed show of support for his boss, and I was glad he said it.

"So let's break this down," I said. "I guess the first thing we should do is take it literally, that we should take it to mean that Ada's child killed her. Let's not think about how it got on my desk, let's just think about the message."

"Okay," said Goldfarb, "so why should we believe the message?"

"First of all, I'm guessing that Ada's child is probably somewhere between eighteen and twenty years old by now."

"How are you guessing that?" said Shepherd.

"Because I think that Dr. Janssen and Dr. Tan are probably right when they say they would have noticed if Ada had been pregnant while she'd been teaching at OCCC. I know it's possible that they wouldn't have, but right now I'm going with what I think is the most probable scenario."

"Okay," said Beth, "but what does his, or her, age have to do with it?"

"I'm thinking that this is about the time when he'd start having angry feelings about his mother deserting him. I mean, even if I assume that the natural father kept custody of the child and eventually married; and even if I assume the step-mother was loving and kind, my experience tells me that adopted children, at least most of them, go through a phase where they feel anger."

"Angry about what?" said Beth.

"That they were rejected, that they just didn't measure up, that they weren't good enough, especially when the rejection comes from the mother."

"But what if the father just told the child that his birth mother died?" said Goldfarb.

"You realize," said Beth, "that we're all of a sudden starting to refer to this child as 'him.'"

"You're right, Beth," I said. "I shouldn't do that." I was probably just picking a personal pronoun and sticking with it for convenience' sake, but unconsciously I might have decided that this was a crime committed by a man. Either way, it was something I had to be careful of. "But anyway, even if the child was told that his or her mother died, this is the age of the Internet. By the time the child was in his or her teens, he or she would be able to find out the truth."

"Let's just stick with 'he,'" said Shepherd. "We all know what you mean."

"Right," I said.

"The only problem is," said Goldfarb, "this doesn't feel like a murder committed by an angry teenager."

"What do you mean?" said Beth.

"I mean it was too well-planned, and too perfectly executed," said Goldfarb. "We didn't find a single scrap of physical evidence at the scene of the crime. Do you know how rare that is?"

"You're right, Steve," I said. "So let's put that theory aside for a minute, and think of other ways to read the note."

"The note seemed pretty straightforward to me," said Eddie.

"You're right, Eddie, it was," I said. I had to say it. "But remember, the note didn't say, '*My child is my killer,*' even though it would have been easy to say that. It just said that if we find the child, we'll find the killer."

"So, what are you saying?" said Beth, "that it could have been the child's father? But why didn't she just say that if that's what she meant?"

"Because it could mean a lot of other things," I said. "Maybe all it means is that once we know who her child is, we will understand why she was murdered and who did it."

"Or, we can believe that it's just is one big joke that somebody's playing on us to distract us from the real murderer and make us look like a bunch of fools in the meantime," said Eddie.

"I don't discount that, Eddie," I said, "I really don't. All I'm saying is that we have to look at this from all the angles. That's all."

"But we can't forget that we already have suspects," said Beth.

"You're right, Beth," I said. "So why don't you tell me who you suspect."

"Well, first, I suspect Ada's brother, Joseph."

"Why?"

"Because he was just so angry, that's why. And who could blame him? He's right: Ada messed up his parents' lives, and she messed up his life. People have killed for less. And on top of that, he's an electrical contractor."

"What does that have to do with anything?" said Chief Shepherd.

"I'm just thinking," said Beth, "that he knows how buildings are constructed. If anyone could figure out a way to get in and out of Matt's building and leave those notes without being detected, it would be Joe Danforth, that's all."

"You're right, Beth," said Eddie. "I'm sorry, that's good thinking." Eddie isn't famous for his modesty, and that surprised me. Eddie should probably have more women working for him.

"I agree," I said. "Who else?"

"Jeremy Carter. He can't control his jealousy, and he can't control his temper. I think he needs to stay on our list."

"And that's a toxic brew in a man," I said. "But I still can't make this feel like a murder that was committed in a fit of temper, and that's how Jeremy is. And don't forget that discussion we had about Jeremy's pattern of violence being against other men, not women."

"I don't disagree, Matt," said Beth, "but I just don't think we should count him out. He's really smart, and as far as we know, he could've been planning this murder since that episode with Ada and Kevin at the Latitude."

"And speaking of Kevin Waldron, what about him?" said Goldfarb.

"No," said Beth.

"Why not?"

"Because Kevin Waldron is just a harmless dweeb. Annoying for sure, but not a killer."

"People can fool you," replied Goldfarb.

"I just don't think they can fool me that much, sir."

"Probably not," said Goldfarb, smiling at Beth. "But let's not discount him completely, okay?"

"Okay, sir," said Beth, smiling back.

"Who else, Beth?" I said.

"Well, I guess we ought to consider Paul Janssen and Justine Tan."

"Why don't you tell me why," I said. I was beginning to like the way Beth Gardner thought, and I was beginning to understand why Steve Goldfarb had decided that she was the pick of the rookie litter. Somewhere along the line she had packed a lot of maturity into a short life. Someone else could issue the parking tickets.

"Well, from what you've told us, Ada Danforth seems to have pushed all of Dr. Janssen's buttons, no matter what he says."

"You're not buying the 'I was in love with the idea of her' tale?"

"Not for a second. He was infatuated with her, even obsessed with her, regardless of what he felt for Justine Tan. I think his feelings for Dr. Tan are genuine, and they're more rational and mature than his feelings for Ada Danforth, but Ada kept on getting in the way of those feelings."

"And Dr. Tan?" I said.

"Justine Tan is tougher because we know so little about her."

"What would you like to know about her?"

"I'd like to know if she's ever been married before, if she ever had a family. And I'd really like to know more about what she hinted to you about possibly being sexually abused in some way when she was a graduate student – or at least at some point in her life – which may or may not have damaged her academic career, even though in the end, I guess it doesn't really matter all that much."

"What do you mean?"

"Well, she pretty much is who she is, right? She's a woman in her fifties, maybe sixties, whose best academic years are behind her, and who probably looked at Paul Janssen as her last chance to escape the loneliness of her life."

"And you think she was lonely enough to kill Ada Danforth?"

"I think people have killed for less, sir."

"Yes," I said, "yes, they have. And on top of that, Justine Tan has all the brains in the world. She could easily have planned and carried out all of this."

"And what do you think about Paul Drake here's cockeyed theories about his cockeyed letters?" said Chief Shepherd. I didn't respond. He deserved a shot back at me, and I didn't want to interrupt the flow of the discussion. I also wanted to see how Beth would handle it.

"I don't think anything about them right now, sir," she replied after only a brief hesitation. "Right now, they're just a data point. My mom always taught me not to be afraid to admit that you don't know something; and right now I don't know what to make of the letters, just like I don't know what to make of Joe Danforth's story about seeing his sister in two places at the same time."

"You actually believe that story?" said Shepherd.

"I believe that he believed it," said Beth. "That's all I can say." Eddie didn't have a comeback for that, and he sat back silently in his chair.

"Beth?" I said.

"Yes?" she said, locking her eyes on me, knowing what I was going to ask.

"What about Ada's parents?"

"Sir," she said, not breaking eye contact, "I come from a loving family. I was raised by loving parents. I simply cannot understand how a parent would murder his, or her, own child, for any reason."

"But it's happened, Beth," I said, "more often than either you or I would like to believe."

"I understand that, sir," she replied. "Maybe I'm just too young to think about that."

"Fair enough," I said.

"Matt?" said Detective Goldfarb.

"What?"

"What do you think?"

"I think that Vincent Danforth is a hopeless drunk who at this point in his life is physically and mentally incapable of planning and executing anything more complicated than a visit to the bathroom, never mind a near perfect murder."

"And what about Barbara Danforth, Matt?"

What was I supposed to say? I hadn't told anyone but Doreen about the details of my encounter with Barbara Danforth, not out of any sense of shame or guilt on my own part, but because I simply couldn't force myself to humiliate the woman like that unless it became absolutely necessary. But I had to say something, and I had to be honest.

"If either one of them could have done it, it would have been Barbara. I know it looks on the surface like they've both bought into the Good Ship Lollipop routine, but my sense is that Barbara only goes along out of loyalty to, and maybe pity for, her husband. She actually drinks very little, and the household would collapse without her. She is also intelligent, observant, and physically fit. But at the end of the day, I can't make myself believe that she'd murder her daughter."

"But why not?" said Goldfarb. "You just convinced me that she *could* have done it."

"Because I think she sees her and her husband's situation as lot more complicated than just having a controversial daughter. And I know that she has good reason to be angry at Ada because of the way her son turned out, but let's face it: Joe Danforth may be angry and troubled, but he's smart, highly skilled, and in most ways leads a successful life. I don't see much of a motive for murder there, at least on Barbara's part."

"Okay, then," said Chief Shepherd, "where do we go from here?"

Goldfarb, Beth, and I stared at each other briefly, but in the end Steve Goldfarb and Eddie Shepherd had put me in charge of the investigation, so I spoke up.

"I think Joe Danforth and Jeremy Carter are the two most likely suspects that we have so far, and I think we also need to dig more into Justine Tan. She just keeps on worming herself back into my mind the more I think about this."

"Do you think that she's a more likely suspect than Joe Danforth or Jeremey Carter?" said Goldfarb, sounding a little incredulous.

"My problem with both Carter and Joe Danforth," I said, "is that they're both so damned angry, and I don't know whether anyone that angry could have planned and executed such a perfect murder. I'm sorry; I know I'm contradicting myself, but I'm just thinking out loud."

"That's okay," said Goldfarb. "That's what we're here for. But then what about Dr. Janssen?" said Goldfarb. "Why isn't he on your list? He's a man, but he's not young and impulsive; and he has the oldest motive in the world."

"What's that?" said Beth.

"Being rejected by a woman he's in love with," said Goldfarb.

"You're right, Steve," I said. "We can't forget about him."

"But," said Beth, "Justine is angry, too. Maybe just as angry as the rest of them."

"You're right," I said. "And she's also not a young man. Joe Danforth and Jeremy Carter are both hot-headed young men who would have acted on impulse, and that crime scene didn't look like the work of an angry, impulsive young man."

"But Justine Tan would have been careful and methodical," said Beth.

"I can't disagree," I said.

"Now it sounds like you're moving away from Jeremy Carter and Joe Danforth," said Chief Shepherd.

"I'm not eliminating them at all," I said, "but you guys are convincing me that perhaps they should be moving down on my list."

"Do you think Dr. Tan also might have been behind those letters?" said Goldfarb.

That one made me sit up; it hadn't even crossed my mind. And I had to admit, at least to myself if to no one else, that the reason I hadn't thought of it was because in my heart of hearts I believed that Ada Danforth had cracked some little piece of God's code, and had written those letters and put them on my desk herself. But there was no way I was going to say that out loud.

"I don't know," was all I said.

CHAPTER THIRTEEN

"I THINK I'LL JUST HAVE THE PHO," said Justine Tan, pronouncing it "fuh," and handing her menu back to the waiter. I had tried to convince her to try one of Richie Glazier's steak sandwiches, along with his unbeatable onion rings, but she wasn't having it. Pho was the only Asian dish that Richie offered on his menu, but as with everything else about him, anything he did he did well or not at all, and I knew that the Pho was one of his most popular menu offerings. It was the first time I'd seen Dr. Tan out of her lab coat. She'd also let her silver-streaked hair down from the tight bun that she kept it in at school, and I detected subtle signs of makeup. She wore snug-fitting jeans and a silk blouse with a floral pattern. Her slender body was wiry and looked strong, but also completely feminine. The effect was startling, leaving me to conclude that Paul Janssen was an idiot.

When I'd contacted Dr. Tan the previous evening and asked her to meet me for the lunch the following day, she'd agreed without hesitation despite the short notice; but she'd said that she didn't want to meet on the OCCC campus, and she didn't want to meet me in Middletown. She also didn't have Dr. Janssen in tow, so I concluded that she wanted to make sure that this meeting would be held in complete privacy.

"I'll have the steak sandwich and onion rings," I said to the waiter, handing him my menu. I tend to stick with what works.

"And I'll have the fish taco," said Beth Gardner. I'd asked her to wear civilian clothes instead of her uniform, and I couldn't help noticing that she'd drawn looks when she walked into the restaurant. I'd asked her to come along because I wanted to have a second pair of ears to hear everything Justine Tan had to say, and also because I wanted Beth to get a sense of the woman.

"Well, aren't we eclectic," I said, trying for a little levity.

"Yes, aren't we," said Justine, staring back at me, expressionless. So much for levity.

"I'd like to thank you for agreeing to see us, Dr. Tan," I said.

"I believe you've already said that at least once," said Dr. Tan, "so let's dispense with the chitchat, shall we? We all know that the reason you're here is because you suspect me of murdering Ada Danforth, and I know that I'm here to clear my name. I'm a private woman, Mr. Hunter, Ms. —"

"Gardner," said Beth.

"Yes," said Justine, "Gardner. You look young enough to be one of my students, Ms. Gardner. Are you here on some kind of training program?"

"She is a full-fledged police officer with the Town of Devon-on-Hudson Police," I said, "and she is here at my request. I hope you don't mind."

"Oh," said Justine, "I don't mind at all, and I'm sorry if I gave you that impression. As I was about to say, I am a private woman, but I am willing to answer any questions that you may have of me, no matter how personal, if that is what is necessary to clear my name."

"Thank you, Dr. Tan," I said.

"Stop thanking me."

"You're right," I said, "so let me start off by asking the obvious question: Where were you on the night that Ada Danforth was murdered?"

"I have no alibi, and I have no corroborating witnesses, Mr. Hunter. I was home alone the entire night, and I communicated with no one. I was grading lab practicals, which is tedious, time-consuming work, and I devoted the entire evening to it. And to answer your next question, I live in the next town over, Cornwall, which also borders on the Hudson River. My home is only a few miles from Dr. Danforth's home, so I could have gotten over there, murdered her, and been back in my own home in plenty of time to complete grading my exams."

"Then Dr. Tan?" I said.

"Yes?"

"Why did you agree to meet us? You just said that you came here to clear your name, but now you just told us that you can't do that. I don't understand."

We were interrupted as the waiter came over with our meals. Dr. Tan's pho, along with a side plate of pungent condiments, diced scallions, and peppers, looked and smelled delectable, and I made a mental note to myself to try it sometime. Beth's taco also looked delicious, as did my reliably tasty steak sandwich and onion rings. Richie's food had a way of stalling conversation, and we all took a few minutes to dig in to our meals.

"Now," said Dr. Tan, putting down her chopsticks and spoon, "I believe you wanted me to tell you why I agreed to see you - and why I thought I could clear my name – when I've already told you that I have no alibi."

"I guess that about sums it up," I said, putting my plate aside even though there were still a couple of onion rings on it, a tribute to my will of iron. Beth, who ate her food the way all young people do, had already polished off her taco, and she, too, pushed her plate to the side. She cast a hungry glance at my leftover onion rings. I gave her a quick nod, and they disappeared.

"Please tell me if I'm wrong, Mr. Hunter, but it is my assumption that you suspect me of killing Dr. Danforth out of jealousy, that I was in love with Paul Janssen, and I felt that Ada had robbed me of his affections. And, of course, being a woman of a certain age, I had few options to exercise, if any."

"Okay," I said, deciding not to beat around the bush, "let's go with that."

"Good," said Dr. Tan, "so let me get straight to the point: Yes, I am in love with Paul Janssen, and yes, I felt as though I had lost him to Ada Danforth."

"How did you feel about that?" I said. I hate it when people ask me that question, but I wanted to know.

"I felt angry. I felt betrayed. I felt humiliated. Shall I go on?"

"I think I get the point," I said. "But who were you angry with? And who did you feel betrayed you?"

"Paul, of course."

"So you didn't feel that Ada deliberately tried to take Dr. Janssen from you?"

"Of course not. As a matter of fact, I don't think Ada reciprocated any of Paul's feelings."

"Why not?"

"First of all, let's keep the time sequence in mind. When I arrived here five years ago, Ada Danforth was about thirty, and Paul was nearing sixty. I was fifty-five. I don't think anyone but Paul thought a relationship between two people with that kind of a difference in age was appropriate."

"Okay, let's take a step back, Dr. Tan," I said. "I thought that you and Dr. Janssen had some kind of a relationship that went beyond mere friendship, that you perhaps had some kind of an understanding."

"You are correct, Mr. Hunter. Paul and I met at the first faculty meeting I attended after I arrived here. Paul went out of his way to seek me out, and shortly after that we began to date."

"Don't answer this if you don't want to, but did you and Dr. Janssen have a, uh, romantic relationship?"

"If you are asking if we were sexually intimate, the answer is 'yes.'"

"Then I'm confused. When exactly was it that you began to feel that Dr. Janssen was infatuated with Ada? I mean, she'd been here for almost ten years before you arrived. You'd think if he was in love with her, it would have been apparent by then."

"You'd think, but that's not the way it was. All I saw between them when I first arrived here was a friendship based on professional respect and, at least for Paul, professional admiration. I mean, who wouldn't admire Ada Danforth? No one had ever seen the likes of her around here before, that's for sure. Of course, we all knew about the controversies, but we didn't care about that. All we knew was that we had a world-class physicist at our little school, and we'd leave the rest of the nonsense to the folks at places like the Fermi Labs to squabble over."

"Did you like her?"

"To the extent that I had any contact with her, yes, I did. Our paths didn't cross often, but when they did, all I saw was a quiet, modest, incredibly shy young woman, walking around with that amazing mind locked inside her head."

"You said, 'to the extent that you had any contact with her.' Does that mean that you avoided her, or that she avoided you?"

"Not at all, Mr. Hunter. It's just that we inhabited two different worlds, and our paths didn't cross that often."

"But you taught at the same school, and it's not that big. And you even belonged to the same department - STEM – right?"

"Yes, that's all correct, but when I said we inhabited two different worlds that's not what I meant."

"Help me, here, Dr. Tan."

"I am a biologist, Mr. Hunter. I care about things that breathe. I care about things that rot, and smell, and make noises; things that are born, and that die. The stars are someone else's concern. So we had very little in common intellectually. But it was even more than that."

"In what way?" I said, but I could already feel what was coming, and I started to feel goosebumps. I looked over at Beth, and I could tell she was feeling the same way.

"Sometimes," said Dr. Tan, staring down at her hands, "it felt like we were literally inhabiting two different worlds. At faculty meetings I'd sometimes look across the table at her, and I'd get this frightening feeling that she wasn't really there, that I was only looking at a hologram of her that was put in place so that she could go elsewhere. I'm a scientist, Mr. Hunter, and it embarrasses me to say that, but that was how I felt."

"You're not the first person to say that," I said, "if that makes you feel any better."

"It probably doesn't," she replied.

"Have you talked to Dr. Janssen about that?" I said.

"I brought it up once, in passing," said Dr. Tan, "but as you know, Ada Danforth was a subject we tried to avoid."

"What did he say?"

"He basically dismissed it. He said that sometimes Ada's mind was so inwardly focused that she really wasn't there, for all practical purposes, and that was probably what I was sensing."

"But you didn't buy that."

"No, I didn't. But I also didn't want to have yet another extended conversation about Ada Danforth with Paul, so I just dropped it."

I could sense Beth's discomfort as she sat beside me, so I decided to get the conversation back on track. The waiter helped by coming over and asking us if we wanted dessert or coffee. We all ordered coffee, but passed on the dessert.

"So, when was it exactly that you began to feel that Dr. Janssen was starting to feel something more than friendship for Ada?" I said, once the waiter left to get our coffee.

"It's hard to say," said Justine. There was a quick interruption as the waiter came back with our coffees, which gave her a chance to gather her thoughts. "I'd say it was about a year ago at this time. I remember that it was the Holiday season, and I was hoping that we might perhaps be able to announce our engagement. But instead, I began to feel Paul start to pull away. At first, I thought nothing of it. I knew that his first marriage had ended disastrously after almost twenty-five years, and that he'd been devastated. I thought that he was just getting a case of cold feet, and the best thing that I could do was to give him a little space to get past all that."

"Did you talk to him about it?" I said.

"No, not at first. I decided that if I gave him the breathing room he needed, he'd eventually come back to me. But then the holidays came and went, and nothing happened."

"Did you try to talk to him then?"

"No, I didn't, because that was when I realized that the real problem I was confronting was that he was spending more time with Ada Danforth than with me."

"Did you bring it up with him?" I said.

"Not at first," said Dr. Tan, taking a sip of her coffee. "Remember, I'm a scientist, so I decided to approach it that way."

"So what did you do?"

"I did what any scientist would do: I observed; I collected data, and then I formulated my hypothesis."

"Which was?"

"Which was that Paul was infatuated with Ada, but that not only was Ada not infatuated with him; she was completely unaware of his feelings."

"And you were pretty sure of that?"

"Oh, yes," said Dr. Tan. "By that time, from what I could tell, Ada Danforth was spending almost all her time inside her own head. She was the quintessential absent-minded professor, oblivious to what was going on around her."

"Was Dr. Janssen aware of that as well?" I said.

"Yes, he was. I think most of the faculty in the STEM department were aware of it."

"Did that diminish his infatuation with her?"

"No. If anything, it just magnified it. He followed her around like a puppy follows its master. It was pathetic, and to make it worse, everyone noticed it."

"That must have been humiliating for you," said Beth, breaking her silence.

"Yes," said Justine, turning her gaze to Beth. "Yes, it was."

"So, did you finally confront him?" said Beth.

"Yes, I did."

"When?" said Beth.

"It was early this past spring. I told Paul that I'd finally had enough, that he had to realize the humiliation that I was suffering. I told him that we would have to end our relationship if he couldn't change his behavior."

"What did he say?"

"He begged me to stay with him. He said that I didn't understand. He insisted that he wasn't in love with Ada. He said that it was his belief that Ada was preparing to announce to the world the most astonishing development in physics, maybe in all human knowledge, since Isaac Newton, Albert Einstein, and Nils Bohr all rolled up together, and that she was doing it all inside her own mind – no labs, no computers, no nothing. He said that being able to witness that process was what had him so enthralled, not Ada personally."

"Did you believe him?" I said.

"What did it matter?" said Dr. Tan. "His behavior was the same, no matter what his explanation for it was, and it was his behavior that was humiliating me."

"I understand, but did you believe him?"

Justine Tan stared at me, and then gazed around the restaurant for long seconds, as if she were reminding herself of where she was, and then back at me.

"Yes," she finally said. "I guess I did."

*　*　*　*　*　*

"She still could have done it, you know."

"I know," I said, looking over at Beth in the passenger seat. I think she liked riding in my Accord.

"I mean," said Beth, "she did exactly what I would have done in the same circumstances: She openly admitted that she didn't have an alibi, and that she had a motive for murdering Dr. Danforth. The honesty is compelling."

"You're right," I said. "It gives her the halo of innocence."

"'Halo of innocence', huh?" said Beth, looking over at me with a smile of her face.

"What?"

"Nothing," said Beth, looking straight ahead, but still smiling.

"So you still suspect her then?" I said, getting the conversation back on track.

"Like I said, I still think she could have done it."

"I could have done it, too, Beth, but that doesn't mean that I'm a suspect."

"Okay, you're right. Yes, she is still a suspect in my book. In fact, maybe I suspect her now more than I ever have."

"Just so you know," I said, "so do I."

"But what about that 'finding her child' note? Where does Justine Tan fit into that?"

We were nearing the police station where I was going to drop Beth off, and I wanted to clear the air while we were still alone. "I don't know," I said. "What do you think about that note?"

Beth folded her arms across her stomach and looked straight ahead. Her long, dark hair was tied back in a ponytail, and she looked too small and too young to be involved with any of this. She sat for a long time, and I was afraid that we'd get back to the police station before she had a chance to tell me what she thought. She was apparently thinking the same thing.

"Do you think we could stop off at McDonald's or something, some place where we can have some time?"

"I know just the place," I said.

We were passing through the village, past my office, and I made the next left-hand turn, just past Cuccina della Torino, Devon-on-Hudson's most popular, and most expensive, restaurant. Apparently, folks thought it was worth the money, because it never had less than a two-week waiting list for a reservation. I pulled into a small parking lot behind the restaurant, next to a dumpster. Beth gave me a puzzled look, a look that grew more puzzled as we got out of my car and walked over to a heavy metal door that looked like a service entrance. I knocked on the door, and waited. It took a few minutes, but soon the door opened slowly, and the visage of my brother-in-law, Anthony Fornaio, peered out. His dark, curly hair was just showing a hint of gray, as was his almost permanent five-o'clock shadow, but his face was still boyish, his smile still shy, and as always, he smelled faintly of rising dough.

"Matt," he said, giving me a warm smile and a hug, "come on in." If he had any hesitation about letting Beth in, he didn't show it. This was Anthony's private space, and I knew I was stepping out of bounds by inviting a stranger without his prior permission. Besides, Anthony's uncle, Tommassino was the organized crime boss of all of New York State north of the five boroughs of New York City, and Anthony didn't make it a habit of inviting unvetted cops into his domain. "And you must be Beth Gardner," he said, turn his warm smile to her. "Lacey's told me all about you, and you're welcome here any time."

"Thanks," said Beth. Anthony must have seen the puzzled expression on her face as she looked around the tiny space we'd entered, dominated by an ancient pizza oven, a short counter, and three small tables. A soda machine sat tucked behind the tables.

"When Matt and I were kids," he said, "this town was a lot different than it is today. It was pretty much a lower-middle-class place, and a fine dining restaurant like Cuccina della Torino wouldn't have lasted a week. So my Dad, may he rest in peace, came to this town and opened a pizzeria that he named after himself, 'Franco's.' It was where all of us hung out when we were in high school, and it's where I learned how to make a pizza. But times changed, and my Dad knew it, so after I graduated from high school he turned the pizzeria over to me, and with his blessing I hired a world-class chef and opened up Cuccina della Torino. It's a wonderful success, and I'm very proud of it, but a little part of me couldn't let go of that pizzeria. So, I carved out this little place, a place for just me and my friends, where we can still sit down and enjoy a Franco's pizza. I run the business end of Cuccina della Torino, but otherwise I leave it to the chef. Can I make you a pizza?"

"Well, we..." I began to say.

"Sure," said Beth. "Pepperoni, green peppers and anchovies, please." I should have known.

Anthony beamed. Anyone who liked anchovies on their pizza was a friend for life as far as he was concerned.

Just as Anthony went to make the pie, the back door opened with a bang. I didn't even have to turn around to know it was Lacey. I'm usually happy to see my sister, but my first thought was that her presence might get in the way of the private conversation that Beth, and I, wanted to have.

"Lacey! I'm so glad you're here!" said Beth, her eyes lighting up. I should have known that, too. Beth was rapidly forming strong bonds with the two most important women in my life, and I couldn't help but think that was a good thing.

Lacey walked over to Anthony, said, "Hi, hon," and gave him a light kiss on the cheek. They were the oddest couple I had ever known, but they were clearly smitten with each other. I'd spent a lot of time puzzling over the chemistry between them, but I'd given up. All I knew what that Anthony's presence in Lacey's life tamed her without breaking her, and Lacey brought out the passion hidden for so long inside chubby, quiet Anthony.

"Anybody mind if we add some mushrooms and sausage to this bad boy?" said Lacey.

"Fine with me," said Beth.

"Fine with me," I heard myself saying, even though I'd promised myself I wasn't going to have any.

Lacey poured herself a Coke from the soda machine and filled a glass for Beth, too. She gave me a look, but I shook my head. I was going to stick with water, dammit. We made small talk until Anthony brought the pizza over and placed it on the table.

"Thanks, hon," said Lacey, giving her husband a smile and reaching for a slice of the pizza, only slightly ahead of Beth. Lacey usually won that race hands down. I was impressed.

"Look," said Anthony, after giving her a smile in return, "I've got some business to take care of up front, so I'll leave you guys alone. If you need anything, just give me a shout."

Lacey and Beth just nodded, their mouths too full to reply. I said, "Thanks."

"*Di nenti*," said Anthony, giving me a wink as he left the room.

I didn't really have a chance to exercise my widely renowned self-control, because Lacey and Beth demolished the pizza before temptation had much of a chance to get a toehold. Lacey brought the empty tray over to the counter and said, "Do you guys need some alone time?"

"No," said Beth before I had a chance to open my mouth. "I really want you to stay for this."

"Stay for what?" said Lacey.

"Why don't you sit down," I said. "We'll explain it to you."

And so we did. I told her about finding the note in my office that Linda Morris had sworn wasn't there just moments before I'd found it, and Beth took her through our subsequent conversations with Chief Shepherd and Detective Goldfarb, and with Justine Tan.

"First of all," said Lacey when we'd finished, "I wouldn't sweat about where the note came from for now. I agree with what you said to Goldfarb and Shepherd, Matt. You should just take the note at its face value. The note is just there, no matter who put it on your desk, or how."

"But actually," said Beth, looking at Lacey, "that's what I want to talk about: where did the note come from? We're already taking it literally to see where that leads us. But I think we're making a mistake if we keep dodging the question of who wrote these notes. I think it affects how we approach the investigation. I mean, if we think someone is gaming us, I guess we approach it one way. But if we really think that Ada Danforth may have found some cracks in time, that will lead us in a different direction."

"The problem is," I said, "that there's no way for us to know, Beth, so I don't know what good it would do us to waste a lot of time trying to find out."

"I'm not talking about 'knowing' anything, Matt," said Beth. "I'm talking about what we choose to believe going forward."

"Beth," I said, "how would that affect our investigation?"

"Because if we don't believe that Ada Danforth wrote those notes, then we're going to have to spend a lot of time chasing down who did, because that person is almost definitely our killer. And we have to stop believing that there is some child out there, because that's probably all part of a huge misdirection scheme that goes all the way back to the original note. And it also affects who we think our most probable suspects are."

"How so?" I said.

"Because if someone other than Ada wrote those notes, then we are looking for a really smart person who spent the better part of a year putting this whole plot together and executing it perfectly, all for reasons we're not even close to figuring out. But if we choose to believe that Ada actually wrote the notes, then our suspect list can grow, because now we have to include people who may have committed the murder maybe not on an impulse, but who may have decided to do it pretty recently."

"You know, Beth," said Lacey, "you have a point. But I think we all have to admit that, as much fun as it is to think otherwise, it's pretty likely that someone else wrote those notes."

"I know that," said Beth. "Occam's Razor and all that."

I felt for Beth. One of the charms of youth is the willingness to embrace the improbable. It's what makes being young almost worth all the pain, confusion, and humiliation. It's what made me a Mets fan. And by making her an integral part of such an emotionally charged murder investigation at such a young age I was forcing her to question those cherished remnants of her youth. It was cruel. But being a part of this investigation was something she had wanted badly to do, so I knew that some part of her, at least, was ready to take that step. At least I hoped so.

They both turned to look at me.

"Matt?" said Lacey.

"I think Lacey's right, Beth," I said. "But I also know that no matter what we think, it's time to do something. I know that all this analysis is probably necessary, but I also know that solving a crime involves putting your feet on the pavement and chasing down clues."

"Okay," said Beth, the light in her eyes dimming only a little, "so, where do we start?"

"We start with Justine Tan."

"Why her?" said Beth.

"Because she has told us enough for us to know that there is an awful lot we don't know about her."

"Like what?" said Lacey.

"I want to know where she was born and raised. I want to know about her family. I want to know where she went to college, and where she worked and taught before she came to OCCC. I want to know if her life ever intersected with Ada Danforth's, and why, in her fifties, she wound up at Orange County Community College."

"You think it may have been a sexual assault? Or maybe an affair?" said Beth.

"What we think doesn't count for much right now," I said. "Let's dig for some facts."

"Let me get started on that," said Beth.

"Tell me if you need any help," said Lacey.

"Don't worry, I will," said Beth, looking gratefully at Lacey.

"What are you going to do, Matt?" said Lacey.

"I'm going to have another chat with Barbara Danforth."

"Do you really think she's a serious suspect?" said Beth.

"I'm not sure if she is or isn't," I said, "but I think her son is, and I think I have a better chance of getting more information about him out of her than out of him."

"I can't disagree with you about that," said Beth.

"Good," I said. "I tell you what. Why don't you guys plan to swing by my place tomorrow night. We'll order some Chinese or something, and hash over what we've learned."

"Sounds good," they said in unison.

*   *   *   *   *   *

I went back to my office to clear a little of my ever-expanding backlog, so I got home a little late.

Doreen and I had a drink and a quick dinner together, and then we both went back to work. Doreen went upstairs to her office, and I sat down on the sofa in the sitting nook in the kitchen with my laptop.

I couldn't come close to dredging up the stuff that Lacey could find on the internet, but I was getting a lot better, and in a couple of hours I was glad that I'd decided to go back and see Barbara Danforth.

*   *   *   *   *   *

CHAPTER FOURTEEN

I FIGURED that the safest bet would be for me to meet Barbara Danforth at a place other than her home. I suggested the Latitude, and she said that sounded fine. It may have been me, but I thought she sounded eager to get out of the house for any reason. I offered to pick her up, but she said, no, she had a car and she knew where the Latitude was. We agreed on one o'clock because Barbara said she was pretty sure Vince would be safely tucked away in the marital stateroom by then.

I almost didn't recognize her when she walked into the Latitude. Of course, it was the first time I'd seen her decently dressed, but it was more than that. She was wearing a pair of gray woolen slacks that hugged her still slim hips, and under her smart lambswool jacket she wore a white cotton blouse that clung to her torso in all the right places. Her silver hair shone, and her face was subtly made up. I couldn't help but notice the looks she got as she walked up to me and gave me a warm hug and a light kiss on the cheek. She noticed, too, and she was clearly relishing being ashore after an extended cruise on the Good Ship Lollipop. I doubt she ever got out for much more than grocery shopping and booze runs, and I couldn't blame her.

"Thank you so much for agreeing to see me," I said, after Richie Glazier had escorted us over to my usual quiet corner of the dining room and took our orders. Richie raised his eyebrows when I ordered the fish taco, and smiled in approval when Barbara ordered the Pho. We both ordered iced tea.

We engaged in small-talk as we ate our meals. We both needed that after the intensity of our first encounter. I told her a little bit about my former careers as a cop and a lawyer. She mostly listened in silence, except to say, "Sorry, I can see you as a policeman, but I can't see you at all as a lawyer." "Neither could anybody else," I replied, which made her laugh. It was a nice laugh. She told me about her career as a CPA. She tried to make it sound boring, but I could tell that she had enjoyed her life in the business world, and it wasn't hard to conclude that she missed it. Barbara Danforth was clearly a social creature, and she was charming in her own quiet way. I didn't know what that boded for her and Vincent's marriage, but I knew I didn't want to think about it, and I was almost relieved when the waiter cleared our table.

"Now," she said, as the waiter disappeared after bringing us each a cup of coffee, "what is it you wanted to talk to me about, Matt? Is it too much to hope that you're getting close to solving my daughter's murder?"

"I'm afraid it is," I said. "Your daughter's death is turning out to be a puzzling matter, Barbara. The police have searched her house and the surrounding area a second and a third time, and they have come up empty. It's as though no one was ever in that house except your daughter. No finger prints, no footprints, nothing out of place, no sign of a struggle, nothing."

"I hope you're not giving up, Matt," she said, and the tone of her voice made me believe that her hope was genuine.

"No, we're not, and we're not going to, Barbara. But we're going to have to solve her murder with literally no physical evidence to go on."

"And how will you do that?"

"By getting to know all of the people in Ada's life a lot better than we do right now."

"Does that mean that you still suspect one of us - me or Vincent or Joe?"

"Let's not worry about who's on our suspect list right now, Barb, because that can always change. I guess instead I'd like to ask you a few questions."

"Please, go ahead," she said, and I could hear the worry in her voice.

"Barbara, did you know that Ada had a baby?"

Barbara's face went white and lost all expression. She slowly put her coffee cup down. She stared at me for long seconds without speaking.

"That is impossible," she finally said. "Whoever told you that is lying, Matt."

"Barb, the medical examiner told me that. She found out as a result of the autopsy she performed."

"Then she is wrong," said Barb, her face still devoid of expression. "She is obviously incompetent. Have someone else redo the autopsy."

"I've done a lot of work with our medical examiner, Barb, and there is no one better. She also had her work reviewed by experts at the Columbia College of Physicians and Surgeons, and they agreed with her conclusions."

"Maybe she had a miscarriage," said Barbara.

"There was no miscarriage," I said. "There are unmistakable changes to a woman's body when she gives birth to a full-term baby." I said that with more conviction than I probably had, but my research on the internet the night before left me feeling on pretty firm ground.

"Matt," she said, after taking a few seconds to digest what I'd said, "I would have known if my daughter was pregnant. We hardly ever saw Ada, but my daughter simply would not have born a child without telling her mother. It is simply impossible that I wouldn't have known. And before you ask the next question, let me tell you that it is utterly unthinkable that Ada would have had an abortion, especially a late-term abortion that would have left her body looking like she carried a child to term and given birth, for any reason. My daughter was a devout Christian, a devout Catholic. The idea of abortion was abhorrent to her."

"People change, Barb," I said, trying to be gentle. "You told me yourself that you never really knew her all that well."

"Now you listen to me, Matthew Hunter," she said, looking straight at me. "You are correct: my daughter was in many ways a stranger to me, but if there is one thing I know, it is that she never, ever, would have had an abortion. Do you understand me?"

"Please, Barb, I'm sorry to have upset you like this. But I have to ask: If you never saw her pregnant, and if she didn't have an abortion, then how do you explain the autopsy results?"

"I can't. But what I do know is that I don't want to discuss this anymore. And if the next thing you are going to do is ask me to incriminate my son, don't bother. I told you once before, I don't believe he is capable of such a thing."

"Okay, Barb," I said, "I won't do that, and I'm so sorry that I've upset you. But I guess I still need to ask you if you have any reason to believe that Joe has any knowledge, or any suspicions, about who might have done it?"

"I wish I could tell you that, Matt," said Barb, visibly making an effort to calm herself, "but I just can't. Joe hardly ever comes over anymore. Usually when he does it's for a quick supper. His father is usually passed out for the night by then, so I have a chance to put on something decent and at least try to create the pretense that things are fairly normal. But Joe's way too smart for that, so our visits are usually pretty awkward, and we keep the conversation to chitchat. He's a good son, and he visits me more out of a sense of obligation than anything else."

"But you're his mother, Barb. You probably have a more personal knowledge of him than anyone in the world. Have you sensed any change, any change at all, in him lately?"

"I wish you would understand what I'm telling you, Matt: I've lost my son, almost as completely as I've lost Ada. And I've lost my husband. I lose sleep every night wondering what I could have done differently, what I could have done that would have changed how all our lives turned out, but it's hopeless. All I know is that I'm not sure that I ever knew Joe any more than I knew Ada." Her eyes started to fill with tears. "I am very alone, Matt. I'm sorry that I can't help you," she said, as she picked up her napkin and dabbed at her eyes.

I felt awful. I had ruined Barbara Danforth's day, a day that clearly had meant a lot to her. It wasn't my job to worry about her happiness, but I was human, and I'd gotten too much of a glimpse into her life not to feel terrible for adding to her misery.

"You're right, Barb," I said. "Thank you for being so patient with me. I really appreciate it." I was about to ask her if she might like a little more coffee when a man looking about Barb's age walked over to our table.

"Barbara? Barbara Danforth?" he said.

"Why, hello, Howard," said Barbara, a smile transforming her face. "Matt, this is Howard Barker, and old friend of ours. We went to the same church all our lives."

"Pleased to meet you," I said, feeling about as awkward as I've ever felt.

"Barb," said Howard, "I can't tell you how sorry I was to hear of your loss."

"And, oh, Howard, I haven't seen you since you lost Anne Marie. How are you holding up?"

"Oh, as well as can be expected," he said. "You know how it is."

"I'm afraid I do," said Barb. "Are you here with anyone else?"

"No," said Howard. "I was here for a quick business meeting. I was going to retire this year, but after I lost Anne Marie, I thought it would be best to keep myself busy. But the meeting ended, and the guy I was meeting with just left. I'm on my way out myself, but I didn't want to leave without saying 'hi.'"

"Are you sure you wouldn't like to sit down and have a cup of coffee before you leave?" said Barb. It was an offer that was tough to refuse for a lonely widower, and it was also an offer that told me that she'd had enough of me. I could hardly blame her.

"Look," I said, looking at Howard, "we were just here for a quick business meeting ourselves, and I was about to leave. Why don't you sit down and have a cup of coffee?" I stood up to emphasize that my offer was sincere.

"Barb?" said Howard, their lonely eyes meeting.

"That sounds wonderful, Howard," said Barb. She looked at me and said, "Thank you, Mr. Hunter. I'll be sure to stay in touch."

"That would be great," I said. "Look, I'll take care of the tab. You folks have a nice visit, okay?" They both said, "Thanks," and I turned to leave.

I didn't know what to make of that chance encounter. All I knew was that it was none of my business, and I was no one to judge.

*　*　*　*　*　*

I was driving back to my office from the Latitude when the thought struck me.

"Dammit!" I shouted, to no one but myself.

I drove past my office and headed straight for the police station, hoping someone would be there.

CHAPTER FIFTEEN

STEVE GOLDFARB and Beth Gardner were both at the station when I got there. I wanted Chief Shepherd to be there, too, but he was at the annual town Holiday luncheon hosted by the mayor, who happened to be my wife. The thought made me smile.

"So what's this all about, Matt?" said Goldfarb. "It would have been nice to have a little heads up."

"That would have required me to have a head, which apparently I don't," I replied. I'm not usually that modest, but right then modest felt about right.

"Look, it's okay," said Goldfarb. "Why don't you just tell us what's going on."

"You guys remember how we found Ada, right?"

"You mean at her house the night she was murdered?" said Beth.

"Yes, that's right," I said.

"She was lying on the floor in her office," said Beth, "wedged between her desk chair and her desk."

"And what did we conclude from that?"

"That she was sitting at her desk working on her PC when she was murdered," said Goldfarb. "What are you getting at?"

"Where is the PC now?" I said.

"It's in the evidence room, right here," said Goldfarb. "What, are you afraid we lost it?"

"Of course not, Steve."

"If your next question is, did we do a forensic examination of it," said Beth "then the answer is 'yes.' We had it examined the day after the murder, and it's been locked away in the evidence room since then."

"And what did you find?" I said.

"We found what we expected to find, I guess," said Beth. "She had no email service, no internet service, and the only software on the hard drive was an ancient version of Microsoft Office."

"Were there any documents saved in Word?" I asked.

"No," said Beth. "But remember, there was no printer either, so any documents she wrote were probably written on another machine, perhaps at school."

"Perhaps," I said. But that wasn't why I was there, so I decided to move on before we got bogged down. "How did you get into the computer?" I said.

"That was easy," said Beth. "It wasn't even password protected."

"So you just turned it on and you were in."

"Yes," said Beth. "And just so you know, the forensic exam of the hard drive was done by your sister, and she said that nothing else had ever been on the hard drive. It had never been wiped."

"Do you remember who removed the device from the house?" I said.

"Sure," said Beth. "I did."

"And did you look at the computer right there at the home?"

"No, of course not. We brought it back here to examine it. We dusted it for prints first, of course."

"And it only had Ada's prints on it?"

"Yes," said Beth. "And we dusted the entire thing, including every single key."

"And you dusted it for prints at the crime scene, right?"

"Yes, of course," said Beth. "That's just standard procedure."

"Okay, then," I said. "So you just turned the machine off and brought it back here."

"Yes," said Beth, but then she hesitated. "I mean, no. I didn't have to turn it off. It wasn't on in the first place."

"Are you sure about that?" I said.

"Yes," replied Beth. "I'm positive." She hesitated for a moment, and then she said, "Oh."

"Matt," said Detective Goldfarb, "what are you getting at?"

"The machine wasn't on, Steve. For all we know, Ada had *never* turned it on."

"Okay," he said. "So?"

"Steve, why was Ada Danforth sitting at that desk in front of her desktop computer when she was murdered when the computer wasn't even turned on?"

"Maybe she'd just sat down, and she hadn't had the chance to turn it on yet."

"What, for the first time since she bought it?"

"You can't know that, Matt," said Goldfarb.

"Steve, there were no documents on Word. She didn't have any email. She didn't have any internet. She *never* used that computer."

"So what are you saying?" said Goldfarb.

I turned to Beth. "Beth?"

"What he's saying, sir, is that Ada Danforth had no reason to be sitting at that desk, so maybe she wasn't sitting there at the time of her death."

"Then why was she there?" said Goldfarb.

"Because she was put there, sir. She was not murdered in that room."

"Do you think she was murdered somewhere else in the house?"

"No, sir, I do not," replied Beth, after only a brief hesitation.

"Why not?"

"Because if she were murdered somewhere else in the house, there would have been no reason to move her; and I think it would have been impossible to do that without leaving at least some physical evidence somewhere, and you know we didn't find anything like that."

"Are you saying that she was murdered somewhere other than her home, and then brought there and carried into her office by her murderer?"

"I'm saying," said Beth, "that we at least have to consider that possibility."

"Okay, let's assume she was," said Goldfarb. "How do you think she was brought there?" said Goldfarb.

"I think –" she said, and then she hesitated. "Okay, I think she was brought there in her own car, because we found absolutely no evidence of there being another car in the immediate vicinity, at least not recently."

"And you examined the car, right?" I said.

"I didn't examine it personally, sir, but it was examined, carefully."

"And what did you find?"

"There was no blood anywhere, but that's not surprising, because Ada's fatal wound didn't produce any blood."

"Did you examine the trunk?"

"Of course we did. Matt...sir, we've been over all this before. We examined the entire house and the immediate vicinity surrounding the house, and that included the car and the carport."

"And the only prints in the car were Ada's?"

"No, sir."

"What?" I said. I'd seen the reports, but I wanted this all repeated to me, just in case I'd missed something.

"We found the fingerprints of both her parents, but all of the mother's prints were on the passenger side of the car, and all of her father's prints were in the rear seat, behind the passenger seat. Nothing from either of them on the driver side. There is absolutely no reason for that to be suspicious. She's owned the car for years, and I would have been surprised *not* to find her parents' prints."

"And what about her brother, Joe?"

"None, sir. And, sir, we vacuumed the car – the entire car including all the seats - to check for any residual matter that might have been left by another person, and we found nothing that couldn't be traced back to either Ada or her family members."

"Okay, what about lividity?"

"Dr. Heath's report only records that blood had pooled in her body consistent with the position she was in when she was found, sir."

"You've got good recall, Officer Gardner," I said.

"I've been pretty much living this case, sir."

"It shows," I said. "But I have one more thing I need you to do. I need you to call Dr. Heath at the medical examiner's office and ask her to confirm her lividity assessment, and ask her how long Dr. Danforth's body could have been in another position immediately after her murder without any blood pooling that would show that."

"What are you after here, Matt?" asked Detective Goldfarb.

"I'm just dredging up memories of other murders I've investigated. I seem to remember that a body can only rest in a position for a very short period of time before it shows up in lividity analysis."

"Which makes you think what?"

"Which makes me think that if Ada Danforth were murdered anywhere other than her house, it had to be somewhere very nearby."

"Like Justine Tan's house," said Beth, "which is only a few minutes away from Ada's house."

"Yes, Beth," I said. "Like Justine Tan's house."

*　*　*　*　*　*

I had just gotten back to my office when my cell phone started ringing. "Hello?" I said as I sat down in my desk chair.

"It's Beth, sir."

"Cut the sir stuff, okay, Beth? I'm not your boss, and I consider ourselves colleagues on this case."

"Yes, sir," she replied. I let it pass.

"So, what have you got?" I said.

"I spoke to Dr. Heath at the Medical Examiner's office."

"And?"

"It's basically what you said. She said she could have only rested in one position for a very few minutes, maximum, immediately after death, without showing any signs of it in a lividity exam. She said the overwhelming likelihood was that Ada was murdered where she was found. The timing for any other scenario is so tight it makes it almost impossible. So I think that makes it Justine's house or nowhere, and even that's a really close call. Other than that, she died where we found her, for reasons we don't understand yet. And Matt?"

"Yes?"

"Let's say she *was* killed somewhere else, and that somehow the murderer got her back to the house before lividity set in."

"Okay."

"I can't believe that someone could have carried her into the house, walked through the living room, and deposited her on the floor in the office without leaving any trace."

"I can't argue with you on that," I said. I looked at my watch. It was already after five. "Look," I said, "it's getting late. Why don't you and Goldfarb swing by my house. I want to hear what you've learned about

Justine Tan's past. Doreen's been out all day and we were just going to get takeout anyway, so I'll just order some extra. I'd rather sit in Doreen's kitchen and chat rather than the police station."

"So would I," said Beth almost before I finished talking. "What about Lacey? Do you think we should invite her over? She gave me a lot of help doing the research."

"Sure," I said. "I'll just double the takeout order."

"Perfect," said Beth. "When do you want us over?"

"I'm leaving the office right now, so get there as soon as you can."

"Will do."

I remembered at the last minute that Goldfarb kept kosher, which eliminated Chinese takeout. So I scrambled over to Sally's, which served kosher meats, just before he closed and ordered an assortment of sandwiches and deli salads for all of us, including the roast beef sandwich, Utz pretzels and Doc Brown's cream soda that I'd promised Steve what now seemed like so long ago.

I spent the drive back to the house thinking about lividity, and about the computer that wasn't turned on. After hearing what Dr. Heath had said, I had to face the fact that Ada Danforth had most likely died where we found her. But why? Why had she been sitting at her desk, in front of a computer that she hadn't been using, and probably never had?

Why?

I didn't have a clue. But I had the certain sense that the answer to that question would lead me to Ada Danforth's murderer.

*   *   *   *   *   *

Doreen's enormous kitchen felt warm and welcoming in the chill December darkness, as we all sat around the dining room.

"So, what did you learn about Justine Tan?" I asked Beth.

Beth was busily getting the best of an enormous tuna salad and provolone sandwich on rye, but she put what little was left of it aside. Lacey sat next to her, and although I knew that she had given Beth an enormous assist, she deferred to the young cop and concentrated on her meal, something she was awfully good at.

"It's an interesting story, actually," said Beth, "but I'm not sure how much it helps us."

"Let's decide on that later," I said.

"Right," she replied. "Justine Marie Logan was born in Council Bluffs, Iowa, in 1960 –"

"Not Tan?" asked Goldfarb.

"I'll get to that," she said. "She was the only child of Timothy Logan and Binh Hanh Nhu. Her father was one of the first wave of American soldiers that were sent to Viet Nam in the late 1950's. He met and fell in love with Miss Nhu in Saigon while he was on R&R, and they were married in a Catholic ceremony there with the blessing of her parents, who probably saw where their country was headed before most people did. Of course, the marriage made it easy to get a visa for Binh Hanh, and he brought her back to Council Bluffs, his home town, when his tour was over. By the way, once Binh Hanh got her citizenship she sponsored her parents, who eventually settled in Los Angeles after briefly experiencing an Iowa winter.

"Justine's father was a carpenter by training, and her mother eventually opened up her own hardware store, of all things, and they settled into a prosperous, middle-class life. Justine was their only child."

"That makes her about sixty," I said, "which seems to fit."

"Yes," said Beth.

Just as Beth was about to continue, Doreen walked in and greeted everyone. Beth lit up at the sight of her as Doreen grabbed a sandwich and sat down.

"I'm sorry to interrupt you, Beth," she said.

"No problem," said Beth, who had used the interruption to polish off her sandwich and her last few chips. She wiped her hands and mouth on her napkin before continuing her recitation. "So, anyway, Justine grew up a typical midwestern American kid. She excelled in school, and was offered a full scholarship to the University of Iowa, where she stayed for eight full years, eventually earning a Ph.D. in biology."

"No Ivy League schooling for Dr. Tan?" I said.

"The University of Iowa is an absolutely top-flight university, sir. We here back East just don't hear much about it."

"That's not what I meant," I said. "I guess I thought that maybe she and Ada Danforth may have run into each other during their university years."

"Not much chance of that," said Beth. "Even if they'd gone to the same school, they pursued different academic specialties, and the chances are they never would have met in any event. And, of course, there's the age disparity."

"You're probably right," I said. "I guess that was just wishful thinking. So where did she go from there?"

"Well, before we move on from there," said Beth, "there's one more thing we have to cover. During her undergraduate years, she met and fell in love with a fourth generation Chinese-American student from California, a young man named Albert Tan, who was at the University of Iowa pursuing a doctorate in mathematics. They got married when Justine was twenty, but they were divorced after only two years."

"Any children?" asked Detective Goldfarb.

"None, sir."

"Do you know why they were divorced?" I asked.

Beth glanced at Lacey.

"No," said Lacey. "I scrounged through the divorce records, but all the divorce documents said was 'mutual incompatibility.'"

"No hint of abuse or adultery?" said Goldfarb.

"None," said Lacey. "All I was able to find out was that Albert Tan moved back to California after he got his doctorate, and almost immediately married a young Chinese-American woman."

"Could have been pressure from his family," I said.

"That's probably a pretty good guess," said Lacey.

"Any idea where he is now?"

"Yeah," said Lacey. "He's a professor at UCLA. Still married to the same woman, three grown kids, a half-dozen grandkids. I reached out to him, but he wouldn't talk to me. He just said it was 'ancient history' and hung up. He didn't even ask why I wanted to know."

"If it comes to it, we can always ask Justine," I said.

"Sure," said Beth, "although the only thing of any consequence that came from the marriage was that it may have been why she moved on from the University of Iowa after she got her doctorate, even though it appeared that Iowa had offered her a position on their faculty."

"Where did she go from there?" I asked.

"She spent the next thirty years at SUNY Buffalo," said Beth, "which is one of the major university centers of the State University of New York. She received her tenure ahead of the normal schedule, and she was made a full professor after seven years. Buffalo sits right on the eastern shore of Lake Erie, and she made a specialty out of the rehabilitation of the lake – identifying biohazards and facilitating the re-creation of healthy wildlife habitats. She made quite a reputation for herself. Pretty impressive stuff."

"But I'm guessing she wasn't on the same level as Ada Danforth," I said.

"Nobody was, sir," said Beth. "But she had a solid academic career there. She was very popular with the students, and she published regularly about her work on the lake."

"Which makes you wonder why she would ever give that all up to come to OCCC."

"We'll be getting to that, sir," said Beth.

"Did she ever remarry?" asked Detective Goldfarb.

"No, she didn't sir," said Beth.

"That seems odd," said Goldfarb.

"Why is it odd, Steve?" I said.

"I don't know," said Steve. "Maybe it's just my prejudices showing. But it just seems to me that she is a very attractive woman, highly successful in her profession, and she had demonstrated an interest in marriage earlier in her life, that's all."

"Was there any anecdotal evidence of any romantic attachments?" I asked.

Beth hesitated, and then looked over at Lacey.

"No, there wasn't," said Lacey, "at least not publicly. But there were rumors for years of something between her and another professor on the faculty there."

"Another biology professor?" I asked.

"No," said Lacey, her expression impassive. "A physics professor."

"Physics?" I said.

"Yes, physics," both Beth and Lacey replied simultaneously.

"Okay, okay," said Goldfarb. "Let's take this back a step. First, how good is this information? Is it just faculty lounge gossip, or what?"

"It's more than that" replied Lacey. "I found out about it because there was a complaint filed with the university's faculty ethics committee about twenty years ago. The committee primarily focuses on inappropriate faculty interactions with students, but in this case, the complaint was brought by a faculty member against two other faculty members."

"So what happened?" said Goldfarb.

"Nothing," said Lacey. "The committee didn't even look into whether there was actually anything going on or not. They just interviewed Dr. Tan and the physics professor – his name was Dr. Michael Fielding, by the way, – and concluded that whatever, if anything, was going on was completely consensual, and they dropped the whole thing."

"Was Dr. Fielding married at the time?" asked Goldfarb.

"No," said Lacey. "In fact, he was a lifelong bachelor. Still is."

"Okay," I said. "That's all really interesting, but you said that all took place twenty years ago. Dr. Tan didn't come to OCCC until five years ago."

"Right," said Beth, "but here comes the interesting part. The professor who brought the complaint was another physics professor, a guy named Donald Porter. And years later, just a couple of years before Justine Tan left SUNY Buffalo and came to OCCC, she filed a sexual harassment complaint against *him*."

That got everyone in the room sitting up.

"And what was the upshot of that complaint?" I asked.

"Well," said Beth, "first you have to know that it seems this guy had quite a reputation in faculty circles for this type of behavior."

"Was *he* married?" asked Doreen, sounding a little scandalized.

"Oh, yes," said Beth. "He was married with four kids."

"But he still fancied himself quite the catch, huh?" said Doreen. Doreen had been betrayed in marriage once before, and she tended to take this type of behavior personally.

"Oh, yes," said Beth.

"So, why hadn't he been fired?" asked Goldfarb.

"You know," said Doreen, "we all tend to forget, because things are so intense these days with the *#metoo* movement and all, that the sensitivity we have to sexual harassment is a very recent phenomenon. Just a few years ago, if you were an influential politician, an important corporate executive – or a high profile, tenured professor at a major university – things like that were all swept under the rug."

"So, what happened with Justine Tan's complaint?" I asked.

"Well, with Dr. Tan's complaint, things were different," said Beth.

"In what way?" I said.

"This was not a matter of sly comments full of sexual innuendo, or even outright propositioning. According to the complaint, he literally sexually assaulted her."

"You mean, he raped her?" asked Doreen, visibly paling.

"No," said Beth, "but everything but. From the text of the complaint, it sounds like the only reason he didn't rape her was because Dr. Tan was strong enough and able enough to defend herself physically. I guess she left him pretty bruised up."

"Good for her!" said Doreen.

"Yes, good for her," said Lacey, "except nothing ever works out perfectly, does it?"

"What do you mean?" said Detective Goldfarb.

Lacey glanced over at Beth.

"After a couple of years," said Beth, "and multiple appeals, Dr. Porter was stripped of his tenure and dismissed from the faculty."

"That's a career death sentence for an academic," I said.

"You're darn right it is," said Beth. "And by all reports he left angry and unapologetic."

"But I don't get it," said Goldfarb. "If Dr. Tan won the case, why did she leave her hard-earned tenured position at a major university to come to Orange County Community College, which is not exactly a big-league school?"

"Because..." said Doreen, but then she stopped. "I'm sorry, Beth; it's your story to tell."

"No, please," said Beth, "go ahead."

"Well, tell me if I'm wrong, Beth, but I'll bet she left for two reasons: Academic politics are vicious, and the victim always gets blamed. Despite everything, Dr. Porter was a long-term and probably well-liked member of the faculty, probably much more popular that Dr. Tan, who can be distant and, well, prickly from what I've heard. Dr. Tan was expected to go along and get along and sweep things under the rug just like all of Dr. Porter's other victims. And frankly, in situations like that, there is always a vague suspicion that the victim must have done something to invite the offending behavior. Dr. Tan was in a no-win situation, so she had to leave."

"From everything we've learned," said Beth, "you are exactly right."

"Okay, then," said Detective Goldfarb, "we all know what happened to Justine Tan, but do we know what ever became of Donald Porter?"

"In fact," said Beth, "we do. Lacey, would you like to do the honors on this one? You're the one who found him."

"Dr. Donald Porter," said Lacey, with what looked to me like a wicked grin lighting up her face, "is now gainfully employed by the New York State Department of Higher Education. He is also, if you can believe this, an adjunct professor of Physics at SUNY Albany. And he currently resides with his lovely wife in the Albany suburb of Latham, which, to answer your next question, is about an hour's drive from here."

"Okay, you're saying that the guy landed on his feet," I said. "So, I get it that he's only an hour from here, and that makes him a person of interest, but let's face it, everything you told me has absolutely *nothing* to do with Ada Danforth. Don't get me wrong, it's really important to have this kind of background information on a suspect in a murder case, but it doesn't give anybody a motive to murder Ada Danforth."

"Did you find *any* connection between Dr. Porter and Ada Danforth?" asked Doreen.

"Not really," replied Beth. "He was born and educated in California, and never had any connection with Cornell or the Fermi labs."

"Then why did you say 'not really'? said Goldfarb.

"Because the one connection we found," replied Beth, "isn't much of one, and it's kind of iffy."

"Why don't you tell us about it anyway," said Goldfarb, as he popped the last of his Utz pretzels in his mouth. "It's not like we have anything else to go on."

"As you can imagine," said Beth after a slight pause, as if the what she was about to say didn't even warrant retelling, "Dr. Danforth was a recluse, and obviously a pariah in the scientific community, so she never attended any professional conferences or symposiums."

"That makes sense," I said.

"But there was one recent exception," said Beth. "About a year-and-a-half ago, the administration at OCCC persuaded her to attend the annual meeting of the Association of New York Professors of Science, which is held on the campus of Siena College near Albany."

"Why would she ever do something like that?" asked Doreen.

"I think," said Beth, "that she got a lot of pressure from the OCCC administration. They felt that it would raise the school's profile across the state, and they somehow convinced Dr. Danforth that, since so much time had passed, the chances of conflict or recrimination were pretty slim."

"And she bought that?" said Detective Goldfarb.

"Apparently she did," said Beth.

"Any indication of how it went?"

"No, said Beth, "there isn't. All we know is that Dr. Danforth stayed for the entire meeting, and said nothing to anyone about it when she returned."

"Do we know if Dr. Porter attended?" asked Goldfarb.

"Yes, he did," said Beth. "But we have no idea if he and Ada had any contact."

"Do you know if Paul Janssen attended the conference?" I asked.

"As a matter of fact," said Beth, "yes, he did."

* * * * * *

CHAPTER SIXTEEN

"**T**HIS IS PRETTY GOOD," said Paul Janssen, as he dug into the ham and Swiss cheese omelet and home fries that he'd surprised me by ordering. The only food I'd ever seen him consume was the bird food at the OCCC cafeteria. The Central Diner, in tiny Central Valley, New York, didn't have bird food on its menu, apparently to Dr. Janssen's delight.

But my first surprise of the morning had come when I'd called him at his home at about seven o'clock, and a sleepy sounding Justine Tan had answered the phone. I'd tried to sound unsurprised, but I'd obviously failed. Far from sounding embarrassed, I thought I detected a hint of triumph in her voice as she replied, "He's in the shower right now," to my request to talk to Janssen.

I had called him at home early, wanting to catch him before he headed off to school. I badly wanted to speak to him privately, so I hoped to get to him before he had Justine hovering over him like a mother bear over her cub.

"Okay," I'd replied, trying to sound unruffled. "That's fine. Could you just ask him to ring me back when he has a moment?"

"No," said Dr. Tan, sounding distinctly proprietary, "I'll just hand him the phone. I think he's out of the shower and shaving now."

"That would be great," I said. There was a muffled sound of what sounded to me like ribald chatter for a few seconds before Janssen came on the line, sounding pretty self-satisfied himself.

Once I had him on the phone I told him briefly what I wanted to talk to him about, and I made it as clear as I could that I would like to talk to him alone and away from the campus, hoping he understood that meant away from Justine. I heard some whispered conversation for a few seconds, and then I was surprised once again when he got on the phone and said that would be fine. He said that Justine had a semester-end make-up class and lab session that would take up the entire morning, so she wouldn't be able to come along in any event. I wasn't sure I bought that, but I took it. I'd suggested the Central Diner in tiny Central Valley, a place I occasionally frequented when I wanted to prove to myself that I wasn't stuck in a rut, and, just to add one more surprise to the conversation, he'd accepted immediately.

I'd ordered a plain breakfast of scrambled eggs, bacon, and toast, since I'd wanted to focus on the conversation more than the breakfast. My usual Central Diner order of their special omelet stuffed with corned beef hash and cheddar cheese with a side of link sausage along with an English muffin would have consumed all my attention. The waitress, whose name I knew was "Ginny," gave me a disapproving stare.

"I'm glad you like it," I said to Janssen, as I stared enviously at his plate, wondering if his shared bed the previous evening had whetted his appetite.

"But we're not here to discuss breakfast cuisine, I imagine."

"No, sadly not," I said, smiling unenthusiastically at my poor attempt at humor. I moved on. "We learned yesterday that Dr. Danforth and you attended an annual meeting a little over a year ago of the New York State Professors of Science."

He stared at me, fork midway between his plate and his mouth.

"If you think anything went on between me and Ada during that conference, you're dead wrong. We didn't even stay at the same hotel."

"Was that on purpose?"

"Of course not," said Janssen, "we just made our plans separately, and we never consulted with one another, that's all."

"Anyway, the thought hadn't even occurred to me until you brought it up just now, so we can just let that go, okay?"

"Fine with me," said Janssen, in between bites of his rapidly disappearing omelet. I hadn't even touched my scrambled eggs yet. "So, what did you bring me all the way over here to talk about, then? Trust me, the meeting, as usual, was a non-event."

"Did either of you happen to run into a man named Dr. Donald Porter?"

Janssen's fork stopped midway between his mouth and his plate once again.

"As a matter of fact, we did," he said slowly, as he put the fork down. "It was at the welcoming reception on the first night."

"So you knew him then? Both of you?"

"If you could call it that."

"Could you tell me more?"

"Okay, look. I think Ada and he vaguely knew each other professionally at one point, because they seemed to recognize each other pretty quickly. That wouldn't surprise me, of course, since I believe Dr. Porter was already at SUNY Buffalo when Ada was getting her doctorate at Cornell. I'm sure a man the likes of Porter would have made sure to get himself introduced to the young woman who was already making so many waves in the scientific community."

"What do you mean, 'the likes of Porter?'"

"Please, Mr. Hunter, I'm sure we wouldn't be sitting here if you hadn't heard about what went on between Justine and that man."

"You're right," I said. No sense beating about the bush. "Did he somehow bring that up?"

"Not somehow. He looked right at me, gave me a snide grin and said, "And how, may I ask, is the lovely Dr. Tan?"

"Did he seem to know that you and she were in a relationship?"

"Of course he did. The scientific community within the State University is small and, let's say, incestuous. The telegraph wire is highly efficient, and vicious. He knew he'd ruined Justine's career, and he had the brass to stand there and throw it in my face."

"What did you say to him?"

"I just said that Dr. Tan was fine, thank you, and then I left."

"You mean you left Ada alone with him, knowing what you knew?"

"I know, I know," said Janssen, what was left of his omelet suddenly forgotten. "I acted impulsively out of anger, and I felt terrible about it almost immediately, so I turned around and went back, but by that time Ada was already walking away from him, too."

"So you never heard anything they said to each other?"

"All I heard Porter say, was, "It was so darn good to see you after all this time." But the way he said it made me certain that it was not spoken with any good will in mind."

"What did you make of that?"

"Nothing more than we've discussed before, Mr. Hunter. People take great delight in seeing the mighty fall, nowhere more so than in academia."

"Do you know if there was any reason for Dr. Porter to feel any hostility toward Ada?"

"I really don't think so. Porter was never even close to Ada's level. He's never made any significant discoveries or even written any important papers, at least to my knowledge. To put it bluntly, he was a lot closer to my level than he was to Ada's, so I can't imagine any professional hostility or jealousy."

"To your knowledge, was that the only time they met at the conference?"

"I know it was," replied Janssen, "unless Ada was lying to me, which is something that Ada never did."

"Are you saying that you asked her?"

"Yes, I did. I wanted to make sure that she was all right. I had questioned the wisdom of her attending the conference in the first place. I told her it would be fine with me if she wanted to leave."

"What did she say?"

"She just laughed it off and said she'd be fine."

"And was she?"

"She seemed to be. I saw her speaking to a couple of other people from time to time, but mostly she kept to herself. I must say, though, that I was encouraged by even the small amount of interaction that she had. She was still young, you know, and my dream was that someday she would be once again recognized for what she was, and maybe even offered a position at a large institution again."

"Do you think that was Ada's hope?"

"I'm afraid that was my dream but not hers. I think she was perfectly content exactly where she was. As I've told you before, she had no need for the equipment or the resources of a large institution. Her mind was the only laboratory she needed. I also think she found her teaching mission at

OCCC personally fulfilling, and she loved her little home on the Hudson. No, I don't think she would take an offer, even to go back to the Fermi Labs, if it were offered to her."

"Did you recognize any of the other people that Ada spoke to?"

"No, I didn't," said Janssen. "I'm at the end of my career, and even though the community is small, I just don't get around that much anymore. And frankly, I wasn't paying that much attention. But she didn't speak to any real celebrities, you know, the people on the cutting edge these days. I would have recognized those folks. But look, if you are asking whether Ada came away from the conference feeling threatened or disturbed by anyone, the answer is 'no,' at least not as far as I know."

The waitress came by and stared dolefully at our half-eaten meals before asking if she could clear anything away. She looked at me with an "I expected better from you," expression on her face as she asked if we wanted our coffees topped off. We both declined.

As I headed back to my office, I couldn't escape the feeling that I was right back where I'd started: Nowhere.

* * * * *

CHAPTER SEVENTEEN

ONNIE CHANDLER was sitting in my office when I got back. It was the first time I'd seen him since he'd shown up completely unexpectedly two weeks ago. We'd all had a great Thanksgiving together, and Donnie and my daughter, Emma, who was in her freshmen year as an engineering student at SUNY Stony Brook on Long Island, had seemed to be getting along well. Admittedly, Emma had spent most of the short break immersed in her Calculus and Physics textbooks, but that was to be expected of a first-year engineering student. Engineering is a brutally tough program, but Emma is an extraordinarily bright young woman, and she would do just fine. Donnie, a sophomore business major at Stuyvesant University in New York City, on the other hand, didn't even bring home a book. I hadn't worried though; he'd made the Dean's List both semesters of his freshman year. The biggest challenge for any young student going to Stuyvesant was learning how to manage your academics with the siren call of life in Manhattan, where the school's main campus was located, constantly beckoning, but he'd seemed to be managing that successfully.

I had worried about Donnie, though. Even though he was bright, of the four kids he was the least intellectually gifted. His twin, Laura, was pre-med at Princeton on a full academic scholarship. She'd also won the NCAA women's tennis championship as a freshman while getting straight A's in her courses; and just for icing on the cake, she'd skipped a four-man sailboat from New York to London the summer before she'd headed off to college. She, not her brother, had inherited her father's athletic talents, and she, not her brother, had also inherited her mother's prodigious intellectual gifts. And my son, whom my ex-wife, Marianne, had insisted on naming

Carroll Matthew Hunter, Jr., but whom we had been mercifully calling "Cal" since he came home from the hospital as an infant, was a senior majoring in math at Boston College and destined, I was pretty sure, for a Ph.D. and a life in academia.

But despite their differences and the awkward family circumstances, they all seemed to get along well. Doreen's enormous five-bedroom house swallowed everyone up comfortably. The boys shared a room, and the girls each had their own rooms, leaving the fifth bedroom exclusively for Doreen's office. The other felicitous aspect of the house's design was that the master bedroom suite was in a completely separate wing of the house from the other bedrooms, so Doreen's and my precious privacy was protected, even with a full house.

But that was all beside the point now. I had to clear my mind of my murder case and focus my attention on the young man sitting in the chair opposite my desk.

"Donnie," I said, always the master of the clever opening conversational gambit, "how are you?"

"I wouldn't be here if I was okay, would I, Mr. Hunter?" he replied, his face, which so much resembled his father's, and his voice betrayed sadness, but not hostility.

"I guess you wouldn't," I said. "Donnie, I have to ask you, have you seen your mother yet?"

"No, I haven't," he said. "I'm sorry."

"I'm going to be blunt, then, Donnie. That puts us both in a really awkward position. Your mother loves you a great deal, and she has always felt that you and she could communicate, even about difficult things. It would hurt her terribly if she felt that there were things that you were willing to talk to me about, but not her."

"Don't you think I know that, Mr. Hunter? I love my Mom, and right now I want to talk to her more than anyone else in the world."

"Then why are you here?"

"Look, Mr. Hunter, this isn't easy. I mean, you married Mom after she and my dad got divorced. No matter what else my father is, he's still my dad, and that still hurts. And no matter what you ever are to me, you'll always be, you know, the man who replaced my father in my mother's life. That'll always be, like, our elephant in the room, I guess."

"Is that what you came here for Donnie? Just to clear the air? Just so you know, I never expected to replace your father in your life. I never wanted that."

"No, that's not it," said Donnie, sounding a little frustrated. "Please, just let me talk, okay? Let me just talk until I'm done."

What was going on here? Was he ill? Was he coming out as gay? Had he committed a crime? I wasn't sure I wanted to know the answer.

"Okay," I said, trying to sound unruffled.

"I love my mom, Mr. Hunter. She was the best mom anybody ever could have had. But she's also, like, you know, Mom. She's always been the smartest, the prettiest, the most popular, the best at everything she ever set her mind to do. And Laura's like that, too; and so's Emma, who I, like, really, really like. And they've always been, so, you know, *directed*; they always knew what they wanted to do, and what they wanted to do after that. And then there's me. I was supposed to be the next great quarterback at Devon Central High, just like Dad. But I wasn't. We were barely a .500 team during the whole three years I was starting quarterback. Mom and Laura were both valedictorians, but I was barely in the top ten percent. So, anyway, I know you weren't like that. I mean, you were an incredible athlete in high school, but you've been honest about the fact that, since then, you've had your ups and downs. You know, you've had your successes, but you've had your failures, too. So I thought that you might be easier to talk to, at least at first. I mean, I'm gonna talk to Mom, don't worry. And I'm gonna talk to Laura and Emma, too. But first, I wanted to talk about things with you, if that's alright."

"Donnie, I don't know if I can help," I said, "but I take it as one of the nicest compliments I've ever received that you would want to talk to me. So, what's on your mind?"

"Aw, Mr. Hunter, I don't want to major in business, and I don't want to be a businessman."

"Is it because you're finding it too difficult?" I asked, hoping the relief I felt wasn't too obvious.

"Heck, no. The stuff is stupid easy. I mean, I keep making the Dean's List, and I'm not even trying that hard."

"So, what's the problem, then?"

"Well first of all, the courses are boring, at least to me. But that's not really the problem. If I thought the courses would qualify me to do something I really wanted to do, I'd take the courses and not complain. But, jeez, Mr. Hunter, I just can't picture myself being a corporate guy, you know? I'm afraid I'd wind up being just as big a failure as Dad was."

"Donnie, you should never fear failure, and you should never let the fear of failure prevent you from pursuing something you really want to do. And, by the way, you're not your father. You're you. Don't ever forget that. But let's look at it another way: Is there something else you'd really rather do?"

"Well, I guess that's the whole point, Mr. Hunter. Yes, there is something else that I really want to do."

"What's that?"

"I know this sounds stupid, but I want to be a high school teacher."

"There's nothing stupid about that, Donnie, nothing at all. I think what this country needs right now more than anything else is more good teachers. It certainly doesn't need more lawyers and private investigators, I can tell you that. But tell me, what makes you think you want to teach?"

"Well, it's kind of like I said. I was never valedictorian. Sure, I did okay, but I think I can relate to the kids who really need the attention: the kids who would do just fine if they just got a little help. Heck, it wouldn't have mattered who taught Laura, or Mom, or Emma; they just basically taught themselves. But most kids aren't like that."

"What do you think you might want to teach, Donnie?"

"I want to teach history. You know, Laura took nothing but AP courses from 10th Grade on, but the only AP course I ever took was History, and I aced the exam. I always loved it, and I don't think kids get enough of it in high school."

"Have you ever thought that you might want to coach, too?"

"Yeah, I have," said Donnie, his eyes lighting up. "Sometimes I think that I'd be a better coach than I was a player. It was, like, I always knew exactly what I should do when I was on the field, I just didn't have the talent to do it like you and Dad did."

"Donnie, all I can say is that your mother would be awfully proud of you if that's what you decided to do, and I think you should talk to her about it."

"I guess, you're right, Mr. Hunter," said Donnie, his face brightening, but only for a second. "Only, there's one other thing."

With kids, there always is. The fear settled back into my stomach. I couldn't begin to guess what the one more thing was; I just had to wait and hear.

"I want to quit Stuyvesant."

"Quit Stuyvesant? But why?"

"First of all, it doesn't really have much of a program to train teachers. But most of all, I just hate it. I hate living in New York City, and I hate the way all the kids who go there think they're so damn special, you know? I grew up in a small town, Mr. Hunter. That's where I belong. And I want to go to college with the same kind of kids I went to high school with, not with a bunch of kids who all believe they're the next big thing, you know?"

"Have you thought about where you might like to go?"

"Sure," he said, surprising me once again. "I want to go to SUNY Oneonta. It's beautiful up there, Mr. Hunter, and there's tons of history in that region. You know, "The Last of the Mohicans" and all that, plus the Baseball Hall of Fame is right nearby."

"Sounds like you've done your homework," I said.

"Yeah," said Donnie, "I have. I've been thinking about this for a long time."

"Donnie, all I have to say is, please, talk to your mother. She'll be awfully proud of you."

"I will, Mr. Hunter, don't worry. And, you know, thanks. You've been really great."

"I'm glad I could help," I said. And I was. My two kids had always been beyond my help, for a lot of reasons. It felt nice to be of use.

But something was bothering me.

Every day I have people come and sit in my office and tell me about problems they want me to solve. Sometimes it's a divorce, or an infidelity they want to prove or disprove. Sometimes it's threats of blackmail. Sometimes it's financial improprieties. They are all profoundly personal problems that require them to tell me a lot more about themselves than they would ever tell anyone under normal circumstances, and they only tell me because they feel they have no other choice. But one thing almost all of these people have in common is that they never tell me the whole story, at least not at first. These are people who are in desperate straits; you'd think they'd open up completely if they were going to open up at all. But they don't. And it's usually the most critical information, the reason they really came to me in the first place, that they hold back.

Last year, a locally prominent man, a member of the Town Council and a lay leader in his church, came to me ostensibly to find out if his wife was having an illicit affair. It didn't take me long to determine that she wasn't. It also didn't take me long to find out that he was – with another man. It wasn't until I called him in to give him the results of the investigation into his wife that he finally came clean: What he really wanted to know was whether his wife knew about his affair, and his true orientation. I told him all I could. No, she did not know about his affair, but that he was a fool if he thought that she didn't know about his homosexuality. She might not have consciously acknowledged it to herself yet, but she knew. Forget about holding back on me, I told him. He and his wife had been holding back on themselves, and on each other, for years, and that was something I couldn't help him with.

That's why something was bothering me with Donnie: He was holding back on me, and I knew it. If it had been a simple matter of wanting to change majors, or to switch schools, he would have immediately gone to his mother, despite all his tortured rationalizations to the contrary. They were as close as mother and son could be, and they would have talked.

And even though our conversation had seemingly come to a conclusion, Donnie didn't budge. In my business, that's called a clue.

"Donnie?" after a silence that was becoming uncomfortably long.

"Yeah?" was all he said, trying to look out the window instead of at me.

"I get the feeling that there's something else you need to talk about."

"No, really Mr. Hunter," he said, still not looking at me, "that was all. Thanks, really." He looked at the door and made a move to get up.

"Donnie?" I said.

He froze, halfway out of his seat.

"Yeah?"

"Please, sit back down. I really think there's something else you want to talk to me about."

"No, really Mr. Hunter. It's okay."

"Donnie, please."

There was another long silence, but this time I let it linger.

"I got thrown out of school."

I've had a lot of practice at maintaining a neutral expression, but I'm not sure how well I succeeded this time.

"Do you want to tell me about it?" I asked. My voice sounded remarkably calm, at least to me. What was he going to tell me? Cheating? An arrest for drunkenness or drugs? A conflict with a faculty member? I just couldn't imagine the Donnie I knew doing those things.

"It was for sexual harassment."

"What!?" My self-control only went so far. "Donnie, what the hell did you do?"

"Hold it, hold it, Mr. Hunter! Please, let me explain. It's not what it sounds like!"

I took a deep breath and blew it out. I counted to five. "Then why don't you tell me about it."

"I guess I shouldn't have said that the way I did. What I'm trying to say is that I got thrown out of school for sexual harassment, but I didn't do it."

"Okay," I said. I took another deep breath. "Perhaps you should start over from the beginning."

"Sure," said Donnie. He hesitated, but not for long. "It was a week after we all got back. The freshmen had already been there for two weeks because of orientation."

"And I'm sure you'd all gotten your indoctrination, or training, whatever they call it."

"Oh, yeah. Returning students get two days, and the freshmen spend almost their whole second orientation week getting lectures, watching videos, role playing, you name it. And I've got to tell you, especially if you're a guy, it's pretty scary."

"What do you mean?"

"It's just so confusing. On one hand, in gender sensitivity training they tell me that just because I look like a male, and just because everybody's always told me that's what I was, that doesn't mean that's what I am, especially if I don't *feel* like a male. But on the other hand, when it comes to sexual sensitivity training, I *am* a male, and I am always guilty. We have to respect the woman's truth, no matter what that truth is, or whether it's like, you know, the truth."

"But you don't get the same privilege, right?"

"Well, we only use the word 'privilege' in terms of race; you know, 'white privilege,' but yeah, we don't, unless our truth is exactly the same as the woman's truth."

"Sounds kind of scary to me."

"It is," said Donnie, nodding his head.

"So, how did you deal with all that?"

"Like everybody else. I kept my head down; I didn't even make eye contact with anyone, because if you do, it's like, you know, a micro-aggression. I did as much of my classwork as I could online. And I never, ever, went into anyone else's dorm room, and my roommate and I agreed that no one was allowed in our dorm room."

"Sounds pretty grim. So, how do you socialize?"

"I don't. I mean, my roommate and me, and maybe a couple of other guys will sometimes go out to grab a burger or something, but if we do, we always take the subway uptown or over to Brooklyn, away from the campus. And I also, you know, stay in touch with Emma. We talk on the phone, and sometimes we FaceTime. And sometimes we'll meet for a lunch somewhere halfway between Stony Brook and Stuyvesant, and it's always just the two of us. But that's not much, because Emma's like really, really busy."

I was glad to hear that; I liked Donnie, and Emma could do a lot worse for a boyfriend.

"So, I'm confused," I said. "Why did you mention the week after orientation? Did something happen then?"

"Nothing," said Donnie. "That's the problem. Except, right at the end of orientation, this girl, this freshman, who I'd never seen before, came up and started talking to me. Ashley, she said her name was. She told me she was from Indiana, and she was really, like, intimidated by New York, and she was wondering if she'd made a mistake coming to Stuyvesant."

"What did you tell her?"

"I said, you know, before you make any decisions, give it a chance. I said it might grow on her. And then – well – then she asked me if I might be willing to show her around."

And you said –?"

"I said, look, I already have a girlfriend, so that might be awkward. And then I said, but, you know, don't worry, you'll be making a lot of friends real soon, and I'm sure that you can all go exploring together."

"And how did Ashley take that?"

"She seemed to take it fine. I mean, thinking back, she may have looked a little disappointed at first, and maybe a little surprised, but then she gave me a nice smile, said, 'Okay, thanks,' and walked away. I never saw her again after that."

"And that was it? Are you sure, Donnie?"

"I'm positive, Mr. Hunter. Positive."

"So why do you think she was the one who brought charges against you?"

"Because she was the only – only, Mr. Hunter – female student I spoke to for the rest of the semester. I mean, we all heard all the stories during orientation, and they were, I mean, truly scary."

"And you received no warning, no indication, no hint, that you were in any kind of trouble?"

"None, right up until Thanksgiving."

"And then?"

"Then, right after I got back from Thanksgiving break, I got a message from the Dean of Diversity telling me that I'd been charged with sexual misconduct for something they said I'd done the first week of the semester. They told me that I had already been tried and found guilty, and that I was expelled from the school. I asked if I was going to have a chance to challenge all that, and the Dean said no. I asked who had charged me, and what the charges were, but the Dean said I wasn't allowed to know that."

"And that's it?" I said. "You mean to tell me that your college career has been ruined, and you were never told why?"

"That's right," said Donnie. "It happens a lot, Mr. Hunter. And you know what?"

"What's that, Donnie?"

"I get it. I really do. You probably know this better than I do, but, up until the past few years, it was always the other way around, right? The guys always owned the truth. If a girl accused a guy of, you know, molesting her, or even raping her, all the guy had to do was deny it. It was, 'he said, she said," you know? And usually, the guy got away with it, and the girl got her reputation ruined, right?"

"That's right," I said. "And the sad part was that most of the time women knew all of this going in, so they wouldn't even bring charges at all."

"Right," said Donnie. "And now the tables are turned. Now the women own the truth, and the guys are the ones who have to pay the consequences. The shoe's on the other foot, and it's making everybody uncomfortable."

"But, you know, Donnie, maybe just like it wasn't fair for women in the past, maybe it's not fair for men now. Maybe the pendulum, for once, has to come to rest at the center."

"Maybe you're right, Mr. Hunter, but that's not going to happen in time to help me."

"Maybe you're right, Donnie, but we still have to do something to try and set the record straight about all of this."

"Mr. Hunter, please. I just want to put it all behind me and move on with my life. I'd already decided that I wanted to leave Stuyvesant before all this came up; I wasn't kidding about that. There's nothing we can do about it anyway, so can't we just drop it?"

"Donnie, you have to understand: We *have to* challenge this, or it will dog you for the rest of your life. It's been done before, you know. There have been successful lawsuits against colleges and universities, so there have been legal precedents set."

"Aw, Mr. Hunter –"

"No, 'Aw Mr. Hunter," I said. "This is something you – we– have to do. But there's one thing you have to do first."

"I know," said Donnie, "talk to my Mom."

"That's right. And you know what else you can do?"

"What?"

"Stop calling me Mr. Hunter. Call me Matt. Please. It'll be awkward at first, but I think we'll both get comfortable with it pretty quickly."

"It's a deal," said Donnie, a smile on his face for the first time. "Mr., uh, Matt."

"Good."

Donnie left my office with perhaps a little more spring in his step than when he arrived. Talking to his mother would help him even more. I'd have to talk to my office mate, Harvey Golub, about mounting a legal defense, but he was in court today, and, besides, I needed to talk to Doreen before I took another step.

"Lechery, lechery; still wars and lechery: nothing else holds fashion."

As usual, Shakespeare was right. And as I sat back in my chair and contemplated Donnie's predicament and poor Ada Danforth's tragic fate, I thought about how similar their situations were. They were two innocents caught up in wars of emotions, jealousies, and sexual desires in which they should have been non-combatants, but one was already a casualty and the other in the line of fire. They were both unlikely victims, not of their own passions, but of the passions they'd aroused in others. For some reason, Donnie's honest response to Ashley's request for help had made something go tilt in her young mind. Who knows? But what about Ada Danforth? She, like Donnie, had been punished for a crime she didn't even know she'd committed, and now there would never be an appeal. She clearly managed to arouse passions in many people around her, also through no fault of her own. But a passion deep enough and violent enough to cause her murder? Had I met that person yet?

I'd have to leave it up to Harvey Golub to handle Donnie's case. But Ada Danforth had called out to me from her grave to find justice. I had no choice but to answer.

* * * * * *

It was good to see Donnie back at the dinner table with us.

Doreen told me that he had come straight home from my office, and they had spent the afternoon talking over his problem and what we were going to do. Doreen had already spoken to Harvey Golub. She had appointed him General Counsel to the town after she had been elected mayor and had since developed a deep respect for Harvey, both as a man and as an attorney. Unsurprisingly to me, they also hit it off personally, which in small town politics is crucial. By all appearances, Harvey was just a small-town lawyer handling a small-town caseload, but he was much more than that. A respected graduate of Columbia Law School, he had escaped the pressure-cooker atmosphere of the large Manhattan firms and was content with his one-man practice in Devon-on-Hudson, a career that allowed him to live a life consistent with his Orthodox Judaism. But he was also heavily sought after by his ex-classmates, who knew that he possessed perhaps the finest legal mind in their class. He was a "lawyer's lawyer," more than willing to work anonymously behind the scenes to guide the large firms through complex, high-stakes cases. My guess is that he was paid a fortune for his services, but he never talked about money, and lived a modest lifestyle. Instead, I guessed he used that income to allow him to take on the cases that were truly important to him: protecting the little guys from the vultures that lurked everywhere, regardless of their ability to pay. If anyone could get Donnie out of his predicament, Harvey could.

We had passed a pleasant dinner, just the three of us sitting at Doreen's enormous, circular kitchen table, feeling cozy nevertheless. We chatted mostly about how nice it would be to be all together when the other three kids got home for the Holidays next week. I asked Donnie what he was going to tell the others about his predicament, and he told me that he'd already been in touch with them that afternoon after he and his mother had talked, and he'd told them everything. Donnie was doing a lot of right things, and I was proud of him.

I was just about to get up from the table to help Doreen with the dishes when Donnie piped up.

"Uh, Matt?"

"Yeah, Donnie?" I said, sitting back down. I thought he might want to talk a little more about his school situation, but he surprised me.

"Could you tell me about the case you're working on? I've read about it in the papers, and Dr. Danforth sounds like she was a pretty amazing woman."

"She most certainly was that," I said. "And you don't even know the half of it. Do you have a little time? It's a long story, but it would probably help me if I could tell the whole thing from the beginning. It might give me a chance to make some sense out of things." I also thought that Donnie might benefit from a little distraction from his woes. Nothing like a good, old-fashioned murder case to shift your focus.

"Sure," said Donnie.

So I did, in all the detail I could muster, from beginning to end. I even recounted my first meeting with Barbara Danforth. Doreen frowned, but Donnie seemed to take it in stride. He asked a couple of brief questions as I talked, but mostly he just listened, and I could tell he was readily absorbing and retaining everything. Good listening skills are just as important as IQ in my book.

"So. What do you think?" I finally said.

"Are all your cases like this?" he asked, his eyes wide.

"No, they're not, thank goodness," I said. "In fact, I've never had a case like this."

"That's got to be the most interesting story I've ever heard, except, you know, somebody got killed."

"Any questions? Criticisms? Observations?"

"Well, first of all, I know about as much about quantum physics as you do, so I don't know what to make of those letters. But I guess I know so little that I'm keeping an open mind about them."

"That's a good way to put it," I said. "That's about where I am, even though I'm kind of all alone on that."

"I bet," said Donnie, smiling.

"What else?"

"I know that this isn't very helpful, but I think basically everybody you mentioned, besides her parents, could have done it. For such a quiet person, Ada Danforth sure gave a lot of people a reason to want to kill her. I can see why you're so frustrated."

"I am, but I'm used to being frustrated on this job. But tell me: what am I missing?"

"I think the only person you might have overlooked is that guy Michael Fielding."

That caught me off guard. All I knew about Michael Fielding was that he was a low-profile professor who may or may not have had a brief romance with Justine Tan.

"What makes you think that?" I said. "I have to admit, I've basically put him out of my mind."

"And I get that," said Donnie, looking serious. "I mean, he might have had something to do with Justine Tan, but there's nothing that says he even knew Dr. Danforth."

"So, what am I missing, Donnie?"

"I'm sorry, Matt, maybe I'm wrong, but I just think there's no such thing as a coincidence. Dr. Fielding knew a major suspect in Dr. Danforth's murder, at a time when he was a physics professor just down the road from where Dr. Danforth was doing some pretty groundbreaking research in, you know, physics. It's hard to believe that he wouldn't have known about her, and perhaps met her. And if that's true, then you have a guy who knew both your victim and one of your major suspects. I guess I just can't get that out of my head."

And now that he'd said it, neither could I. What hadn't even occurred to me before now seemed to be at least a necessary path of investigation that I would have missed.

"Donnie," I said, "if you ever decide not to become a teacher, you might want to give police work some thought."

"Don't you dare," said his mother, glaring at me. But Donnie Chandler swelled with pride.

CHAPTER EIGHTEEN

I WAS BACK AT THE CENTRAL DINER, but this time with someone who put a smile on Ginny's face.

Lacey had ordered three eggs over easy, bacon, toast, home-fries, and a short stack of pancakes. She already burned halfway through it all, and if I didn't hurry up she'd start stealing my hash-and-cheese stuffed omelet, never mind the sausages.

I'd called Lacey after dinner the night before and told her about my conversation with Donnie. She'd clearly been miffed with herself that she hadn't seen the potential Michael Fielding angle, and I guessed that she'd been up half the night chasing it down.

"So, what have you got for me?" I said between bites, determined not to be left behind.

"You're gonna love this," said Lacey, not once putting her knife and fork down.

"Try me," I said.

"Dr. Michael Fielding, who, if I've got the dates triangulated right, is probably about the same age as Dr. Tan, was, still is, a physics professor at SUNY Buffalo. He is not a major figure in his field, but he seems to be a good, solid, faculty member who is willing to work with the second-tier graduate students so the more accomplished faculty can work with the all-stars. He is not, and never has been, married, and I don't think he is gay. He just seems to be one of those people who is perfectly content being single."

"Except the fact that he seemed to be intrigued with Justine Tan at one point."

"Yes, and I don't have much to say about that. You'll have to talk to him directly, or Dr. Tan, if you want to dig into that any deeper."

"I probably will," I said. "So what else?"

"He is also the son of Dr. Lionel Fielding."

It took me a few seconds for the name to register.

"*The* Dr. Lionel Fielding?"

"Yes," said Lacey. "*The* Dr. Lionel Fielding. I could have smacked myself for not making the connection sooner."

So could I. Even I had heard of Lionel Fielding, going back to my youth. He'd won the Nobel Prize in Physics in, I believe, 1961, making him an overnight American celebrity. He'd been born in the Finger Lakes Region of upstate New York, in the tiny town of Victor, right near Lake Canandaigua. He'd attended the University of Rochester as an undergraduate, and then gone on to Cornell for his Ph.D. He spent the rest of his life and career at Cornell.

But aging Nobel Laureates, like aging high school football stars, begin to fade from people's memories sooner rather than later, and it had been years since I'd heard or read anything about him.

"Is he still alive?" I asked.

"Believe it or not, yes. He's 92 years-old, but he is still on the faculty of Cornell, as a Professor Emeritus, and still helps guide some of the most gifted graduate students."

"So don't tell me —"

"Okay," said Lacey, grinning, "I won't."

"He was Ada Danforth's thesis advisor, wasn't he?"

"Yes, he was," said Lacey, as she polished off the last of her breakfast. I'd done a pretty good job on my own meal, and the only thing left for her to steal off my plate was the last link sausage, which I wasn't sure I was going to be able to eat in any event. I made a lame show of protesting when she speared it and put it on her own plate, but what I really wanted to do was get back to the conversation.

"Did they remain close?" I asked, as Ginny came to whisk away our plates and freshen our coffees. She smiled at me as she looked down at my clean plate.

"Yes, they did," said Lacey. "He was maybe the only elite physicist who remained loyal to her. And on the very rare occasions when she left

Devon-on-Hudson, it was to visit him. From everything I could gather, they not only admired each other as colleagues, but they were also devoted to each other personally."

"Perhaps he was a father figure to her," I said.

"Perhaps," said Lacey, "but last night I happened to connect with a man who was a graduate student under Dr. Fielding at the same time as Ada, and he said the murmurs were that if there hadn't been such an age difference – remember, she was still a teenager and he was in his seventies when she was a student at Cornell – there would have been a genuine romance between them. I guess they were inseparable."

"Was Dr. Fielding still married at the time? Do you think that Michael Fielding could have felt hostility or jealousy toward Ada because of her relationship with his father?"

"I haven't gotten that far yet, but I think it's something that you might want to look into."

"I think so, too." I replied. We both got up from the table, and I picked up the check because Lacey never does, even though she's wealthy in her own right. I paid a still smiling Ginny at the counter, but not before Lacey added a glazed donut and a coffee to go to the tab.

CHAPTER NINETEEN

TRIED THE EASY WAY. I'd called Justine Tan to ask her about Dr. Michael Fielding, but she'd just stonewalled me. She said they'd been nothing but casual friends, and anything else was a figment of Donald Porter's imagination. Other than that, she wouldn't talk about him or Porter, no matter how hard I tried. I asked her if she knew anything about Fielding's relationship with his father, but all she said was that I would have to ask him about that. What she told me was all arguably true, so I had a hard time pressing her on it. I thought of going around her and talking to Paul Janssen, but I was almost certain that it wouldn't have done me any good. Even if Justine had told him something more about her possible relationship with Michael Fielding, he wasn't going to spill it to me now that his relationship with Justine was so obviously back on track.

So I'd decided to try the hard way, which was why I was currently on the New York State Thruway headed west toward Buffalo. December weather in upstate New York can be iffy at best, and downright awful at its worst, making driving, even on the well-maintained Thruway treacherous. So I'd borrowed Doreen's all-wheel-drive Lexus SUV for the trip. I'd felt a little guilty leaving my Accord behind, but as much as I loved my Accord, I had to admit it was lousy in snow. And besides, Doreen's Lexus was a pretty sweet ride. So far, the weather was holding up, but you never know.

I'd taken the scenic route, up Route 17 to Binghamton, then I-81 north to Syracuse where I'd met up with the Thruway. It was shorter than just going north to Albany and heading west from there, but most of all, the drive up Route 17 is just spectacular, and I didn't want to miss a chance to drive it one more time. When you utter the words "New York" to most Americans they think of nothing but New York City. Upstate New York is one of the best kept secrets in the country, home to Niagara Falls, the Finger Lakes, the Thousand Islands, the Adirondack Park, and some of the best trout fishing in the world. It's also hard to find an area of the country that's more beautiful. I've always said that if you drove an average American through upstate New York and asked them to guess where they were, they'd guess all day without getting it right. The drive also took me past the Roscoe Diner, which for my money is one of the best diners in the country. I'd timed my departure from home so that I'd get to Roscoe just in time for breakfast, and the inner man was content as I headed down the long, straight highway toward Buffalo.

I'd spent the rest of the previous day making phone calls to arrange visits. In that respect, I'd been lucky. Even though the two Dr. Fieldings were academics and the semester break had begun, they were both going to be at home, and both, perhaps surprisingly, had agreed to see me with little or no pushback. I guessed they were both anxious to hear as much as I would tell them about what had happened to Ada.

I'd also asked Beth Gardner to do some off-the-record snooping into phone records for me, and it turned out that both the Fielding men had been in frequent touch with Ada during the last few months of her life. I didn't know what to make of that. I guessed I shouldn't have been surprised that she had kept in touch with Dr. Fielding the elder, given what we'd learned about their past personal as well as professional relationship. But I was puzzled that the younger Dr. Fielding would have been in touch with her at all. Perhaps he knew her through her father and they shared a common concern for his well-being as he aged. It was something I'd have to find out.

Another benefit of driving Doreen's Lexus was that it had an excellent navigational system. I pulled over at the last rest stop on the Thruway before Buffalo and punched in the address of the Niagara Grill, a breakfast and lunch place near the SUNY Buffalo campus where Michael Fielding had agreed to meet me. I'd hoped he would invite me to his home, since I've always found that you can get a good sense of a person just by stepping into their house, but he'd said that he was going to be on campus to finish some thesis assessments, since he was one of those people who preferred not to bring their work home with them. I was the same way, so it was hard to disagree. I got back on the highway, and the skyline of Buffalo soon appeared in the distance.

The city of Buffalo is usually dismissed by invidious comparison with Toronto, the Canadian city just across the border. I haven't spent much time in that area so maybe I'm being unfair, but I've always thought that Toronto was an overrated city filled with people who aren't overly fond of Americans. Buffalo, on the other hand, is an economically and socially diverse town with plenty to do, both culturally and socially, filled with friendly people, and it has a fascinating history that is largely forgotten.

As the 20th Century dawned, Buffalo was regarded as the most advanced city in the nation, and in 1901 it had proudly hosted the Pan-American Exposition, which, among many other things, highlighted Buffalo's transformation into the nation's first city completely electrified by alternating current electricity, thanks to the gigantic generators installed on nearby Niagara Falls by a company then called "Thomas A. Edison, Inc." The city formerly known as "The Rainbow City" overnight became renowned as "The City of Light."

Sadly, if anyone remembers the Pan-American exposition for anything these days it is as the place where President William McKinley was assassinated on September 6, 1901, by an obscure anarchist named Leon Czolgosz. Ironically, one of the groundbreaking new technical wonders being showcased at the Exposition was the X-Ray machine, which McKinley's doctors refused to use to help them find the bullet lodged in his body, not trusting the nascent technology, thereby dooming our 25th President to die of gangrene the following week.

Edison's electricity notwithstanding, the air was cold as I stepped out of the Lexus and onto the sidewalk in front of the Niagara Grill around two o'clock, and low, gray clouds loomed over the city like an unspoken threat. The warm, damp air, redolent of the aromas of the breakfast they served all day and the Polish sausages they served at lunch felt good as I stepped inside. I knew what Michael Fielding looked like thanks to a photo that Lacey had downloaded from the internet for me, but I really didn't need it. I spotted him right away, sitting in a booth in the back corner of the diner, looking not at all like the two steamfitters sitting at the counter washing down *galumkis* with pints of Yuengling freshly imported from exotic Pittsburgh, who were the only two other customers at that slow part of the diner day.

Fielding recognized me, too, and he stood up to greet me as I approached the booth. He looked professorial in khakis and a white, button-down shirt under a houndstooth sports jacket with the requisite *faux* leather elbow pads and a plaid scarf. He was a slight, mild-looking man with thinning, gray hair and a whisp of a goatee. One thing he didn't look like was a murderer, but you never know.

"Mr. Hunter, I presume," he said with a pleasant smile as he stretched out his hand and grasped mine.

"Hello, Professor Fielding," I replied as I took a seat opposite him. "Thank you so much for seeing me on such short notice."

"Not at all. Anything I can do to assist you in finding Dr. Danforth's murderer is not an inconvenience. Far from it."

"Thanks," I said, as a waitress, a good-looking fortyish woman who looked remarkably like Ginny from the Central Diner, but whose nameplate announced her as "Trisha" put menus in front of us. "I really appreciate it." Trisha asked us if we'd like anything to drink, and we both ordered coffee.

"Please feel free to order something to eat," said Fielding. "I had a late breakfast, but I assume you've been on the road all day, and I can vouch for the food here. Like everything else about Buffalo, this place looks modest, but the food is excellent." That elicited a smile from Trisha. It was a nice smile that I bet earned her a lot of tips.

The aroma of the *galumkis* had whetted my appetite, but I wasn't up for anything that heavy, so when Trisha returned I ordered a tuna sandwich on whole wheat with a side of potato chips and a pickle. She looked a little crestfallen at my order, but you can't please everyone all the time.

"So, tell me," I said after Trisha had picked up our menus and left, "how did you know Ada Danforth? Was it through your father?"

"Only partially," said Fielding, looking at his coffee more than me. "Of course I knew her through my father, but Dr. Danforth became a celebrity in the Physics community in this area long before she became nationally and internationally famous. Everyone had heard of the young prodigy at Cornell, and everyone knew that my father was her mentor."

"But you must have met her personally through your father, right?"

"I am a physicist, too, Mr. Hunter, admittedly nowhere near Dr. Danforth's, or my father's for that matter, caliber, but a physicist nonetheless. I actually first met her at a conference here at UB before she had completed her doctorate."

"Did you become personally friendly?"

"No, I wouldn't say that, but we were cordial."

"But you also must have met her, perhaps on a more personal basis through your father, right?"

"I'm not sure what you're getting at, Mr. Hunter."

"Please, call me Matt, professor."

"If you like…Matt."

This wasn't getting off to a good start, and I was afraid it was my fault. Perhaps it had been the long drive, or the darkening weather outside, but I'd been impatient, and that had made Dr. Fielding suspicious.

"Please, Dr. Fielding. I have no hidden agenda. I'm just very anxious to get to the bottom of Ada Danforth's murder, and, to be perfectly candid, I'm not having a lot of luck. When I find myself in situations like this, I just tend to ask anyone I can find all the questions I can think of. Sometimes it gives me leads I hadn't thought of before, that's all."

"I understand, Mr. – Matt. It sounds a lot like being in a physics lab when your latest hypothesis has just come to a dead end. You'll try almost anything to get back on track."

"Thank you, professor," I replied, noticing that he hadn't invited me to call him "Mike." "That describes my situation just about perfectly. But, to answer your question, the reason that I'm asking you about your father is that I have heard – and please tell me if I'm wrong – that your father and Dr. Danforth were personally as well as professionally friendly, and I figured that you might have met her while you were visiting with your father."

"I'm sorry to disappoint you, but my father and I were never really all that close. But I have visited him sporadically over the years, and, yes, I did meet Dr. Danforth on a couple of those occasions."

"I don't mean to pry," I said, "but can you tell me why you weren't that close to your father?"

Michael Fielding hesitated, and I suspected that what he was going to tell me next might not be entirely the truth. I waited.

"I don't know how any of this will help you," he finally said, "but in the interest of helping you solve a crime I'll tell you what I can." Trisha gave him time to collect himself while she served me my meal and refreshed both our coffees. He took a sip of the coffee before he continued. "Look, my father is, and always has been, a distant man, and I never felt as though I knew him that well, that's all."

"So I take it your mother did most of the parenting while your father was out earning his Nobel Prize?"

"I never knew my mother, Mr. Hunter."

"I'm sorry," I said. "I didn't mean to tread on painful ground."

"Don't worry, it's not really all that painful. Whoever my mother was, my father never discussed her other than to say that he lost her immediately after I was born. He never told me more than that, and, to be perfectly honest, I never tried to find out any more than that."

"I'm sorry," I said, thinking that when someone says, "to be perfectly honest," it usually means they're about to tell a lie.

"Really, it's no problem. I guess if I had really wanted to, I could have nosed around birth records and found out who she was. But what would it have mattered? If she had never bothered to contact me, it could only have been for one of two reasons: she was dead, or she just didn't want to. Either way, I didn't see much point in pursuing it."

"Did your father ever remarry?"

"No, he didn't. As I said, my father is a rather remote man, completely devoted to his work. As far as I could tell, he neither needed nor wanted anyone else in his life."

"So where did that leave you?" I asked, thinking that children who grow up lonely and unloved quite often remain lonely and unloved.

"I was raised mostly by a succession of nannies until I was deemed old enough to be sent off to boarding school at the age of ten. So, as you can hopefully see, to say that I wasn't all that close to my father is probably being kind about it."

"But you do keep in touch with him?"

"Of course I do. He is my father, after all, and he's in his nineties. He is remarkably robust for his age, but I still worry about him. He has permanent homecare, though, and I have to admit that more often than not when I call to check up on him I spend more time talking to the housekeeper and the nurse than I do with him."

"It must have been quite a blow to him to learn of Dr. Danforth's death, particularly given the circumstances."

"I would guess that if he were ever going to mourn someone's death it would be Dr. Danforth's. You were right when you mentioned earlier that their friendship went beyond any professional bond. It was as puzzling to me as it was to anyone else, but it was undeniable."

"Did that bother you?"

"Oh, Mr. Hunter, I thought you were a private investigator, not a grief counsellor." He tried to sound amused as he said it, but I could tell that I'd struck a nerve.

"It's amazing how often my job requires me to be both," I replied, trying to keep things light.

"Touché," Fielding replied.

"Well, then?"

"'Well, what?"

"I guess I'd like to know," I replied, "if your father's relationship with Ada Danforth bothered you."

"Look," he said, his expression turning wary, "I don't know what you're getting at here, but you made a long trip, and I agreed to see you, so to be polite, I'll answer: Yes, it bothered me; it upset me, if you will. For heaven's sake, he was in his seventies, and she was just a teenager. Other people couldn't help but notice, and that was personally embarrassing to me. Don't you think I had reason to be upset?"

"That depends," I replied.

"On what?"

"On whether you thought it was just personal affection, or if it went beyond that. Do you think one of them, or both of them, had something resembling romantic feelings for the other?"

"Oh, really, Mr. Hunter."

"Because if it was just a personal affection, I don't understand why it would have upset you, and I don't understand why you would have cared what other people thought. But it *did* upset you. You said so."

"Mr. Hunter, I have tried to be accommodating. I have tried to be polite. But I'm starting to feel that what you're trying to do here is fabricate a motive for me to want Dr. Danforth dead, which is patently ridiculous. I had only a passing acquaintance with her, and, as I've already told you, I wasn't close at all to my father. So, I think I should terminate this conversation, and I think you should find someone else to pick on, maybe the person who actually murdered the poor woman."

"Professor Fielding," I said, holding up my arms in mock surrender, "I'm not here to accuse you of anything. And I'm not trying to accuse your father of anything. You just have to understand that almost all murders like this involve someone the victim knew, most often a loved one or a relative. Dr. Danforth was a recluse who was close to very few people, at least from what I can tell, so when I do find people who knew her, I have to ask every question I can think of."

"I guess I can understand that," said Fielding, "but you have made me personally uncomfortable, nevertheless."

"I'm sorry if I've done that," I replied. "But my client is dead, and I feel as though I have to advocate for her as forcefully as possible."

"Mr. Hunter, I know you have a difficult job, but I still feel as though I should end this conversation."

"I can't make you stay here, Professor, so please feel free to leave if you want. But I'd like to ask you one final question before you leave."

"Fine," said Fielding, "but please make it quick. I have a lot of work to do, and the weather does not look promising."

I took a look outside. He was right. I was suddenly eager to leave, too.

"You're right," I said, "so I'll make this quick. It seems that you spoke to Dr. Danforth frequently over the last few months of her life. Not to sound skeptical, Professor, but it seems the two of you had a lot to talk about. Can you help me with that?"

I sat silently while he tried to process what I'd just said. He was saved by the bell as Trisha came by to pick up my plate and offer us a refresh on the coffee. We both declined the coffee, and I asked for the check. She gave me a funny look as she walked off with the dishes. The diner hadn't gotten any more crowded while we were there, and she probably couldn't have helped but overhear the tenseness in our voices as we spoke. Fielding bought a little more time as we waited for Trisha to bring me the check. I gave her thirty bucks on a fifteen-dollar bill and told her to keep the change. I also gave her one of my patented winning smiles, but none of it worked. I guessed Fielding was a regular customer and she was being loyal to him; otherwise I was positive my battle-tested smile would have melted her.

"How do you know that?" said Fielding, snapping my attention back to the issue at hand.

"Let's just say I know, okay?"

"I can have you arrested for eavesdropping, you know. I know my rights."

"I doubt that, Professor Fielding. But in any event, you won't, so let's just move on, alright?"

"Those phone conversations are none of your business, and I will not discuss them. Period. Now," he said as he stood up, "I must go. I'm sorry you came all this way for nothing." He turned to leave, just in time for one last question to occur to me.

"Dr. Fielding?" I said. He turned to face me, glowering. He said nothing, so I decided to plow ahead. "Did you attend the New York State Professors of Science conference last year?"

"Yes," he said, turning away again.

"Did you see Ada while you were there?"

"No, I didn't," said Fielding. "I didn't even know she was there." If he hadn't added that second sentence I might have believed him. But I didn't believe that anyone at that conference could have been unaware of Ada's presence.

"How about Dr. Justine Tan or Dr. Paul Janssen?"

He stared at me long and hard. "I don't know either of them."

The lies were coming hard and fast now, but the Niagara Diner was neither the time nor the place for where the conversation would have to go. This time when he turned to leave I knew I'd lost him for good.

"Okay," I said. I took my time getting my coat on, giving Fielding time to get out the door ahead of me.

"Thanks for everything," I said to Trisha on my way out. She gave me a dirty look in return, so I figured I'd save another smile for another time.

The temperature had gone down, and the dark skies had lowered while we'd been in the diner. Tiny flakes of snow were starting to spit from the sky. It occurred to me that I hadn't given any thought to where I was going to stay for the night. I certainly wasn't going to make it home in this weather. I let the GPS guide me out of town and onto the Thruway, headed east. I'd figure something out.

But I left Buffalo with a smile on my face. It was a nice town, and I hadn't made the journey for nothing.

*   *   *   *   *   *

I was just past Rochester when I finally had to admit that, my four-wheel drive SUV notwithstanding, I had to get off the road. The next exit said, "Victor," the town where Dr. Lionel Fielding had grown up. I took it as an omen and got off the highway. There was a Comfort Inn two minutes from the exit, so I pulled off there and got a room.

I don't stay in hotels very often, but if there's one thing I've learned about modern hotels in my life is that they're predictable: no surprises, pleasant or unpleasant. My room featured a king-sized bed that was going to feel way too big without Doreen there to share it with me, a small sofa, cable TV, a spacious and immaculate looking bathroom, a minifridge, and, of course, free Wi-Fi. There were also vending machines in the lobby, and I considered just loading up on snacks and calling it a night. But the tuna sandwich at the Niagara Grill hadn't stuck with me, and there was a diner across the street that looked inviting, and, even better, it looked open. I was too tired for anything to drink, which was a good thing because it turned out the diner didn't have a liquor license. But they did have a Pot Roast Dinner Special, which looked to me like the answer to a prayer and tasted even better. I hadn't had the opportunity to insult any of her other customers, so the waitress, "Betsy," gave me a nice smile when I got up to leave.

CHAPTER TWENTY

I T WAS ONLY 8:30 by the time I got back to my room, so I brushed my teeth, got undressed, and turned on the TV, hoping to catch a weather forecast, after which I planned to call Doreen and then Steve Goldfarb to catch up with what was going on back home. The big mistake I made was climbing onto the bed and propping my head up on a pillow. The next thing I knew, it was 5:30 in the morning and the TV was still on. I heard the weatherman announcing that the storm had passed, and that western New York was going to get "an early present from Santa," as he put it, a beautiful, clear, snowless day.

The hotel offered a buffet breakfast, but I was in the mood for more than that, so after I showered and shaved and checked out I scooted back over to the diner across the street. Betsy was still there, looking a little bleary-eyed. I asked her what kind of shift she worked. She said, no, it was just that the regular night waitress had called up and said that she couldn't make it in because the parking lot at her apartment complex was snowed in, so Betsy had volunteered to pull the graveyard shift, after what had already been a long day.

"It's okay," she said. "It's not like I had to do much waitressing, and with Christmas coming I can use the extra money anyway, y'know?"

At one time in my life, I guess I did know that. But then I got lucky in more ways than I could count, and it took Betsy to remind me. I ate a modest breakfast, but it was hot and tasty, and when Betsy brought me the check, I wrote "Merry Christmas" on it and laid a fifty on top. Then I slipped out before she got back to the table. She missed the priceless gift of one of my winning smiles, but I figured she'd survive the loss.

I was going to get back on the Thruway, but the car's GPS informed me that the quickest route to Ithaca, home of Cornell University, was simply to stay on Route 96, the state road that ran by the Comfort Inn, and take it all the way down. It was a spectacular drive, but it also served as a reminder of the poverty that still persists in that part of New York. There are a lot of families in upstate New York whose only hope of meat through the long winter is to bag a deer, or maybe two if they're willing to flout the poaching regulations which, from what I've heard, is so common it amounts to a pastime. And who's going to blame them?

I also spent almost the entire trip on the phone, which, thanks to Doreen's Lexus, I was able to do hands free through a Bluetooth connection. I always feel a little awkward sitting alone in a car and talking out-loud, but it's a brave new world, and I've learned to deal with it. It turned out that things were pretty quiet on both the home and investigative fronts. The other three kids would all be getting home for the semester break later in the day, and Doreen and Donnie would be having their first meeting with Harvey Golub after lunch, so there would be a lot to talk about by the time I got home. I asked Steve Goldfarb to see if he could get Beth or Lacey to dig up EZ-Pass records on Michael Fielding's car. He was initially hesitant about the request, but after I told him about my conversation with Fielding the day before, Goldfarb said he felt he had enough to justify it.

Unlike his son, Dr. Lionel Fielding had invited me to his home, but instead of giving me an address, saying that an address would do me no good, he gave me some brief directions instead. They directed me to get off Route 96 onto a small back road at "an intersection with a Shell station on the left," a road that was probably impassable through much of the winter without an SUV or a truck. Then I got my first surprise before I even met the man.

Once I'd pulled off the road at "a large green sign that says 'Dew Drop Inn, 5 miles," I found myself in a small parking lot at the base of a tall, snow-covered cliff. There was no sign of a house, and I realized what he meant when he'd said that an address wouldn't help me. Puzzled, I got out of the car to look around and it was then that I noticed a small sign that said, "Take The Cable Car." I looked around and, sure enough, about twenty yards away, was a cable car designed to look like an old English brougham attached to a series of cables that led up to the top of the cliff.

I locked my car, walked over to it, and found another sign that said, "Please Climb In And Close The Door Behind You." I did as I was told, and I found myself in what looked like a Victorian era sitting room, replete with leather chairs and a sofa that could altogether comfortably seat around ten people. I sat down in one of the chairs, and a few short seconds later there was a slight shudder as the cable car started its journey up the steep hill. It only took a few minutes, and when I stepped out I was greeted with the sight of what looked like a large ski chalet, invisible from the ground, overlooking an incredible vista of Lake Cayuga, perhaps the most famous of the Finger Lakes. There was another sign that said "Please Ring The Bell At The Door," with an arrow directing me toward the chalet. I walked to the large, wooden door and was about to ring the bell when the door suddenly opened. I expected that one of the house staff would greet me and take me to meet Dr. Fielding, who I imagined would be a frail, ancient creature sitting in a wheelchair under a quilt. That's what I get for thinking.

Unlike his son, Professor Lionel Fielding was a large man, still standing a robust six-feet tall even though his back was slightly stooped with age. His hair was white, but thick and carefully combed. His face looked like it was carved from granite, with a prominent nose, a strong jaw, and a stubborn-looking chin. But his most remarkable feature was his eyes, deep green and sparkling with intelligence. He was, all in all, the most virile looking nonagenarian I had ever met.

"Enjoy the ride?" he said, an amused grin on his face.

"Sure did," I said, smiling back.

"Good. Well, don't just stand there. I don't want to be heating the whole county now, do I?"

"I guess not," I said, stepping inside into a large foyer whose ceiling went all the way up to the roof. I held out my large hand, and one just as large reached out to shake it. His grip was firm and dry.

"I've got a fire going upstairs, so let's not waste it standing here." He led me over to a long flight of stairs that he hopped up with surprising agility. At the top of the stairs was an enormous room constructed completely of cylindrical, wood-cabin like timbers, and topped by a vaulted roof that reminded me of a European cathedral. An immense fireplace took up most of the east wall, while the north wall was fabricated entirely of glass, overlooking the southern tip of Lake Cayuga. A half-dozen leather-upholstered sofas and chairs faced the fireplace, with a grouping of Adirondack chairs facing the glass and overlooking the lake.

"Winning a Nobel Prize has its benefits," he said, as he watched me gazing around the room.

"I guess it does," I said.

"Take a seat – anywhere – it doesn't matter to me."

I wanted to take a seat that afforded the view of Lake Cayuga, but I was afraid that it would be too much of a distraction, so I sat down in one of the upholstered chairs by the fireplace, which was distracting in its own way, but it would have to do.

"Can I get you something to eat or drink?" Fielding asked.

"A cup of coffee would be great," I said.

"Sounds good to me, too," he replied. "Just a second." He pushed a button on what looked like an intercom and spoke a few brief instructions. In a few moments, a tray arrived with a pot of coffee, a jug of cream, a bowl of sugar, and a couple of muffins.

"Thanks," I said, "this looks great."

"I hope you like bran muffins," he said, as he poured a liberal dollop of cream into his coffee, but ignored the sugar. "They're the only kinds of muffins I eat these days. My nurse seems to think they're just the thing for my superannuated digestive system."

"You look terrific, Professor Fielding," I said. "What's your secret?"

"No secrets, just dumb luck," he replied, sitting down and biting into a muffin. "I've been lucky in so many ways in my life it's almost embarrassing to think about it, but one of them is I seem to have won the genetic lottery. I've always eaten what I want and done what I want, and the old machine just keeps chugging away in spite of me. But look, I know you already had a long day yesterday, and you're looking at a long drive this afternoon, so let's not waste any more time discussing me and my dumb luck."

"Thanks," I said. "But I have to admit, it's a beautiful drive."

"It certainly is that," said Fielding. "I used to like nothing more than taking a long drive, but I can't do that anymore. My eyes get tired, and my hearing isn't what it used to be. There are certain things I have to be practical about." He finished off his muffin and poured himself a little more coffee, and I did the same. He stared into the fire, and it seemed to mesmerize him for a moment, but he snapped himself out it quickly. "So," he said, "ask away."

"First of all," I began, "I'd like to offer my condolences. I've been told that you remained close to Dr. Danforth, and it must be a terrible loss."

"Ada Danforth is a remarkable woman, and it has been a privilege to know her as I have. She is a giant in her field, and I stand in awe of her along with everyone else."

I was puzzled by his use of the present tense, but I also know that it takes people time to start referring to lost loved ones in the past tense. Or, it just could have been a senior moment. I let it pass.

"It must have hurt you to see how she was treated by her peers after that interview she gave."

"First of all," said Fielding, with some real heat in his voice, "those people were not her peers. Ada Danforth has no peers. They were just the usual collection of small minds who fail to honor prophets in their own time. I can tell you that their treatment of Ada didn't bother her in the least."

"But it must have bothered you."

"Of course it did, but Ada taught me to let all that go, although I admittedly have my lapses. The world was not ready for Ada, and she knew that one day she would have to pay the price for that, like so many other prophets."

"But there must have been others, like you. Fellow Nobelists, perhaps –"

"Ada Danforth has no peers," said Fielding again, chopping the air with his right hand. "Not me, not anyone. I was Ada's student from the day she arrived on the Cornell campus. The woman was, quite simply, one of a kind."

I thought of small, shy, unprepossessing Ada. A giant. The woman who elicited powerful emotions from everyone she touched, including the man sitting across from me, while seemingly remaining untouched herself. A being apart.

"Your son tells me that perhaps you and Dr. Danforth had a relationship that went beyond the professional," I said, thinking that there was no sense in wasting any time on niceties with this man.

"I'm sure," said Fielding, "at least if you are half the private investigator that people say you are, that you haven't found a single person – friend, family, colleague – that was capable of reacting to Ada objectively."

"You've spoken to people about me?"

"Oh, please, Mr. Hunter, don't go getting insecure on me. I merely googled your website and found all those wonderful testimonies to your Sherlock Holmes-like skills and professionalism."

"Sorry," I said. "That was stupid of me. Yes, I have learned a lot about how people reacted to Dr. Danforth, and you're right: no one was indifferent."

"I tried to talk to her family over the years, beginning when she first came to Cornell, but it was useless. They felt like they'd given birth to a Martian, and they just couldn't deal with it. How are they doing, by the way?"

"I guess if anything, they're relieved. I know that sounds terrible, but I don't know how else to describe it." I decided Professor Fielding didn't need to know about the whole Love Boat thing if he didn't already know.

"It's not terrible; I'm glad to hear it, and I know that Ada would be relieved to hear it, too."

"Just to backtrack a little, Professor: I know that Dr. Danforth was only a teenager when you first met her, but you seem to have stayed in touch over the years. Did you ever share what anyone might call romantic feelings?"

"I am assuming, Mr. Hunter," he replied after hesitating only briefly, "that if you've learned anything at all about me, it is that I am not a 'romantic' in any sense of the word."

"But you did father a child."

"Yes, I did."

"So I'm assuming that at least once in your life you had a romantic relationship with someone."

"It could have been just a one-night stand, you know," he said, raising one eyebrow.

"Pardon me, Professor Fielding, but you don't impress me as a man who would get involved in a one-night stand."

Lionel Fielding hesitated long enough for it start to feel uncomfortable. His supreme confidence started to falter for just a moment. But then he seemed to recover.

"You're right," he said.

"So, you were in love with your son's mother, then?"

Another pause.

"Yes."

"But you never maintained any kind of contact with her."

"Mr. Hunter, I don't think any of this is relevant to your purpose for being here. It has nothing whatsoever to do with Ada Danforth's death, and I'd rather move on."

"I don't mean to pry, Professor," I said, noting that he hadn't answered my question, when a simple "no" would have sufficed. "It's just that your son seems to have been profoundly affected by the lack of a mother and, frankly, your indifference as a father. And all that seems to have affected how he felt about Ada Danforth. So I'm sorry, but it seems relevant to me. You were aware, weren't you, that your son seems to have been in contact with Dr. Danforth during the last year of her life?"

"I recall that Ada mentioned that to me during one of our conversations, but she never made much of it, so neither did I."

He was lying. I couldn't prove it, and I wasn't about to try, but I knew it. But he was also clearly tiring. He may have been a robust nonagenarian, but he was a nonagenarian nevertheless, and I knew that my remaining time with him would be limited, either by him or his caretakers, so I had to get on with it.

"So you don't think your son had any romantic feelings for Dr. Danforth?"

He wasn't ready for that one, and again he hesitated. He stared into the fire for a few moments.

"I can tell you for an absolute fact," he finally said, looking back at me, "that my son never had any romantic feelings for Ada Danforth."

"Look," I said, "I really appreciate the time that you've been willing to spend with me, but it's probably time for me to get going soon, so, if you don't mind, I'll just ask a couple more quick questions, and then I'll get back on the road."

"I guess you're right," said Fielding. "So ask what you must."

I was pretty sure he knew what I was going to ask, so I plunged ahead.

"We've talked a lot about the powerful feelings that Ada Danforth aroused in the people who knew her."

"Yes, we have."

"Do you know anyone whose feelings were so powerful that they might have made that person capable of murdering her?"

Professor Lionel Fielding stared at me long and hard.

"People tell me that I'm a genius, Mr. Hunter," he finally said, shifting his gaze to the fire. "Who knows? Maybe I am. I have been able to advance humankind's knowledge of the universe in ways that not many other people have been able to do. Ada Danforth was another one of those people. But one thing that has baffled me from the time I was very young is human nature. You know, people have often accused me of being cold and distant. My own son has accused me of that. Maybe those people are right, but I don't think they understand me. You see, from the time I was a child, learning came easily to me. My ego thrived on my ability to master concepts so abstract that few, if any, would ever be able to understand them at all. I not only mastered that kind of difficult knowledge; I created it; I advanced it. But I don't understand my fellow man, Mr. Hunter. I don't understand *people*. And so, in my vanity, I turned away from them, because my ego was insulted by the fact that I could no more understand people than the average human being could understand quantum physics. So, to answer your question: No, I don't know anyone who would want to murder Ada Danforth, but I wouldn't expect myself to. But we both know the powerful feelings she elicited from others, so I guess it could be almost anyone."

"But you were in love with Ada Danforth."

Lionel Fielding eyed me warily. He turned his head to stare out the vast window at the heavenly view. I was starting to worry that I'd lost him, but then he turned back and stared directly at me once again. He looked like a man who'd just made up his mind.

"For some reason I trust you, Mr. Hunter, and I badly want Ada Danforth's murder solved. If I have to open myself up to you completely to help you do that, then so be it. And I guess there's no harm in saying it now, is there? Yes, I am in love with Ada Danforth. I have been in love with her since the day I met her, and I have loved her every day since. And if I'm going to be honest, I'm going to be completely, totally honest. It was not just platonic love, Mr. Hunter. By the time she left Cornell, I desired her; I lusted after her. God help me, you can't imagine the guilt, the shame I felt for having those feelings for that young girl."

"Do you think Ada knew that?"

"Of course, I did everything in my power to hide those feelings, and it goes without saying that I never in any way acted on them, but—"

"'But' what?"

"Yes. She knew how I felt."

"Did she ever tell you that?" I said, trying to keep the disbelief out of my voice.

"No, of course she didn't. It all remained unspoken, but we both knew. And more than that —"

"Yes?"

"She had those same feelings for me."

I tried not to appear shocked by that, but I probably failed. "But neither of you ever acted on them," I finally said.

"Ada and I both knew that in this life, in this world, we could never do that. Both our reputations would have been destroyed. It was out of the question."

"Even after Ada grew to adulthood?"

"I don't know if you have developed any understanding of academic politics during your investigation, Mr. Hunter. By the time Ada had grown to adulthood, she had already been disgraced by the ignorant fools in the scientific community, and I was nearing eighty. I'm sure that you can imagine the tongue-wagging that would have gone on if we had ever made our feelings known."

"But by that time Ada's reputation was destroyed anyway."

"Yes, that's true, but her name would have been dragged through the mud all over again at a time when things were finally starting to quiet down, and my legacy would have been tarnished. Neither of us wanted any of that."

"What about now?" I asked. "Do you have any regrets now?"

"I'm in my nineties. I try to limit my regrets to things that I can change and that I have the time to change, and that's precious little. But let me tell you something as a quantum physicist that I hope you will remember as an everyday lesson in life, Mr. Hunter: Every single thing you do, every single decision you make, you and everyone else in this world, changes the universe forever in ways that no one can begin to contemplate. None of us has the time or the comprehension to regret all the consequences of all our actions. So perhaps regrets are pointless at any age."

"What do you mean?" I said.

"It doesn't matter," said Fielding, sounding resigned and tired. "Look, it doesn't matter how great or small the action; it doesn't even matter whether you're conscious of it or remember it. It can be something as big or small as simply saying 'thank you' to someone, or perhaps it's making love to your wife or lover without bothering to use birth control. All of your actions have consequences, and they change other people in ways that you can never foresee, and that changes the world forever. So, be careful, Mr. Hunter: Every single day you – and I – change the universe forever."

I didn't know what to ask after that, and in any event I never had the chance. As if on cue, a stern looking nurse appeared at the top of the stairs, gave me a hard stare, and then looked at Dr. Lionel Fielding as if he were a disobedient child.

"I have your lunch ready downstairs," she said to Fielding, but frowning at me, making it clear that I would not be fed, "and then you'll need a nap."

Fielding deliberately looked at me and not the nurse. "Would you like some lunch, Mr. Hunter? I rarely dine with anyone these days, and I'd love the company."

"I'm not sure the cook –" began the nurse.

"The cook can manage a second serving," said Fielding. "For heaven's sake, the pantry in this place always has at least six months of food stocked up. And there will be plenty of time for napping once I'm dead, so let's not fret about that. Please, Mr. Hunter, I would truly appreciate your company."

"That sounds wonderful," I said. "Thank you. You keep six month's-worth of food here?"

"This is a beautiful home, and I love living here, but's it's remote, and the winters here are harsh. There are times when we're snowed in for weeks, so some preparation is required."

The nurse stared daggers at me, but I think that anyone who makes it past their ninetieth birthday has earned the right to do what they damn please, and Fielding was clearly hoping for the rare opportunity of company for a meal.

We enjoyed a wonderful lunch of beefy, homemade soup and a fresh salad, served with home-baked bread, over which we chatted about nothing in particular, which I think we both needed. By the time we'd finished our meal, however, Fielding was clearly in need of a nap despite his protests, and I was ready to get back on the road. I thanked the chef for the fine meal, and I thanked the nurse for her indulgence. The chef was pleased to receive the compliment, but the nurse didn't seem mollified.

After bidding Fielding farewell, I took the tram back down the hill and got back into the Lexus for the trip home. I made a brief call to tell Doreen that I'd be back in time for supper, but mostly I spent the trip lost in my own thoughts, thoughts about Michael Fielding, Lionel Fielding, and Ada Danforth. I didn't know what I'd learned from the Fieldings, but I was left with the sure suspicion that they both had told me far from everything they knew. What they were hiding? I didn't know, and I didn't think I'd ever find out from them. But I had to find out somehow, because I knew that I would never solve Ada Danforth's murder otherwise.

CHAPTER TWENTY-ONE

THE FIRST THING I thought of when I woke up the next morning was that it was only a few days until Christmas and I still hadn't gotten Doreen a present. The next thing I thought of was the gift that she had waiting for me after we'd climbed into bed the night before.

I'd gotten home right about dinnertime, and I was treated to the cacophony of dinner preparation in Doreen's kitchen. All four kids were there, talking and joking with each other over the sound of some goofy holiday movie on the Hallmark Channel. Fresh bread was baking in the oven; bolognèse sauce was bubbling on the stove; my son, Cal, was busily turning out fresh linguine from a pasta machine, and Doreen was sitting at the big round table with a glass of red wine in her hand and a contented smile on her face.

"Make yourself a drink," she said to me. "The kids are making dinner tonight."

I mixed myself a martini and brought it over to the table to sit down next to Doreen. Normally, we'd sit in the loveseat in the little seating nook that she had created at the far end of the kitchen and ignore the news on the television while we chatted about our days, but I knew that she wanted to immerse herself in the busy-ness of her family, and so did I.

"Good day?" I asked, just loud enough for her to hear.

"Fine," she said, "but we can talk about it later. How about you?"

"Fascinating," I said, "but I'd like to let that wait, too. I think I'd just like to enjoy the evening with the kids."

"Me, too. It feels like they've been away forever."

Dinner was fabulous – hot, flavorful, and satisfying. The kids cleaned up while we all stayed in the kitchen and talked about everything from school to the Mets and the Jets, to the latest movies, none of which I'd seen or even heard of. It was the most fun I'd had in a long while.

Doreen and I did chat for a while after dinner once the kids had all scattered and we'd retreated to the bedroom, but after she showed up in bed without her nightie conversation came to a halt, and we both fell sound asleep shortly thereafter.

"Good morning," I heard her murmur, as she rolled over to my side of the bed. Because I'm a professional investigator, I immediately noted that she still wasn't wearing her nightie.

"Good morning," I said.

"In the mood for an eye-opener?" she whispered in my ear, sliding one of her delicious thighs between mine.

"Apparently I am," I said, because apparently I was.

Let's just say that my day got off to a good start.

We made it down to the kitchen about eight. It was quiet and empty, and I didn't expect to see any of the kids until at least ten. We put some coffee on, and once we'd gotten our mugs filled we sat ourselves down on the loveseat in the seating nook. At least Doreen was dressed by then, and I was able to tear my mind away from all the lovemaking.

"Why don't you tell me what Harvey had to say yesterday?" I asked.

"Well, the good news is that one of Harvey's Columbia Law classmates is a graduate of Stuyvesant and is also on its Board of Trustees. He's aware of the issue and has been working with the president of the university and his fellow Trustees to make their policy more equitable and transparent. But that's going to take years."

"Donnie doesn't have years."

"No, he doesn't. So the president agreed to expunge Donnie's case from the record on the condition that Donnie doesn't request reinstatement."

"That's great," I said "Donnie doesn't want to go back to Stuyvesant anyway."

"That's true," said Doreen, "but Harvey said that it's important for him to have this whole incident expunged from his record so that when he begins applying to other schools, his transcripts from Stuyvesant will be clean.

"I'm glad for all that," I said, "but I just feel bad that Donnie has to go through all this. The poor kid's endured enough over the past couple of years, and I'm sure that his father's behavior made him wonder if there wasn't something wrong with him, too, despite the facts."

That wasn't something Doreen was ready to talk about, so in her way, she just didn't. She changed the subject and asked me about my visits to Buffalo and Ithaca. I gave her as detailed a summary as possible, both to organize and solidify my own impressions, but most importantly to hear her thoughts. As usual, she didn't disappoint me, but she did surprise me.

"I think you're getting closer, Matt," she said after what seemed like an endless pause.

"I don't feel like I'm any closer," I said. "I mean, yeah, Lionel Fielding confessed that he'd been in love with Ada, but he didn't impress me at all as the kind of guy who would commit murder, especially not her."

"I'm not talking about Lionel Fielding," said Doreen. "I'm talking about his son."

"I've got to tell you, Doreen, I thought the guy was kind of strange, but he didn't come across to me at all like a killer either".

"But think about it, Matt. It's almost like a Greek tragedy, you know, a variation on the Oedipus complex: The mother he never knew, and worse, who possibly never wanted to know him; the cold, distant, but domineering father who not only kept him from his mother, but who replaced her with a completely inappropriate young woman *who was also his intellectual superior.* No matter where Michael Fielding turned, all he found was rejection and humiliation, and after a long life, it just got to be too much."

"Okay," I said, "but why now? I mean, this stuff has been going on all his life. Let's say you're right, and Michael Fielding was involved in her murder, wouldn't there have to be some recent event that caused him to act on all those feelings after all these years?"

Doreen again sat silently for a long time. She never speaks until she's ready, and I'd given her something to think about. That doesn't happen very often, which makes it all the more gratifying when it does.

"You're right," she finally said after she had drained the last of her coffee from her cup, "but I'm afraid I can't help you with that. I'm willing to bet, though, that that was what Ada and Michael were communicating about during the last year of her life."

"But how am I supposed to find out what that was? Michael Fielding certainly isn't going to tell me, and Ada can't."

"That's true," said Doreen, "but you know Paul Janssen, who was in touch with Ada right up to the end, and you know Justine Tan, who's known Michael Fielding for years. They're probably both long shots, but they're what you have right now. If I were you, I'd have another go at them. And I'd also stop by the Latitude."

That one caught me by surprise.

"Why the Latitude?"

"Because if I'm even close to being right about this, I think Michael Fielding would have wanted a personal confrontation with Ada, and I think Ada would have wanted to meet him in a safe place, if she agreed to see him at all. And I think the safest place she knows is the Latitude."

"I don't think I would have thought of that," I said. "Thanks."

"Isn't it amazing just how many of your urgent needs I can satisfy?" she said, giving me a smile that made me feel warm all over.

"You know, I think I'm starting to forget already," I said, smiling back, probably looking hopeful.

"Do you think you might like a reminder?" she said, taking me by the hand and standing up. Her auburn hair was unkempt, she was wearing no makeup, and all she was wearing was the old sweatshirt and a faded pair of jeans she'd thrown on before we'd come downstairs. She was the most beautiful thing I'd ever seen. My throat went dry, and I couldn't have said anything even if I had something to say. It turned out I didn't have to.

"Come on," she said, looking down at me. "We can't have the kids seeing you like this."

CHAPTER TWENTY-TWO

"**W**ELL, don't you look like the cat who just ate the canary," said Linda Morris with a mischievous grin on her face when I walked into the office around ten. There was a large cup of McDonald's coffee on her desk, and the coffee maker was off, which my keen detective instincts told me was because Harvey Golub had picked up coffee on his way in from morning prayers. The Orthodox Jewish community in this part of New York is growing rapidly, but it's still tiny, and Harvey's and Steve Goldfarb's attendance at the prayers was usually the difference between having a minyan and not having one. Harvey almost never missed, and Steve only missed when police work prevented him from attending.

"I don't know what you're talking about," I said, giving her an innocent smile back. Linda was good people, and I never minded her ribbing, just as she never minded mine.

"I hope you saved at least a little bit of energy," she said. "You've got a crowd waiting for you."

"Thanks for the heads up," I said, as I turned to head down the hallway.

When I got to my office, I was greeted by the sight of Steve Goldfarb, Beth Gardner, and Harvey Golub crowded into my small space, all holding large cups of McDonald's coffee. I was about to feel left out until I spotted the unopened cup sitting on my desk.

"To what do I owe the honor of this distinguished company?" I said, grabbing my cup. I took a sip; it was still hot.

"I believe Detective Goldfarb and Officer Gardner are here on business," said Harvey. "I was just in here kibbitzing until you got here. I'll leave you all to your business now that you're here." He turned to leave.

"Before you go, Harvey," I said, "I just want to say thanks."

"Don't thank me yet," he replied, giving me a lawyerly gaze. Harvey and I were about the same age, but his thinning, prematurely graying hair made him look older, without making him look old. "You haven't gotten my bill." I thought I detected a glint of humor in his eyes when he said that, but with Harvey you never know.

"What was that all about?" asked Goldfarb after Harvey had left.

"Oh, nothing," I said. "Harvey's just taking care of a little personal matter for us, that's all." Steve and I usually share just about everything with each other, but it was Donnie's matter, so I had to be careful. "Anything new?"

"Not really," said Beth. Her youthful face had matured noticeably over the past few weeks, and I almost regretted having pulled her into this mess. But I also knew that it was what she wanted, and she had no regrets despite the personal price she was paying. She also had the comfort of knowing that she was doing a damn good job, and that both Steve and I knew it.

"Did you have a chance to look into Michael Fielding's EZ-Pass records?" I asked.

"Didn't need to," said Beth. "He doesn't own a car."

"Then how does he get around?"

"He lives in one of the old neighborhoods in the center of Buffalo, and he just takes buses everywhere. From what we can tell, he's pretty much a hermit, and he spends his life either at the university or in his apartment. We can't find any close personal friends of either sex, and even his colleagues at the university don't seem to know him that well."

"Were you able to find out if he's had any unexplained or unexpected absences from the university lately?"

"The problem is," said Beth, "it's not like anybody really pays attention to him, so we couldn't find anybody who had any specific recollection of his being away. He doesn't teach undergrad courses anymore, and his grad students only meet with him when they have to, and none of them remembered Fielding not being there when they needed an appointment."

"I take it from this discussion," said Goldfarb, "that you're starting to focus on Michael Fielding as a serious suspect."

"You know how it is, Steve. Ada Danforth was murdered over two weeks ago, and we're still basically nowhere. So at this point, I'm looking at everyone as a serious suspect." I also told them about my conversation with Doreen. She may not have been a cop, but they both had tremendous respect for her mind, and they took her observations seriously.

"Okay, then," said Goldfarb, looking at his watch, "where do we go from here?"

"I'm going to clear up some paperwork here," I said, staring at my cluttered desk, "and answer some phone calls until lunchtime, then I'm going up to the Latitude to talk with Richie Glazier."

"You want company?" asked Beth, probably sensing a chance to mix work with pleasure. Beth liked Richie, and she liked his food even more.

"I think I'll take care of that by myself," I said. "In the meantime, I'd like to see if you can find any records of air travel or car rentals in Michael Fielding's name."

"Anything else?" said Goldfarb.

"Then I'm going to have another go at Justine Tan," I said.

"What more do you think you're going to get from her?" asked Goldfarb.

"She gave me the stiff-arm when I tried to talk to her about Michael Fielding before I drove out to visit him. I let her get away with it then, but I'm not going to make that mistake this time. It could get interesting."

* * * * * *

"I work awfully hard to make that coleslaw both nutritious *and* delicious, you know," said Richie, scowling at my plate. He was carrying a small tray with two coffees and a small pitcher of cream.

I hadn't been planning to eat at the Latitude, but the food smells when I got there were irresistible, and I strongly suspected it was going to be a long afternoon. In addition, Richie was hung up on an unexpected business call with a supplier, and I didn't just want to hang around cooling my heals. So I opted for health food and ordered a bacon cheeseburger with French fries and coleslaw from the nice waiter who sat me in my usual quiet corner, probably at Richie's direction, promising myself that I'd only eat a couple of the fries. By the time Richie showed up the fries were gone and I was on the last bite of my burger, but I still had plenty of coleslaw to work on.

"It's really great," I said, wolfing down a few large bites. It really was.

"Don't worry," said Richie, "I'm not your mother."

"My mother never made coleslaw like this," I said. Richie knew I wasn't lying; he'd eaten often at my house when we were kids. Mom is a lovely lady, but as a cook she's an also-ran at best. Luckily, Dad's a completely indifferent eater, one of those people I just don't understand who only eat to stop being hungry. Where Lacey and I got our love of food from I'll never know.

"At the risk of sounding optimistic," said Richie as he passed me my coffee, "can I hope that you're here because you're making progress on Ada's case?"

"I don't know, Richie," I said. "It depends on what you're going to tell me." I pulled an envelope out of my jacket pocket that contained photographs of varying quality of all of the potential suspects in the case.

"It's always good to feel needed," said Richie, but he didn't smile as he stared at the envelope.

I pulled out the picture of Michael Fielding and laid it on the table next to Richie's coffee cup.

"Ever seen this guy?" I said.

Richie is a very deliberate man in everything that he does. He picked up the photo slowly and stared at it for a long time before looking up.

"Yeah," he said. "I've seen him."

"And?"

"And, yeah, I saw him in here with Ada Danforth. It was about two months ago. Look, man, I'm sorry. I can't believe I forgot about this."

"Don't worry, Richie, it happens to all of us. Anybody else with them?"

"No, and no, I didn't go over to the table. I was going to, but Ada caught my eye and gave me one of those 'not right now' looks."

"Okay, but how did they seem? Did it look like they were arguing, or anything like that?"

"Nothing like that. But there *was* something going on."

"Like what?"

"It's hard to say, man. It's not like I was standing over them and staring at them, and I couldn't hear anything they were saying. But the guy, the guy seemed upset about something."

"What about Ada?"

"Ada was fine. If she hadn't seemed fine I would have gone over to the table. But the guy was upset about something, at least that's what it looked like from a distance."

"Okay, thanks, Richie."

"No prob —"

"Hey!" someone suddenly shouted from the far end of the dining room, the end overlooking the parking lot. "A car's burning!"

"I called 911, Richie!" shouted an employee from behind the bar.

Richie and I both ran over to the window, but I already knew what I was going to see. I always park at the far end of the parking lot, as far away from other cars as possible to avoid the dents and scratches that inevitably come from parking in close quarters. And there, at the far end, was my Accord, engulfed in flames. I could already hear the fire sirens in the distance, but it didn't matter. The firemen would put the fire out and avoid further hazard, but my Accord was gone. The gas tank was on fire, and so were the tires, and my beloved little car was disappearing, literally oxidizing, before my eyes.

"Well, Richie," I said, turning away from the tragic sight in the parking lot, "I think we're getting closer."

CHAPTER TWENTY-THREE

I SPENT ABOUT AN HOUR at the Latitude giving my report to the police. Afterward I called Doreen, and she'd come up to get me and bring me home, where I spent another hour on the phone with the insurance company. By that time, it was mid-afternoon and the winter daylight was already starting to dim, but I still had work to do, and it couldn't wait. I picked up my phone and dialed a number that by now was becoming familiar to me.

"Justine Tan," came the voice over the line after six rings. She sounded suspicious, and I figured my number was becoming familiar to her, too.

"Hello, Dr. Tan. This is Matt Hunter, and I need to speak to you in person, right away."

"What's this all about, Mr. Hunter?" I thought I heard a voice in the background, and I would have bet that it was Paul Janssen.

"I'd rather talk to you in person, if you don't mind."

"Look," said Justine as the voice in the background seemed to grow louder, "can't this wait until after the Holidays? Paul and I are leaving in the morning for two weeks in Aruba, and we haven't even begun to pack yet."

"No, it can't wait, and I'm guessing your odds of getting on that plane to Aruba are about 50-50 right now; and if I don't get to see you this afternoon those odds are going straight to zero."

There was a long pause as I heard, but couldn't understand, a whispered conversation in the background.

"Okay," Justine finally said, "we'll talk. We're at Paul's house; do you have his address?"

"I'd like to speak to you alone, Dr. Tan."

"Okay, then, where would you like to meet?"

Before I had the chance to respond, I heard another whispered conversation in the background, and although I couldn't hear what was being said, it sounded angry. The next voice I heard was not Justine Tan's.

"Mr. Hunter? This is Paul Janssen. Would you please tell me what this is all about? Justine and I both have been more than cooperative throughout your entire investigation, and I don't understand why you're suddenly trying to ruin a vacation that is very important to both of us."

"Put Justine back on the phone, Dr. Janssen."

"I feel that I'm owed at least some explanation, Mr. Hunter."

"Tick, tick, tick."

I heard an exasperated sigh, and then Justine was back on the phone.

"Please tell me where you would like to meet," she said.

"My office, your office at school, or your house. Your choice." I knew which one she was going to choose, but I politely gave her time to respond. It didn't take long.

"Meet me at the school in a half-hour. If you don't see my car in the parking lot, wait in your car; I'll have to unlock the door since the school is closed for the Holidays. I assume you'll be driving that little silver car?"

"No, I'll be driving a metallic black Lexus SUV."

"Oh, what happened to your other car?"

"It died a dusty death. Long story. I'll see you at the school. Please, don't be late."

* * * * * *

Justine was waiting for me in the parking lot in front of the School of Sciences building. She was driving one of those sporty looking little Acuras, and it was fire -engine red. People always surprise you. We didn't say a word to each other as we walked to the building, and then to her office. The same key card that opened the front door also opened her office door. She tossed her keys and her purse onto her desk, but she didn't sit down. The look she gave me wasn't friendly.

"What the hell is this all about, Mr. Hunter?"

"What was Michael Fielding doing out here last month, and what was he talking to Ada Danforth about?"

"What are you *talking* about?"

"Michael Fielding made a trip out here last month, and he had a meal with Ada Danforth at the Latitude. But I think you already knew that."

"I don't know anything of the sort."

"Justine, you knew Michael Fielding for years, and I'm willing to bet that it was more than just a professional friendship. The man almost never leaves Buffalo, and I'm positive that if he came all the way out here he would have contacted you beforehand, and probably visited you." I knew no such thing, but sometimes you just have to trust your instincts.

"I don't know what to tell you except that you are wrong. I haven't seen Michael Fielding since I left Buffalo five years ago."

"You've been very helpful with this case up until now, Justine, and I want you to know how much I appreciate that. And that's also why I want to give you every opportunity to be honest with me. I'm going to find out one way or the other, you know that."

"So, what, you think Michael Fielding and I, for some unfathomable reason, entered into a secret conspiracy to murder Ada Danforth, is that it?"

She said it, I didn't, but I wasn't ready to go there yet.

"So," I said.

She stared at me for a long time, and I couldn't help noticing, once again, what an attractive woman she was. Paul Janssen was going to be one of the most envied men in Aruba if they ever made it there, which I sincerely hoped they would. I was willing to bet that Justine was thinking along the same lines. A lot depended on what she was going to tell me next.

"Look, okay. I didn't see Michael, but we spoke on the phone. He wanted to see me, but I told him now wasn't a good time, what with everything that was going on with Paul. It was the first time we had spoken in five years. As I have tried to explain to you, there was never anything serious between us, and there was no reason to keep in touch."

"Then why did you lie to me about knowing that he had come out here? Would it have been so hard just to be honest?"

"Because Ada Danforth keeps messing with my life, even now that she's dead, that's why! Paul and I are finally finding some happiness, and I just want to move on while I still have the chance, but that woman won't let me go, and I'm sick of it. Can't you understand that?"

It was one of those moments. I actually believed that she was telling me the truth. I knew from painful personal experience how hard it was to escape the relentless pull of the past and not be defined by it forever. I was running out of reasons to ruin her vacation, but I still had a couple more questions.

"Do you know if Michael Fielding and Paul Janssen ever met each other?"

"I'm sure they must have met at academic conferences in the past. It's hard not to. But other than that, I don't think so."

"Okay. Did Dr. Fielding know that you and Paul were in a relationship?"

"I really don't know why he would have."

What was I supposed to do? Everything she had said sounded reasonable and, frankly, honest. Michael Fielding had obviously lied to me about a lot of things, especially involving his relationships with Justine Tan and Ada Danforth. If I should be grilling anybody, if I should be ruining anybody's Holiday season, and if there was anyone who had revealed himself as a legitimate suspect in the murder of Ada Danforth, it was Michael Fielding, not Justine Tan. And I was about to say just that and wish Justine a bon voyage to Aruba when my cell phone buzzed. I was going to ignore it, but when I looked down I saw that it was Steve Goldfarb, and I always pick up for him, as he does for me. Justine must have seen something on my face as I listened to what Steve had to say, because I saw her eyes start to widen, and her expression turn almost feral.

The next thing I knew I was lying on the floor of Justine's office, and the clock on the wall said that ten minutes had passed since I'd gotten the phone call from Goldfarb.

The other thing I knew was that Justine Tan was gone.

CHAPTER TWENTY-FOUR

SHOULD HAVE KNOWN that Justine Tan, like most smart, single women, would be carrying some kind of defensive spray in her purse, and I also should have known that she would know how to use it. And I should have known that it wouldn't be one of those run-of-the-mill pepper sprays. My head still ached as I sat in Steve Goldfarb's office in the Devon-on-Hudson police station sipping the station coffee which was awful, but helpful. Beth was there, but luckily Chief Eddie Shepherd, like half the town, had left for a warmer climate with his new wife, and he wouldn't be back until after the new year.

I didn't remember half the drive back to Devon-on-Hudson from the school, and I barely remembered calling Goldfarb to tell him what had happened. They'd both expressed concern, but we all knew that this was no time to be fretting over my health.

"Do you have any idea where they could have gone, Matt?" said Goldfarb.

"They?" I said.

"Yeah, I sent a patrol car over to Paul Janssen's house a little while ago. I could kick myself for not doing it sooner. Justine's car was in the garage, but Janssen's car wasn't there, and the house was empty."

"Have you put out a BOLO on Janssen's car?"

"Of course we have, but it's a five-year-old, blue Toyota Camry, and I'm sure he's switched out the plates by now. It'll be like finding a needle in a haystack."

"What about his E-Z Pass?"

"I've got a call into Lacey about that," said Beth.

"If I know my sister," I said, "we'll be hearing back from her pretty soon. What about their phones?"

"Lacey's looking into that, too," said Beth. "But I wouldn't get my hopes up."

"Why not?" said Goldfarb.

"Because, sir," said Beth, "these are two highly intelligent people, and I'm sure that they already thought to ditch the E-Z Pass, assuming Janssen had one, and that they've already disabled the tracking app on their phones, and probably shut them down."

"So, you're telling me that they're in the wind," I said.

"That's my guess," said Beth.

"Great." I said. "Look, before we do anything else I think we ought to take a step back and give ourselves a few minutes to think this whole thing over."

"Okay," said Goldfarb. "You start." Steve sounded discouraged, and a little angry, and I was pretty sure I knew why. The coming evening would be the last night of Chanukkah, and I knew how much he was looking forward to celebrating it with his wife and two kids. But, I also knew that he was too good a cop to walk away from this case.

"Look," I said, "up until an hour ago, I was getting myself convinced that Michael Fielding was our prime suspect. I was getting ready to tell Justine to have a nice vacation in Aruba when you called to tell me that the GPS tracker on Fielding's rental car showed him at Paul Janssen's house after he'd had his lunch with Ada at the Latitude, right after she'd just told me that Paul and Michael didn't know each other. She must have seen on my face that I'd just caught her in a lie, because that's when she nailed me with that spray, whatever it was. So I guess the question is, what would he be going to see Paul Janssen about?"

"It might have something to do with the fact he and Michael Fielding were classmates at Cornell, and that Lionel Fielding had been Paul Janssen's thesis advisor while he was doing his doctoral work."

"What?! How did you find that out?"

"Beth just dug it up while she was going through Cornell's alumni data. Apparently, your sister has been teaching her some of her hacking skills."

My aching head started to reel. I had to put my coffee down before I spilled it. The one person I believed had been open and honest with me throughout my entire investigation had been Paul Janssen. Had I been a fool? It wouldn't be the first time.

"So now," said Goldfarb, "Justine's not only made herself a suspect, but Paul Janssen as well."

"But why?" I said. "I mean, I guess I can come up with a scenario about Michael Fielding suddenly cracking after a lifetime of being alienated from his father, and somehow blaming Ada Danforth for all that. And I guess I can come up with a scenario about Justine Tan finally deciding that she wasn't going to lose Paul Janssen to Ada at this point in her life. But what's going on with Paul Janssen? The guy practically worshipped Ada, and he was fascinated with whatever work it was that she was doing. It never occurred to me to suspect him of anything."

"And what reason on Earth," said Beth, "would they have to collude together to kill Ada?"

"I don't know," I said, "but that has to be our working theory right now, and the only way we're ever going to find out what's going on between them is to find them."

"And that's not going to be easy," said Beth, looking down at her phone. "I just got a text from Lacey. No E-Z Pass registered to Paul Janssen's car, and their cell phones have gone silent. She's also checked all the airline reservation systems, and she can't find any flights booked in either of their names."

"Except for the flight to Aruba," I said.

"Not even that," said Beth. "They either cancelled it, or it never existed in the first place."

"Why would it never have existed?" asked Goldfarb. "Why would they have made something like that up?"

"Maybe as a way to give themselves a chance to get out of town without people wondering where they were," said Beth. "By the time anybody realized that they hadn't gotten back, they'd be long gone."

"Okay, then," I said. "What about money?"

"What about it?" said Goldfarb.

"I'm just thinking that if there was some grand plan to murder Ada Danforth and disappear, even if disappearing was just a contingency, wouldn't we be able to track money moving from one place to another? They'd have to have money, no matter where they went. And from what

I understand, the world banking system has really tightened up over the last couple of decades. People can't hide money anymore the way they used to."

"Maybe they can't hide it, "said Goldfarb, "but they can make it pretty damn hard to find, and we don't have that kind of time."

"And not to pile on," I said, "but what does any of this have to do with my car getting torched?"

"Probably just more misdirection," said Goldfarb. "We've been getting misdirection thrown at us from day one on this case."

"Justine asked if I was going to show up at the school in my Accord," I said. "If she or Janssen had anything to do with destroying it, why would she have brought it up?"

"Just more misdirection," said Goldfarb.

"You're probably right," I said. My head starting to throb again, but I didn't think it had much to do with Justine Tan's spray, whatever it was.

Goldfarb's phone rang. I thought he was going to ignore it, but he stared at the caller ID and suddenly held his finger up, then picked up the phone. He said, "Goldfarb," into the phone, and after listening for a few seconds he said, "Thanks," and hung up.

"What was that all about?" I asked.

"It was the Buffalo police," he said. "I called them up before you got here to see if they could find Michael Fielding."

"And?" Beth and I said at the same time.

"Gone," said Goldfarb. "No trace of him anywhere. Not at his home, not at the school."

"I guess we shouldn't be surprised about that," I said.

"No, we shouldn't," said Goldfarb.

"So I guess that means we have to resort to our final option," I said.

"What's that?" said Beth.

"We're going to have to think."

CHAPTER TWENTY-FIVE

T HINKING WASN'T WORKING TOO WELL.
Steve Goldfarb had run back to his house briefly so that the last night of Chanukkah wouldn't be completely ruined for his kids. Beth had changed out of her uniform, and we had headed over to my house because I needed aspirin and some hot food.

Dinner was over by the time Beth and I got back to the house, and the kids had just finished loading the dishwasher and putting the left-over food in the fridge. The other three had gone off to wrap Christmas gifts, but Cal had hung back.

"So, Dad, do you guys want something to eat?" he'd said.

He said, "Dad," but he was looking right at Beth, and she was looking right back. The Sicilians have a word for moments like this that translates roughly as "thunderclap." Boom. Suddenly, it felt like all the oxygen in the room had been replaced by pheromones. Beth was a couple of years older than Cal, but he got his size from me, his dark good looks from someone in the gene pool who was definitely better looking than me, and he exudes maturity. Any age barrier between the two was going to collapse like the Maginot Line.

"I didn't know you knew how to cook," I said, mostly because I wanted them to remember that I was still in the room.

"Oh, yeah," said Cal, shaking himself out of it, at least momentarily. "I got tired of the cafeteria food pretty quick, and our dorm has a kitchen area on every floor, so I just started cooking for myself. I eat better, and it helps me get my mind off my schoolwork."

"Well, if you don't mind, all I want right now is a grilled cheese sandwich and some potato chips, with maybe a dill pickle."

"Sure thing," said Cal, his eyes returning to Beth. "Officer Gardner?"

"You can make me one of those bad boys, too, if you don't mind. And you can call me Beth."

"Sure thing," said Cal, giving Beth a look that said, "And you can call me anything you want."

In just a few minutes, he served us up the perfectly grilled sandwiches. He'd used Velveeta cheese and added slices of bacon and tomato to each one. I'm pretty sure they serve those sandwiches in Heaven, and I was also pretty sure that Cal and Beth thought they were already there. Cal stayed while we ate, but I felt like I was dining alone as they began what was starting to sound to me like a lifelong conversation. He knew that Beth and I had work to do, though, and he quietly left us alone after cleaning up the kitchen.

The food and aspirin had helped clear my head, but I was still having trouble thinking the whole thing through.

I kept coming back to the letters. I'd tried to bring them up before Steve left, and again with Beth while he was gone, but they had both dismissed them, Steve more vehemently than Beth. I knew Beth harbored her own personal thoughts, but she'd decided to side with Steve on the theory that, no matter what they were or where they came from, they weren't going to help us solve the case. But they still bothered me, especially the one about Ada's child. Maybe I wouldn't have been so obsessed with it if Ada hadn't indeed born a child. That was an indisputable fact, and I couldn't help but think that the fact of the child lent at least some credence to the letter. So when Steve got back, looking more contented than when he left, and perhaps more receptive to thinking outside the box, I took one more shot at it.

"Look," I said. "Let's forget any of the wild theories about those letters, okay? I get it: Just because we can't figure out how Ada or somebody else pulled it off, it doesn't mean it was impossible or requires some science fiction explanation."

"But you still haven't let go of it, have you?" said Goldfarb.

"No, I haven't. And after everything I've learned in the past couple of weeks, I don't know why I should. But that's irrelevant right now.

Let's just focus on the facts that Ada Danforth undoubtedly had a baby, and somebody – let's not worry about who, or when, or whatever – wanted to let us know that finding that child was the key to solving the murder."

"But, Matt," said Beth, "we think we're on the verge of solving the murder without figuring out the baby angle. Either Justine Tan, Michael Fielding, or Paul Janssen, or some combination of the three, murdered Ada Danforth. That's our working theory. Our biggest problem now is finding them, and figuring out the mystery of Ada's baby isn't going to help us with that."

"Okay," I said, "but what happens when we do find them? By that time, they'll have had plenty of time to put together a solid alibi, and don't forget: we have no physical evidence to link them – or anyone else for that matter – to the crime. I still think we're going to have to solve the child angle in order to figure out a motive for the murder."

"Okay, okay," said Goldfarb, "but let's take first things first. Before any of this other stuff even begins to matter, we have to find all of them."

"You're right," I had to admit.

"And here we are," said Beth, "the night before Christmas Eve, with a blizzard headed our way."

"What?" said Goldfarb and I, in unison.

"Don't you guys ever read the news?" said Beth. "There's a huge storm coming that's going to bury all of upstate New York. It's supposed to start overnight tonight and go well into tomorrow. We're going to get hit pretty hard here, but north of us is going to get walloped."

And that's when it hit me.

"I think I know where they might have gone," I said.

Beth and Steve both stared at me for a second, then Steve said, "Where?" But I could see on both their expressions that they already knew the answer.

"Lionel Fielding's house," said Beth, her eyes widening.

*　*　*　*　*

"That's what I'm thinking," I said. "It's completely isolated, and you can only get to it by taking the cable car – which, if I remember, is only controlled from the house – and it's a perfect place to wait out a storm."

"But if they went there," said Steve, "they're creating a problem for themselves, right?"

"What's that?" I said.

"Well, we may not be able to get into the house, but how the hell are they going to get out without walking right into our arms when they try to leave?"

"They won't have to leave for a really long time," I said. "I remember Fielding telling me that they always had a six-month supply of food there, and it's powered by its own generator. And I'm just guessing now, but Lionel Fielding is a smart guy, and I'm willing to bet that he built an emergency escape route into that property so that he could always get out no matter what the weather, even if the cable car broke down."

"Why do you think that?" said Steve.

"Because he's an old man, and he'd want to make sure that he'd have access to emergency medical care, no matter what the weather."

"That would cost a fortune," said Steve.

"He has a fortune," I replied.

"Hold it, hold it," said Beth, reaching for the soft-sided briefcase that she always carried with her now, a habit that she'd picked up from Lacey. She withdrew a laptop, set it on the table, and started typing in the same rapid, staccato fashion as my sister, though not quite with Lacey's speed.

"What are you doing?" I said.

"Google Earth," she said.

I'd heard of Google Earth, but I'd never used it.

"Are you telling me that you can see an individual house on Google Earth?" I said.

"Sure you can," said Beth, "but it's a satellite image, so you can only see it from the top. But we're just looking at the terrain, so that doesn't matter to us."

"And why are we looking at the terrain?" I said. "If Fielding built some kind of escape route, it'll probably be underground, like an elevator connecting to a tunnel or something, right?"

"Yeah, you're right," said Beth, "but I'm hoping we're going to get lucky."

"Lucky, how?" said Goldfarb.

"I'm thinking that there has to be an egress somewhere that exits directly onto a main road. Maybe, if we're lucky, we can spot that."

"Sounds to me like a needle in a haystack," I said.

"Sure," said Beth, "but at least when you're looking for a needle in a haystack, you know there's a needle, and you know it's in a haystack, so it's just a matter of how long do you want to look, right?"

"I never thought about it like that," I said.

"Well, let's not get our hopes up," said Beth. "Google Earth is great, but it's a pretty crude tool when you're looking for a needle. But anyway, here we are," she said, turning her eyes back to her screen.

Steve and I both moved in behind Beth so that we could all look at the screen.

"I can't even tell what I'm looking at," I said.

"Sure you can," said Steve, who was no doubt well trained in the art of looking at digital images during his days with the Navy Seals. "Look," he said, pointing his finger at the screen. "The first thing you have to do is get the big picture. So, there's Lake Cayuga, right?"

"Okay," I said.

"Do you remember his address?" said Goldfarb.

"He never gave me one," I replied.

"Hang on," said Beth. I saw her open a new screen and start scrolling. "Crap," she said.

"What?" said Goldfarb.

"The only mailing address he has is a post office box."

"Okay," said Goldfarb, "that means we're going to have to do this the hard way. You said that Fielding's home was on the southern shore of the lake, right?"

"Okay."

"Good. Beth, can you zoom in on the south shore of the lake?"

"Sure."

"Okay," said Steve. "And you said that Fielding's house had a huge window that looked out on the lake, right Matt?"

"Yes, it did," I said.

"So, from your view out that window, can you guess roughly where the house was located along the south shore?"

I stared at the image in front of me, and tried to remember the view that I'd had from inside the house.

"I think," I said, after studying the image for a few minutes, "that it was right near the southern tip, but just a little bit to the east."

Beth zoomed in without prompting and refined the image.

"Recognize anything?" said Steve.

"Holy crap," I said, pointing at the screen, "I think that's the house."

Beth zoomed in more. I couldn't believe how clear the image was.

"See?" I said. "There's the cable car, and there's the road that led me there."

"Okay," said Steve, "I'm thinking that any emergency egress wouldn't be on the same side of the house as the cable car."

"Why not?" said Beth, craning her neck to look at Steve.

"Because – tell me if I'm wrong, Matt – but that road that leads to the cable car looks like it's barely a road; it's more like a path."

"Yeah, you're right," I said, thinking back to my drive to the house. "And Route 96 is over a mile from the side road."

"Right. But look at the other side, the side that faces the lake. That road that runs by the lakeshore looks wide and well-paved, and I bet the county keeps it cleared if there's a storm."

Beth zoomed in even closer to the area directly below the house and adjacent to the road.

"This is about as close as I'm going to be able to get," she said. "But look, right here."

Steve and I both looked to the spot where Beth was pointing her finger."

"Am I imagining things," said Beth, "or does that look like a driveway?"

"Could be," said Steve. "It's hard to tell. But if it is, it's an odd place for a driveway, because there are no houses within two-hundred feet either way of it."

"That's a driveway, alright," I said. "And it's right where we should expect it to be: directly below Fielding's home. Now the only question is how we're going to get there in this weather."

"Are we *that* sure that's where they went?" said Goldfarb.

"I can't think of anywhere else they'd go," I said. "And if I'm right, we have no time to waste. And if I'm wrong, we'll be no worse off than we are just sitting here. We can always keep working on our phones and Beth's laptop if anything else comes up."

"Beth," said Steve, "when is this storm supposed to hit?"

"It's already started upstate, and it's going to get here in just a few hours."

I looked at the clock on the wall, and was shocked to realize that it was already ten o'clock.

"Look," I said, "I know that they can hunker down in that house for as long as they want, but they're not going to do that. They have to know that we'll figure out where they are sooner or later, so they're only going to stay there long enough to regroup and hatch a long-term plan."

"So we have to leave now," said Steve.

"Yeah, we do," I replied. "It's not like we can just call and ask. We have to go there. The question is, how do we get there in this mess?"

"It's not as tough as you might think," said Steve. "Thanks to your wife, the mayor, the police department just took delivery last month of a brand-new Ford Explorer Police Special. It's got all-wheel drive, and it came outfitted with heavy-duty snow tires, stabilizer bars and a scrape plate."

"And," said Beth, "it's got one of those Eco-Boost V6's that makes that puppy drive like a Ferrari."

"Okay, then," I said. "I know that we've all had a long day, but I think we have to get going asap. Why don't you guys swing by your houses and pick up bad-weather clothes, then come back here and pick me up. We can sleep in shifts on the way. Even with that new Explorer of yours, it's going to be a slog, and it'll probably be daylight by the time we get there."

"Good," said Steve. "And, Matt?"

"Yeah?"

"Why don't you give our old buddy Andy Pilcher a call. We might need his help, and I bet he wouldn't mind lending a hand."

"Good idea, Steve," I said. "I'll get right on it."

"Who's that?" said Beth.

I explained to Beth that Andy was an ex-Army Ranger Steve and I had met during our search for an Episcopal priest named Peter Lucky, a case that still mystified me and would forever haunt me. Andy lived in Canajoharie in upstate New York, was a one-man arsenal, and drove a tricked-out Ford F-350 that could climb Mount Everest. I'd heard that he had reconciled with his previously estranged wife, and they and their two children were now all settled together in Canajoharie, Andy's home town.

Steve and Beth left, and I went about getting myself ready. I wound up borrowing a pair of Cal's Xtratuf boots that he'd picked up on a trip to Alaska, along with some thick woolen socks. I'm not a big fan of outdoor winter activities, but Cal is, and he's equipped for it. He also loaned me a heavy woolen watch cap, insulated gloves which would keep my hands dry and warm while leaving me able to use my old NYPD issue .45 if I had to. He also gave me a balaclava, just in case.

When Steve and Beth returned they were both wearing their winter uniforms, and they had also stored heavy coats, hats, and gloves in the back of the Explorer. Cal had made sandwiches that he'd stored in a cooler, and a huge thermos of coffee. His jaw dropped when he came into the living room to hand me the provisions and got an eyeful of Beth in her uniform. I decided we'd better leave before the two of them decided to mate on the living room floor.

"Okay," I said, "let's get loaded up and get going."

I said good-bye to Doreen, and when I bent to give her a kiss, she whispered, "The elves and I will be waiting for you."

When Cal handed Beth the cooler and the thermos, she looked him straight in the eyes and said, "I'll be back soon."

"I'll be here," said Cal.

"Good," said Beth, and then turned to Steve and me and said, "Let's get going. You guys can fight over who rides shotgun. I'm driving."

CHAPTER TWENTY-SIX

THE SLEEPING IN SHIFTS IDEA hadn't worked out so well. We were all too keyed up to sleep.

We'd decided to take Route 17, since we figured the weather and the road conditions were going to bad no matter which route we took, and Route 17 was more direct. Plows were doing a heroic job, but we were driving through at least a few inches of snow on the road, and in some places it had started to drift and pile up, while visibility was so bad I never even noticed when we drove by the Roscoe Diner. Beth, however, turned out to be an expert driver, and she appeared completely unfazed as she drove through the storm, one hand on the wheel and one hand holding either a sandwich or coffee. She showed no signs of fatigue, and gave no indication at all that she wanted to give up the wheel. Still, we were averaging 35 miles-per-hour at best, and we'd be lucky to get to Fielding's home before daybreak.

I'd called Andy Pilcher, and despite the fact that Christmas Eve was approaching, he agreed to meet us at the Fielding house. In addition to being a former Ranger, Andy was an expert hunter, fisherman, and woodsman who had spent his life in the wilds of upstate New York, and his presence would be invaluable.

Steve and I decided on a strategy of divide and conquer: He and I would drive up to the front of the house where the cable car was and try to get ourselves invited in. We would not indicate that we had Beth and Andy on the other side of the house locating the driveway that we thought might be the egress from the escape path, whatever that was. If we were wrong about Janssen, Justine, and Michael Fielding being there, perhaps

Lionel Fielding would invite us in and we would be able to question him further, but I didn't think we were wrong.

*   *   *   *   *   *

By the time we got to the Ithaca area day should have been breaking, but the storm was still raging around us, and it remained pitch-dark. We'd agreed to meet Andy at a spot around five miles from the Fielding house where Route 96 intersected with a local road. When we got there Andy's enormous truck was already pulled into the parking lot of a gas station that showed no sign of being open, and Andy, all six-foot-four of him, was standing outside the truck waiting for us like it was a Spring day. A heavy woolen cap covered his unruly head of hair, but his thick, sandy colored beard overflowed the collar of his coat, giving his face all the protection it needed. We pulled in next to him and got out of the Explorer. After we'd all shrugged ourselves into our overcoats and gloves, I introduced Beth, who still looked fresh and alert despite the long, treacherous drive.

"Pretty ugly out, huh?" I shouted over the wind.

"I've made camp in worse," replied Andy, not raising his voice and not needing to, "but yeah, your right. It should work to our advantage, though. I can't see three sixty-something professors getting anywhere in this."

"I hope you're right," said Goldfarb. "Okay, look. You and Beth try to find that driveway we saw on Google Earth, and Matt and I are going to try the direct approach. Everybody keep your phones on."

Beth hopped into Andy's truck, looking tiny, and they took off for the southern tip of Lake Cayuga while Steve and I got back into the Explorer and headed the other way, toward the cable car that led to Lionel Fielding's house. Steve drove while I moved from the back seat to the passenger side in front.

It had gotten light out by that time, if you could call it that. The sun was up somewhere, but all it did was make the whiteout a little brighter. Visibility was almost zero, and we crept along at about five miles-an-hour while I searched for the turn-off for the small parking lot that led to the cable car. The road leading in was almost impassable, and there were moments when I wasn't even sure if we were still on it, but Goldfarb, whose instincts and eyesight were hopefully better than mine, plowed ahead.

Almost miraculously I spotted the turn-off. We were almost by it when I spotted it. Steve backed up the Explorer and turned in. There was about six inches of snow on the parking area, but at the rate that the snow was falling that meant that it had been recently plowed. I looked at Steve, and he looked back at me with a shrug of his shoulders. Maybe, we were both thinking.

We got out and headed over to the cable-car and got in.

"I don't think this is going to work," I said, at the same moment that the car shuddered and started up the hill.

"Good thinking, Tex," said Goldfarb as he gazed curiously around the interior of the car. "Interesting," was all he said.

"It gets better," I said. "Wait till you see the house."

The cable car soon shuddered to a halt, and Steve and I got out and headed to the front door. Unlike the last time, though, Lionel Fielding was not at the door waiting. Instead, a voice came over a speaker. It was Lionel Fielding's voice, and he sounded tired. "Let yourselves in and come upstairs," was all he said, sounding like he'd been expecting us.

We stepped into the foyer and unburdened ourselves of our coats, hats, and boots before we headed up the stairs.

Dr. Lionel Fielding was not the same man I had met such a short while ago. Then, he had looked like a vigorous man in perhaps his mid-seventies, a man who still might mow his own lawn, and perhaps even hike in the summer and ski in the winter.

The man who greeted Detective Goldfarb and me didn't even bother to rise from his chair, instead he merely nodded his head listlessly in our direction before returning his gaze to the wall of white that obliterated any view of the lake. He was wearing a worn bathrobe that might once have been blue, but was now a depressing shade of purple. He was unshaven, and his hair was uncombed and still matted from his pillow. A cup of coffee sat on the table next to him, but it was only partially consumed and it looked like it had been sitting there a while.

"I've ordered some coffee and muffins for you," he finally said. "You've had a long drive, and I thought you might need some refreshment."

"Thank you," I said and nodded toward Goldfarb. "Professor Fielding, this is Detective Steven Goldfarb of the Devon-on-Hudson Police. I'll let him explain to you why we're here."

"No need," said Fielding, waving his hand listlessly. "By the way, they're not here, so you can invite your two colleagues to come in. I'm impressed, by the way, that you found my emergency exit so quickly. Of course, it was never meant to be hidden; it was just meant to get me to a hospital quickly in an emergency. A cable car down a mountainside isn't exactly an emergency conveyance."

"I understand," I said, as Goldfarb phoned Beth and Andy.

In a few minutes, I heard a bell ring, which I assumed was the signal to bring the cable car up, while the maid brought a pot of coffee and a large tray of breads and pastries. The nurse also arrived to inform us that, "The Professor had a bad night's sleep, and is under a great deal of stress." She didn't say directly what she wanted us to do about that, but she obviously wanted us out of there. I guess I couldn't blame her for putting the professor's health ahead of the need to solve a murder; everyone has their priorities. My priority was to find my three prime suspects, and if they weren't there I would be more than happy to comply with the nurse's wishes. But first, I needed some answers.

Andy and Beth came up the stairs and entered the room, looking like they'd just returned from a relaxing morning stroll. Beth actually had a smile on her face. Kids.

"Professor," I said, once I'd performed the necessary introductions and we'd finally gotten ourselves settled, "you said, 'they're not here.' I assume you're talking about your son, Michael, Paul Janssen, and Justine Tan."

"Yes, I am."

"And I further assume you know why we are looking for them."

"Of course I do," replied Fielding, sounding like he was responding to a question from a particularly obtuse student. "You suspect them of conspiring to murder Ada Danforth."

"Did they?"

"I didn't ask."

"That wasn't my question."

"I'm a scientist, Mr. Hunter; I don't guess."

"Of course you do, Professor," said Beth. "They're called hypotheses."

"And you received your Ph.D. from which prestigious institution, young lady?"

"That's Officer Gardner to you, sir," said Beth, "and with all due respect, you don't need a Ph.D. to know what a hypothesis is."

I was a little shocked by Beth's interruption, but perhaps it was what Dr. Fielding needed. He seemed to deflate, and let out a sigh.

"You're right, you're right, Officer –"

"Gardner, sir," said Beth, with a deft touch of deference in her voice.

"Yes, Gardner." He paused, and I began to worry that the exhaustion and stress of the previous night had taken their toll, but he rallied. "Look, I know you're in a hurry to get out of here and chase the three of them down, but they're not going to get far in this," he said, gesturing to the window.

"What's most important right now," I said, "is for you to tell us what you know."

"Look," said Detective Goldfarb, "there's four of us here with two vehicles. There's no reason for all four of us to stay here; we can stay in touch by phone. Professor, do you know where they're going, and what kind of vehicle they're driving?"

"I know that they are driving my car, a white Jeep Grand Cherokee. I don't know the plate numbers. Where they are going, I'm not sure. I'm not even sure they know. But my guess is that they would try to get over to Route 81 and either go north to the Thruway, or south to get out of the storm. My guess is that they would go south, because according to the forecasts, the weather is clear by the time you get to Pennsylvania, and they'll have plenty of options once they get there."

"What options?" I asked. I'm not big on Pennsylvania geography.

"They can get on I-80," said a voice behind me. It was Andy Pilcher. "And head either east toward the Poconos, or west into Ohio. They could also head down to the Pennsylvania Turnpike. Or they could just stay on I-81 into Virginia."

"Sounds to me," I said, "that the most logical thing for them to do is to head south."

"Except," said Goldfarb, "that north is the way home."

"What do you mean?" I asked.

"Both Michael Fielding and Dr. Tan spent most of their adult lives in Buffalo," said Steve, "and Beth learned from the Cornell alumni records that Janssen grew up in Syracuse. These people are not professional criminals, and they're going to panic. And when people panic, they run to what they know. They run home."

"I told you," said Professor Fielding, looking at me with an amused glint in his eye, "that I know nothing about human nature. So I would recommend that you listen to the detective here."

"Okay, look," said Andy, "I'm a hunter and a tracker, not a cop. Why don't you let me get in my truck and find them? How long ago did you say they left, Professor?"

"Only about twenty minutes before you arrived."

"Good," said Andy. "I can track them down. I know I can."

"You're right," said Steve. "But you're going to need some law enforcement with you, someone authorized to make an arrest. If you try to do that yourself, you'll just be kidnapping them."

"I'll go with him," said Beth, who clearly craved action over warmth and comfort.

"Maybe I should go, Beth," said Steve. "If you catch them, it'll be three against two."

"No," said Beth, "it'll be the three of them against Andy and me. It won't be a fair fight any way you look at it."

"You're right," said Goldfarb, after only a moment's hesitation. "Okay, you guys get going." But that wasn't necessary; they were already both getting their coats and hats on.

"I'll drive if you want," was the last thing I heard Beth say as they headed down the stairs.

*　*　*　*　*　*

Steve and I both grabbed a muffin and refilled our coffee cups. The nurse came in and glared at all of us, but Fielding waved her away. Her face turned red, but she said nothing as she headed back down the stairs.

"Can I get you anything, Professor?" I said before I sat back down.

"What I want is a chance to talk," he replied, "but I guess you can give me a refill on the coffee while you're up."

I grabbed his cup and poured more coffee in, and I put another muffin on his plate, just in case.

"We're listening," I said before biting into my muffin.

"This may take a while, but please be patient. I have to tell this in my own way." Steve and I both nodded. Fielding stared out the window for a few seconds, gathering his thoughts, but not for long.

"My son, Michael, was an unhappy child from the time he realized that other kids had mothers but he didn't. And he just got unhappier and angrier the older he got. He would constantly badger me to tell him about his mother, and it made him even angrier when I told him the truth: that I just couldn't."

I started to say something, but I bit my tongue. He must have noticed the expression on my face, though.

"I know what you're thinking," he said. "What do I mean, I couldn't? After all, I knew Michael's mother well enough to make love to her and produce a child, so you'd think I could have told him something, right?"

Steve and I both nodded.

"So let me tell you what I knew, what I know. She told me her name was Alice Sterling, but I don't even know if that's true. She was not a fellow faculty member, and, no, she was not a brilliant young protégée. She was a waitress at a local coffee shop where I used to go each morning for a cup of coffee and an English muffin before my first class of the day. I thought I knew all of the waitresses there, but you know how it is – waitresses come and waitresses go. I remember that she came over to take my order, and all I can tell you is that the moment I laid eyes on her I knew I was in love with her, that my search for human happiness after a long, sterile academic life, was over, and that all I wanted in this world was her."

"Was she beautiful?" I blurted out. "Was she young? Was she old?"

"It's hard for me to recall, because it was so long ago now – over sixty years ago. What I can remember was that she was not at all what anyone would call beautiful, but she was pleasant looking. She was small and trim. Her hair was brown, but she kept it cut short, and she really didn't do anything with it. I don't think I ever saw her wear makeup. I was in my early thirties at the time, and I remember having the impression that she might have been a year or two younger than me."

"So what caught your attention?" I asked.

"That's the thing," Fielding replied. "I don't remember, and I don't think I ever really knew. All I knew was that I couldn't take my eyes off her. I didn't take my eyes off her the entire time I was eating my breakfast and drinking my coffee, and when she came over to give me my check, I asked her if I could see her again, away from work. My recollection is that she didn't hesitate, but that might be just my memory fooling me. All I remember clearly is that she said, 'Sure.' I said, 'How about tonight?' And she said, 'Sure.'"

"But she didn't even know you," I said. "Didn't you find that odd?"

"All I can tell you is that it didn't feel like that. It felt like I'd known her all my life, and she looked at me like she'd known me forever, too. And that was what it felt like the entire month that we were together."

"A month?" I asked. "That's all?"

"That's all, but it was the most wonderful month of my life. We went out to dinner that night at an out of the way place on the edge of town, a place where I figured I wouldn't run into fellow faculty or, God forbid, students. And after dinner, we went back to my home. I lived in a small house in town back then, not here. And we made love that first night. I don't remember asking her to come home with me. It was like we'd agreed on that long ago. And I don't remember ever trying to seduce her or, for that matter, her me. We just made love like we'd been waiting for that moment all our lives. And it went on like that for a month. I never knew where she lived. All I knew was that she was there in the morning when I left, and she was there in the evening when I came home."

"Did you see her at the coffee shop?"

"No, I didn't. I assumed that she continued to work there, but I went somewhere else, because I knew I couldn't trust myself to behave indifferently around her. It was like there was some magnetic attraction between us. I think we made love every single night we were together, like we were afraid every time might be the last time."

"And then what happened after a month?" I asked.

"She disappeared," said Fielding, a look of grief on his face as though it had just happened yesterday. "She never told me that she was leaving. Just, one morning, she was there when I left, and she was gone when I got home."

"Did she leave you a note?" I asked. "Anything?"

"Nothing," said Fielding. "She left my life the way she entered it: suddenly and without any warning."

"Did you go back to the diner to look for her?" asked Goldfarb.

"Of course I did, but she wasn't there. When I asked after her, the waitresses looked at me like they didn't know who I was talking about. And the guy who owned and operated the place ran a cash business, and he wasn't about to go talking to some stranger about who he did or didn't employ. So I just assumed that she'd only worked there a day or two when we met, and she never went back afterwards."

"And you never heard from her again?"

"I received a note from her a few months later. It merely said that she was pregnant, that I would be notified when she the child was born, and that she hoped that I would have the heart to adopt and raise him for her. She called it our 'quantum child.'"

That sat me up.

"Why did she call it that?"

"Oh, it was just an extension of a little joke between us. At one point early on, Alice had asked me what I did at the university. I doubted that she had much more than a high school education, so I described my work in simple terms, but I have to say I was amazed at how quickly she caught on. Anyway, after that she would sometimes call me her 'quantum man.'"

It seemed to be a straightforward enough explanation, and Goldfarb was giving me one of those, "don't go there," looks, so I moved on.

"Was there a return address on the envelope? Anything?"

"Nothing. The envelope was blank. Alice must have just placed it in my mailbox herself."

"Do you have any photographs of her?" asked Goldfarb. "Anything?"

"Yes, I do. Just before she left we went out for a picnic together. I had an old Kodak Brownie camera with me that I think my folks gave me as a college graduation present, and I brought it along with me. I took some pictures of Alice, and she took some pictures of me, and then we asked a nice young man to take a couple of pictures of the two of us."

"What ever happened to the pictures?" I asked.

"Most of the pictures are lost, and so are the negatives. The poor little Brownie didn't have much of a lens, and I didn't know how to use it properly. I had one framed, though, but I haven't seen it in ages. I suppose I could look for it, but I wouldn't know where to begin."

"So I guess you heard from someone after Alice had the baby, right?"

"Yes, I did," said Fielding, looking and sounding awfully tired. "It was about a year after Alice left. I got a phone call from a local attorney. He told me that Alice had delivered a healthy boy about three months earlier. She had been caring for him up to that point, but that now it had become necessary for her to leave, and she hoped that I would have mercy on the child, if not on her, and bring him home and care for him. The attorney said that he had a list of suitable candidates for at-home caretakers for me if I so wished."

"Have you told all of this to your son?" I asked.

"For the most part, yes, I have. I felt as though I owed him that much. I was such a terrible, distant father; I hoped that it might help him to know that he was conceived in a passionate, loving relationship."

"But it didn't help," I said.

"No," said Fielding. "Poor Michael."

"That's an interesting story, Dr. Fielding," said Goldfarb, "but what does it have to do with anything?"

"I'm afraid it might have everything to do with why you're here," said Fielding, looking at Goldfarb with an inexpressibly sad expression.

But we never got to hear the rest of his story, because just as he was about to speak, my phone rang, and when I looked down at the Caller ID, it was Andy Pilcher.

"They didn't get far," said Andy, still sounding like he was out on a summer stroll. I had put my phone on speaker so Goldfarb and Dr. Fielding could hear what was going on. "They thought they were on Route 13, heading over to I-81, but instead they were on Route 34, which hugs the eastern lakeshore, going north. They ran off the road near something called the Cornell Sailing Center and got stuck in the snow. The Jeep's engine stalled, so they're all pretty cold, but otherwise they're fine. Never did trust Jeeps. I'm going to throw them all in the truck and bring them back to Fielding's house. We can decide what to do from there. We should be back there in about twenty minutes."

"Sounds good," I said, and hung up.

"So, now," said Goldfarb, looking at Fielding, "perhaps you can tell us the rest of the story."

And he did.

CHAPTER TWENTY-SEVEN

"**T**HE WORST THING I ever did to my son was keep him," said Professor Lionel Fielding.

"I had no business being a father, and in most ways – all of the important ways– I wasn't. Michael would have been better off if I'd just put him up for adoption and given him the chance to be raised in a loving family. The only reason I didn't was because Alice had asked me to keep him. I was completely ill-equipped for the job. I didn't have friends; I had colleagues. I didn't have a social life; I had my work. I had never even been on a date, never mind felt love for anyone, until Alice came along. And what was I supposed to make of that? A month of bliss, and then nothing. I vowed that I would never allow myself to love anyone, ever again. And poor Michael paid the price. He was raised by a succession of nannies who were all very good, but they were young women. Eventually they all met young men, got married, and left to start families of their own. So Michael was constantly being deserted by the only meaningful parental figures he had in his life, none of whom was me. He was only ten when I sent him off to boarding school. So I guess I shouldn't have been surprised when he became obsessed with his mother."

"When did that start?" I asked.

"It's hard for me to tell, I guess. I rarely saw him. He was away at school most of the year, and I sent him off to one camp or another during the summer months. Thanksgivings and the Christmas holidays were a disaster. I stayed at work while he stayed at home with caretakers or went to my parents' home."

"Did he get along with your folks?"

"Yes, he did. My parents were wonderful people, but of course I didn't have much of a relationship with them, either. Like Ada Danforth's parents, my folks were more puzzled by me than anything. I know they were proud of me, but they had no way of understanding what I was doing, and I really didn't make much of an effort to stay in touch. I think they loved Michael because he was someone they could understand. So it wasn't until he came to Cornell to do his graduate work that I started seeing him on a regular basis, but even that was awkward."

"Why was that?" asked Goldfarb.

"Frankly, because he didn't really belong there, and the only reason he was accepted was because he was my son."

"So he wasn't a very good physicist?" I asked.

"Cornell is not in the business of churning out 'very good' physicists, Mr. Hunter. Cornell is in the business of creating Nobel Prize winners. Michael is an adequate physicist, and people like him have a role to play, even at major universities like SUNY Buffalo. Someone has to teach the undergraduate classes and the graduate seminars while people like me – and people like Ada – focus on our research. So I wasn't surprised when he latched onto Paul Janssen."

"Janssen was a student of yours, too, right?"

"Sadly, yes. Young Janssen came highly recommended, and had displayed some early talent, so I took him on. But after his first year or so here, it became obvious that bringing him to Cornell – and especially assigning me as his thesis adviser – had been a mistake. But by then I was stuck with him, mostly because no one else wanted him, and he wasn't doing poorly enough to flunk him out of the program. So Michael and Paul had their mediocrity in common, I guess you could say. And one thing I'll say for young Janssen: What he lacked in gifts he made up for in loyalty. He was slavishly devoted to me, and he was always willing to do whatever I asked him to do, no matter how menial the task. So, in any event, they became close and stayed close. Even though their work took them to opposite sides of the state, they always stayed in touch." Fielding's eyes drifted off toward the window. Seeing what? Looking for what? I couldn't tell.

But I was starting to see where this was heading, and from the looks Goldfarb was giving me, so was he. Now, however, was no time to interrupt.

I didn't know how much longer Professor Fielding was going to last, and I needed him to finish his story.

"And that's the way it went until about twenty years ago. I'd see Michael off and on, mostly in the summer when he came to Ithaca to see old friends and sail on the lake. Usually Paul Janssen would come out about the same time, and I'd suffer through an afternoon cookout with them. That was actually when I met Justine Tan for the first time. Michael had brought her out with him for some sailing. I thought she was a charming woman, and I thought that Michael might finally have a chance at some happiness with her. But that was about the time Ada arrived at Cornell, and it didn't take long for her to become a celebrity. The university community treated it all like a 'Pygmalion' story, you know: 'Celebrated Cornell Nobelist Cultivates His Successor,' that kind of stuff. Of course, I didn't help. It had been quite a few years since I'd won my Nobel, and the shine was starting to wear off. It felt good to be in the limelight again." Just reliving those memories seemed to enliven Fielding. His color improved, and he sat up straighter in his chair.

"And, of course, you became infatuated with Ada personally."

"Yes, Mr. Hunter, I did, as I've already admitted to you. It was like meeting Alice all over again, and I just couldn't help myself. But it wasn't just me, it was the entire academic community. The only person totally oblivious to Ada's celebrity and charm was Ada herself."

"And Michael?" asked Goldfarb.

"As I've already explained to Mr. Hunter, Detective Goldfarb, Michael never had anything even remotely like romantic feelings for Ada. But he did become obsessed with her, completely obsessed, and that's what ruined his relationship with Justine Tan, and eventually ruined his entire life."

"I'm not sure I'm following you, Dr. Fielding," said Goldfarb.

"Please remember, Detective Goldfarb, that I was past my seventieth birthday by then; Michael was forty, but Ada was still a teenager. It was perfectly obvious to Michael how I felt about Ada, and he thought it was disgraceful, as did I, for that matter. He felt that I was not only going to humiliate myself, but tarnish my legacy in the process. And by inference, that would reflect on him. But he might have gotten over it; after all, Ada would be here only a few short years, and then she'd be out of my life, and Michael's, for good."

"But he didn't get over it, did he?" I said.

"No, he didn't, and it was my fault."

"How was it your fault?"

"He'd come out to visit one weekend. I'd made the mistake of inviting Ada over also. What was I thinking? So we'd had dinner, just Michael and Ada and me."

"Not Justine?" I said.

"No. Michael and Justine were still together, but Justine had tired of the tension between Michael and me, so she stopped accompanying him on his visits, which I thought was sad, because I liked Justine. Anyway, we made it through dinner, most of all because we didn't want to create a scene in front of Ada, but Ada must have sensed the tension, because she left early. And then, of course, it started up again. 'She's a child,' he said. 'She's young enough to be your granddaughter. You ought to be ashamed of yourself.' And on and on he went. I told him that my feelings were what they were, and I couldn't help them, but that didn't mean that I would ever act on them. I was a grownup, after all."

"And of course you sensed that she had similar feelings toward you," I added.

"Of course, and that made it exponentially more difficult for me," said Fielding. "But she was still a teenager. The whole situation was ludicrous, and I told Michael again and again that I would never act on those feelings, and that that was the only thing that counted in the end. But then I made my big mistake. I told him – and I think these were my exact words – 'In a different time, in a different place, maybe things would be different. If Ada and I were closer in age, if she weren't my student, perhaps I would allow myself to act on my feelings.' But that was all idle speculation, I said, so nothing would ever come of Ada's and my friendship other than exactly what it was."

"It sounds to me like that was a pretty reasonable thing to say," said Goldfarb.

"I thought so, too," said Fielding, "but I was wrong. Those were the words that finally sent him over the edge. As I have told you, Michael is not much of a physicist, and quantum mechanics is not his area of specialty, but of course he was just smart enough and just knowledgeable enough to make him dangerous, at least to himself. And I guess all the years of loneliness, all the years of rejection by his own father, all the years of wondering what life would have been like if he'd only had a mother, finally came crashing down on the poor young man and broke him."

"He started to believe that Ada was his mother, didn't he?" I said.

"What?!?" said Goldfarb, loud enough to make both Professor Fielding and me jump.

"Yes," said Fielding, looking at me like I was a not particularly bright student who had just made an unexpectedly keen observation. "He began to conjure up a fantasy that somehow Ada had found a way to go back in time, and the woman I knew as Alice Sterling was really Ada. And it just got worse from there –"

We were suddenly all distracted by the sound of the bell for the cable car ringing. I'd completely lost track of time, and when I looked down at my watch I realized that Beth and Andy should have been back long ago. The maid went down to unlock the front door, and soon after we heard her yelp along with the crash of the door being flung open, and then the sound of Andy's boots pounding up the stairs two at a time. In seconds he burst into the living room. He was carrying what for an instant I thought was a rolled-up carpet. But it didn't take me long to realize that it was a large, heavy, black woolen blanket, with an unconscious Beth Gardner wrapped inside.

"Water! We need warm water!" shouted Andy. "Where's your tub?"

"Follow me!" said Professor Fielding, jumping up from the sofa with surprising agility.

The nurse – I never did learn her name – must have heard the commotion, because she was suddenly just a step behind me.

"Get out of my way!" she yelled at me as she squeezed by. "Put her in the tub just the way she is, with the blanket on," she ordered Andy, who recognized a direct order when he heard one. She turned on the water and left her fingers under the spout to gauge its temperature. "Now, open up that medicine cabinet above the sink. There are two thermometers in there. Give me them both. And beneath the sink there's a blood pressure cuff. Get that, too." She turned to Andy. "Okay, big boy, you're going to have to do. The rest of you, get out of here and close the door behind you, and tell the maid to bring up some warm tea or coffee; it doesn't matter which."

"Should I call the EMT's?" I said.

"It doesn't matter," said the nurse. "She'll either be dead or past the crisis by the time they get here. But yes, do that. Now, get out!"

We all – Goldfarb, me, and Professor Fielding – stumbled back down the hall as the maid – who was apparently a step ahead of all of us – went racing by with a large carafe of warm liquid.

We'd momentarily forgotten about the others. Justine Tan, Paul Janssen, and Michael Fielding, who was standing shivering with a blanket around him and dripping water on the floor, all stood in the middle of the room looking miserable.

"Michael," said the professor, sounding distinctly paternal, "go to my room and get a dry bathrobe on yourself." Michael left without uttering a word, passing by the maid, who went racing back down the stairs. In what seemed like a few short seconds she was back up with two large carafes of piping hot coffee, cream, sugar, and a huge plate of pastries. She disappeared as soon as she put the tray down on the coffee table.

"Justine," ordered the professor, "please tell me why I have a half-dead young woman in my tub."

"I'd like to wait until Michael is back in the room," replied Justine, "if you don't mind."

"You're right," said the professor. "Get yourselves something to eat. You must be starving."

It didn't take long for Michael to return, wrapped up in a robe that was three sizes too big for him and made him look like a recalcitrant child. He headed straight for the food tray.

"Dad, let me explain," he said while he filled a mug and a plate.

"I asked Justine to speak for all of you."

Michael looked momentarily stunned, but then took a seat and ate silently.

"Justine?"

Justine Tan looked exhausted but alert as she took a sip of coffee and composed her thoughts. Her eyes were clear, her unlined skin bore no signs of makeup, and her hair was down. She was wearing thigh-hugging jeans and a gray sweatshirt with "OCCC" printed across the front, and if it weren't for the heavy streaks of silver in her long hair she could have passed for a student rather than a sixty-ish professor. She held her head high and stared right at me, as did Paul Janssen. Michael Fielding stared glumly at the floor, still slightly shivering.

"First," she finally said. "I need to say that none of us killed Ada Danforth, and none of us knows who did. If you're looking for a confession then you can look elsewhere."

"Then why, for the love of God," I said, "did you taser me?"

"Because I was scared, that's why!" said Justine. She paused for a few seconds to calm herself down. "And it wasn't a taser, it was a mild neurotoxin, and I'm sorry. I panicked, and I'm sorry. Look, we knew you had spoken to both Michael and Professor Fielding, and your questions to me were becoming increasingly, let's say, suspicious, as were your questions to Michael." She shifted her gaze to Detective Goldfarb. "We are not crooks, and we are certainly not murderers. If we were, perhaps we would have behaved more cleverly; but we're not, and we panicked. We felt that we had to go somewhere together and think this whole thing through, maybe figure out on our own who may have killed Ada, if for no other reason than to defend ourselves. This house seemed like a good place to meet halfway, that's all."

"But when you saw us coming," said Goldfarb, "you ran."

"We'd only just gotten here. We were exhausted, and we still needed time. It was a stupid thing to do. Like I said, we're not crooks."

"Where were you headed?" asked Goldfarb.

"Where we should have gone in the first place. Paul still owns his parents' home in Syracuse, but we were afraid it might lose power in the storm, and we knew this place wouldn't. Anyway, that's where we were headed."

"But that didn't work out," said Goldfarb.

"No," said Justine, shooting Michael Fielding a look. "Michael argued that he knew the roads around here better than Paul or I did, and he insisted on driving. He thought he'd gotten on Route13 going east, which would have taken us over to Route 81, but instead he got onto Route 34 going north, and before we knew it we were stuck in a four-foot drift right next to the lake, and the engine was stalled. If it weren't for the drift, we probably all would have wound up drowned in the lake. We eventually pushed the car out of the drift, but we still couldn't get it started, and then Officer Gardner and this guy showed up."

"This guy," was Andy, who had appeared in the hallway, looking like he'd just gotten back from an afternoon at the beach.

"Knucklehead here," he said, nodding his head at Michael, "decided he was going to make a run for it. I don't know where he thought he was going, but he wound up sprinting down a forty-foot dock and right into the lake. I was under the hood of the Jeep, but Officer Gardner saw the whole thing, and she followed him, right into the lake. I heard the two splashes, but when I looked up, all I saw were footprints heading down the dock and the coat Beth had thrown off before she jumped in. It's too early in the winter for the lake to be frozen over, even on the shoreline, but the water is killing cold. I ran to the end of the dock, but by the time I got there, Officer Gardner was pulling Fielding over to the side. I reached down and pulled him out, and then dragged him over to the truck and told Janssen and Justine to put him in and turn on the heat. I thought Office Gardner was right behind me, but when I turned around, she wasn't there. I ran to the end of the dock, but I still couldn't see her, so I dove in. Luckily, the water was only about ten feet deep at the end of the dock, and it only took me a few seconds to spot her. But by the time I got her out, she was unconscious."

"What about you?" Goldfarb asked Andy.

"My outerwear is waterproof, and I'm, you know, me. But Beth is tiny, and she was soaked to the skin. I got her into the back seat of the truck and stripped her clothes off, and then I got her wrapped in a thermal blanket I always keep with me. Fielding was in the front passenger seat under another blanket, and I told Janssen and Justine to get in the back. I put Officer Gardner on Justine's lap and told Justine to keep rubbing her with the blanket as hard as she could. Then I drove back here. The Jeep is still out by the lake."

"So here we are," I said. "Justine, you knocked me out with whatever that thing is that you had; Michael, you made a run for it right into Lake Cayuga in the middle of a blizzard, and Janssen, you're standing there looking like you just swallowed a frog. But you're all innocent, is that what you're telling me?"

"Where did you think you were going, Michael?" asked Justine.

"I don't know," he mumbled.

"You have to do better than that," said Justine. "You're making us all look like murderers."

We were interrupted by the appearance of the nurse in the hallway.

"The young woman is fine," she announced, giving us all accusatory stares. "She's young, strong, and lucky. I have her tucked into the bed in the spare room, and she's resting comfortably. I've already called the EMT's and called off the emergency. She said she wants to see you, Mr. Hunter. Only you." And with that, she stalked out of the room.

"I'll be right back," I said as I hurried down the hallway.

*　*　*　*　*　*

The room was in shadows when I first peered in, and for a moment I thought I was in the wrong room because the bed looked empty. But as my eyes adjusted I was able to make out a small form beneath a mountain of quilts. I walked over to the bed, and I saw Beth's pretty face looking up at me. She looked pale but alert, and she surprised me with her first question.

"Who undressed me?" she asked.

"What?" I said, thinking that I may not have understood.

"Who undressed me?" she repeated.

"It was Andy, Beth. He had to. You were –"

"Good," she said. "That's all I needed to know."

I was puzzled for a moment, but then I understood. Steve Goldfarb was her boss, and I was the father of the young man with whom she apparently intended to become romantically involved. Beth was a modest young woman, and she would have been humiliated if her boss, or her potential father-in-law, had seen her naked, especially me. It's funny the things people think about in times of crisis.

"I want to get up."

"Beth, you've just been through a lot. Don't you think you should rest a little more?"

"No, I want to get up."

"Okay," I said, "let me see if I can find the maid. I don't know if your clothes are dry yet." But I didn't have to go anywhere. As if on cue, the maid showed up with Beth's uniform, carefully dried and pressed, with the exception of her leather belt, which was still soaked. She laid everything at the foot of the bed and quietly left.

"I'll get out of here so you can get yourself ready," I said, standing up.

"Mr. Hunter? Matt? Could you wait just a minute?"

"Sure. What's up?"

"I need to say something, and if I don't say it all now, I don't think I'll ever have the nerve to say it again."

"Okay," I said, wondering what was going on. I sat back down. Beth waited until I was settled before she began to speak.

"I never lost consciousness while I was in the water," she began. "I remember being cold, colder than I thought it was possible to feel, and then my muscles stopped working, and then I remember starting to feel warmer after my body settled on the lake bed. And then I felt this enormous power lifting me up and out of the water, and that's when I lost consciousness."

"That 'enormous power' was Andy Pilcher saving your life."

"Yes, it was. And I'll always be grateful to him, and I'll never forget him. But that's not what I wanted to talk about."

"I'm listening."

"I had thoughts going through my head the entire time I was down there. But the first thing I want you to know is that I wasn't afraid of dying."

"It would have been nothing to be ashamed of if you had been, Beth."

"I guess not, but I just wasn't. What I thought about was living. I'm only twenty-two years old, and all the time I was growing up I always dreamed of having a fulfilling life. I love my job, and I want it to be my career. But most of all, I've always wanted to know what it's like to love someone, and to be loved back, and to make a life with that someone. To have kids, all that. And there I was lying on the bottom of that lake, thinking that I was never going to have any of that. I'm still a virgin, Mr. Hunter. I couldn't believe I was going to die without even having that one basic experience. But what was worst was when I thought of all the young men, in all the wars all through history, who must have died thinking exactly the same thoughts I was. That was the saddest thought I ever had, and, more than anything, I didn't want to die feeling that sad, you know? And that's when Andy came and got me, and that's when I passed out. The next thing I remember was being in the warm tub wondering who took my clothes off."

"Beth," I said, "all I can tell you is that I've never had an experience like that. I've known fellow police officers who've had near death experiences just like you had, and I've also held a brother officer in my arms while he died. I can't tell you much, but what I can tell you is that experiences like that change you forever, sometimes for better, and sometimes for worse. That part is up to you."

"You're right," she said. "And that's why I have to get back to work. So please tell everyone that I'll be right out, okay?"

"Okay."

"And Mr. Hunter?"

"Yes?"

"I'm thinking that I want to do all those things with your son, with Cal. Something happened between us the minute we met each other, and I don't think that's going to change."

"Believe me, Beth, we all noticed. And I think that would be wonderful, for all of us."

"Mr. Hunter?"

"Yes, Beth? And I really think it's time you started calling me Matt."

"Okay. But what I want to know is, is that what it was like between you and Doreen?"

"Well, it took Doreen and me a long time to get to that moment, but, yes, when that moment finally arrived it was just like that."

"I'm glad," she said, giving me a lovely smile.

"Okay," I said, "I'll get out of here now." But before I stood up, I leaned over and gave her a light kiss on the forehead, for what I guessed was not the last time.

*   *   *   *   *   *

It didn't look like much had gone on when I got back to the living room, except that Professor Fielding had apparently gone off to get dressed. He'd also given himself a quick shave and combed his hair. I remember thinking that he looked like he'd gotten himself ready to go on a trip.

I poured myself a hot cup of coffee, but I couldn't even look at the pastries. If I didn't have some protein, and soon, I might commit a felony.

Beth followed me into the room just a few seconds later. She walked directly over to Andy, gave him a hug, and whispered, "Thank you." She pointedly ignored Michael Fielding. Then she grabbed a cup of coffee and proceeded to act as though nothing had happened.

"So, where were we?" said Detective Goldfarb.

"I believe," I said, nodding in the direction of Michael Fielding, Justine Tan, and Paul Janssen, "that these three were going to explain why we should believe that they're innocent."

"They don't have to do that," came a voice from behind me.

"Professor Fielding?" I said, as I turned around.

"I said that the three of them don't have to explain that they're innocent, because I'll do it for them: They're innocent."

"But how can you know that?" said Beth.

"Because I did it," said Professor Fielding. "I killed Ada Danforth."

CHAPTER TWENTY-EIGHT

"**D**AD!" cried Michael, sounding more like a little boy than any sixty-year-old I'd ever heard.

"Just you be quiet, son!" said Lionel Fielding, sounding more like a father than I'd ever heard him sound. "I'm tired. I'm tired of all the lies, all the evasions. And mostly I'm tired, Michael, of making you pay for all the selfish things I've done. I'm at the end of my life, and for once I want to speak some truth."

We were all too stunned to say anything.

"Do you expect us to believe that?" said Detective Goldfarb.

"I don't 'expect' you to do anything," said Fielding. "I'm just telling you, that's all."

"Professor Fielding," I said, trying to sound calmer than I was feeling. "I think you need to explain yourself." I felt annoyed, annoyed and angry, not with Lionel Fielding, but with myself. Whether he was lying to protect his son, or whether he was telling the truth was irrelevant. I should have at least considered the possibility. My only excuse was that the man was a nonagenarian, and you don't expect ninety-year-olds to commit murder. But I knew that Lionel Fielding was no ordinary ninety-year-old, so shame on me.

"This is going to take a while," said Professor Fielding, glancing at his watch, "and I'm only going to say it all once, so listen carefully."

"Just for the record, Professor Fielding," said Beth, pushing a couple of buttons on her iPhone, "I'm going to record what you're saying."

"Record away," replied Fielding.

"Okay, professor," I said, "we're all ears."

"As I was beginning to tell you a few moments ago, poor Michael had gotten it into his head that he truly was a quantum child, that Ada Danforth had found a way to travel back in time and, under the guise of Alice Sterling, had produced a child with me. As I said, I blame myself partially for that because of things I said, but it was all made infinitely worse by my favorite graduate student here, Paul Janssen."

"Professor, I was just only –"

"Be quiet, Janssen," said Fielding quietly, but it was obvious that he was working hard to contain his anger.

"Keep going, Professor," I said, shooting a glance at Janssen that I hope he understood meant, "shut up." "You'll get your turn, Dr. Janssen."

"As you know, Janssen and my son had stayed in contact over the years. About a year ago, Janssen started to report alarming things to Michael about Ada, things that only made things worse for him. He started telling Michael that he thought that Ada was on the verge of an enormous breakthrough, a breakthrough that would turn not just the world of physics, but the world itself, on its head. He felt that Ada had finally discovered the convergence of quantum mechanics and the physics of larger bodies, and that she was getting ready to make an announcement. As usual, Janssen didn't grasp the real significance of this potential discovery. As I told you before, he made up in loyalty what he lacked in ability, and the only thing he was concerned about was that her discovery would make my life's work irrelevant. He couldn't seem to understand that I – and all true scientists – dream of living to see the day that our work would become irrelevant, because that would mean that we would be witness to the next great leap in human knowledge and understanding. And he also should have known not to talk about it with Michael, because Justine had told him all about Michael's obsession, of course; it was what had broken up her and Michael's relationship. And now, Michael's obsession was compounded, because he became petrified that Ada would once again travel back in time and change history – his history – by *not* conceiving a child with me. In the blink of an eye, Michael was afraid that not only would he cease to exist, he never would have existed in the first place."

"So, Professor," I said, "I'm pretty sure that I don't understand most of what you've just said. But everything you've told us so far seems to be pointing to the fact that all three of these folks – your son, Justine Tan, and

Paul Janssen – had a motive to want Ada Danforth dead: Your son thought his own life was at stake; Paul Janssen, your devoted student, believed that your professional legacy was at risk, and Justine Tan was facing the prospect of losing yet another man to Ada Danforth."

"Precisely," said Professor Fielding, once more glancing at his watch, which made me glance at mine. Incredibly, it was still only 10 AM. "And the conversations I had with Michael and Paul over the past year, Michael in particular, were leading me to that conclusion. There was a collective insanity developing among the three of them, and I was becoming increasingly alarmed about where it might lead them."

"So, what are you telling us, Professor," I said, "that you decided to take things into your own hands to protect those three?"

"Yes," he replied, suddenly sounding tired. "That is precisely what I am saying."

"I'm not sure that's good enough," said Goldfarb. "You're saying that you murdered Ada in order to prevent these guys from killing her. That sounds like nonsense to me. I still think you're just covering up for the real murderers, one of whom happens to be your son."

"Who, by the way," said Beth, "happens to be the one who took the long walk off the short pier. Explain that."

"Oh, Officer Gardner," said Professor Fielding, "I am so sorry about what happened to you. But please, blame me, not my son."

"And why should I do that?" replied Beth. "You're not the one I chased into the lake."

"Because parents are always parents, and children are always children. I always was, and still am, a rotten parent."

"Dad –"

"Please, Michael, let me finish. No matter how old any of us get, all we ever want is our parents' approval, and to be deserving of their love. Michael was beginning to suspect that I was the one who had murdered Ada, and he was going to prove – once and for all – that he was deserving of my love."

"By placing the blame on himself," said Goldfarb.

"Yes, Detective, that's right," said Fielding, looking up at the big cop. "And he was going to go to his grave before anyone could prove otherwise. Isn't that right, Michael?"

"Oh, Dad, I just wanted –" But Michael Danforth could go no further. He sank into a chair, put his face in his hands, and began to sob.

"Michael," said Professor Fielding, "come here."

Michael looked up.

"Come here, son," said Fielding, holding out a hand. "Come sit next to me."

I could tell – I think everyone in the room could tell – that all Michael Fielding wanted to do was run to his father. He lifted his head up, an expression of hope mixed with utter shock on his face. He seemed to begin to rise, but then he sank back into his chair, and turned away from his father.

"Oh, God," said Fielding, "what have I done? I love you Michael. Now that it's too late, I need you to know that." But Michael remained still, and Lionel Fielding's outstretched hand fell to the sofa.

"Professor," said Goldfarb, "maybe it would be easier for me to believe you if you told us how you did it."

"Perhaps I should," said Fielding, sounding relieved to be drawn back from the unrelenting rip tide of emotion into the safe haven of rational thought. "It was easier than you think. First of all, I knew that no one would ever suspect me which, as you know better than I, is half the battle. I simply told my staff that I had been invited to a dinner at the home of another former graduate student who was teaching at Hartwick College down in Oneonta. I said that, because of the distance, I would be his houseguest for the night, and that I would return the following morning. It wouldn't be the first time I'd done such a thing, so they weren't surprised, and I suspect they were relieved to have a day without me to worry over, so they didn't ask me any questions. But instead, I drove out to Devon-on Hudson."

"Did Ada know you were coming?" said Goldfarb.

"I guess I'd have to say 'yes and no' to that, Detective. I'm not trying to be flippant; I'm just trying to answer honestly."

"Okay," said Goldfarb, trying not to sound as skeptical as he looked, "then what did you mean?"

"I wish I could tell you. All I know is that I never told her I was coming out; I didn't think I had to. I knew there was a ninety-nine percent probability that she would be home, simply because I knew that she never went anywhere."

"So, I'm still wondering," said Goldfarb, "why did you say 'yes and no'?"

"Detective, the only way I can answer your question is to continue with my story."

"Okay, go ahead," said Goldfarb, still sounding skeptical.

"Thank you. So I drove out to Devon-on-Hudson, directly to Ada's house, but I stopped at a spot about a mile from her home, where the road is still asphalt. I didn't pull over, because I didn't want to leave any tracks, but I didn't think it would be a problem. There's hardly any traffic on that road, especially in the wintertime, and if anyone did go by, they would probably think that I had broken down or run out of gas, and that I was going to get help. I always keep a fresh hazmat suit at home, because in the course of my work I am sometimes exposed to dangerous substances, and I had brought it along with me. I didn't put it on until I was almost to Ada's house."

"So that's why we never found any tire tracks," I said, "and why we never found any trace of anyone else being in the house."

"Correct," replied Fielding. "And I also brought along with me a wooden mallet that had been sitting on the tool bench in the garage since the day I bought this place thirty years ago. The previous owner had been quite the handyman, and he had actually helped build my little cable car. In any event, I knew that no one would ever miss it."

"Where are the mallet and the hazmat suit now?" I asked.

"The hazmat suit has been incinerated, which is normal practice. I just brought it over to the university incineration site and dumped it in the burn pile along with everything else that had accumulated. They usually do two burns a week, so it's long gone. And the mallet is somewhere in the Atlantic Ocean, I would imagine. I dumped it in the Hudson after I – uh – left the house. It was light, and the river current would have carried it out to sea."

"Hold it," said Goldfarb. "What are you telling us, that you just showed up at Ada's front door with a full hazmat suit on and a wooden mallet in your hand, and she just said, 'Oh, hi,' and let you in?"

"I didn't say that yet, Detective Goldfarb, but yes, that is precisely what happened."

"I don't believe you," said Goldfarb. "You're making this all up to protect your son."

"Remember my 'yes and no' answer I gave you a couple of minutes ago, Detective, the one you liked so much?"

"Yeah."

"That's what I meant. I had hoped to find out where Ada was in the house, and then I intended to sneak in and surprise her. But instead, she was literally waiting for me at the front door, and all she said to me was 'Hello, Lionel. Come in.' Then she opened the door and stood aside to let me in."

"So it was like she knew you were coming all along," said Beth, with dread creeping into her voice.

"Maybe one of these three gave her the heads up," said Goldfarb, pointing his chin at Michael, Justine, and Paul.

"No, no, none of them knew I was coming out. I made sure of that."

"Okay," said Goldfarb, "let's put that aside for now. I don't know about everyone else, but I'm just going to assume that she found out somehow that you were coming out. What did she do once you were inside?"

"She tried to give me a hug, but that didn't work out too well with the hazmat suit and all, so she just took me by the arm and led me into her study. Then she sat down in her desk chair and looked up at me. She said, "I'm so sorry, Lionel, but this is how it had to be all along. You're the only one with the will to do what you know has to be done, and now you must fulfill your destiny. The world isn't ready for me, and I need to be stopped. I've lost control of my own mind, and even I can't make it stop; and it won't let me destroy it by destroying myself. I have committed nothing to paper, and nothing to any form of computer software. So rest assured, it all dies with me. I'm so sorry, Lionel.' And then she turned away from me. I guess you know the rest."

"Professor," said Andy Pilcher in his soft, clear voice. "I'm going to believe you: I believe you killed Ada Danforth. But protecting your son wasn't the only reason you did it, was it? You believed what Ada Danforth was telling you – that she really was on to something, something enormous – didn't you."

Professor Lionel Fielding, Ph.D., Nobel Prize Laureate, stared long and hard at Andy Pilcher, Army Ranger and woodsman.

"Ultimately, Mr. Pilcher," he finally said, "we scientists are amoral creatures. We pursue knowledge simply for the sake of pursuing it. What other people do with it does not concern us. So what would you do, what would any of you do if, for example, in 1945 you were given the power to postpone the basic research that resulted in the development of the atomic bombs that fell on Japan, and, even more importantly, the subsequent development of thermonuclear weapons? Perhaps if human civilization had another century or two to mature, that knowledge would be used more responsibly, perhaps to power the world with utterly clean, perfectly efficient energy without burdening it with the threat of annihilation. *What would you do?"*

"Do you really believe whatever it was that Ada had discovered was such a threat to humanity?" I asked.

"I had spoken to Ada extensively over the past year, and I had come to believe that she had made some breakthrough discoveries about the true nature of time and space. I believe that she had made these discoveries long ago and had often used herself as an experimental subject. But she was the only one, with that spectacular mind of hers, who could explore that knowledge. I think what she was on the verge of disclosing were general applications of that knowledge that would give average people, people like me and you, the ability to use it. Can you imagine the implications of that? I can't, and I'm not sure I want to. But perhaps I am dead wrong, tragically wrong. Maybe I murdered Ada for no reason whatsoever."

"Why do you say that?" said Goldfarb.

"Because what do *I* know? Ada Danforth came to Cornell when she was fourteen. Think about that. *Fourteen.* And there I was, Dr. Professor Nobel Prize. I still remember sitting down with her for the first time. It didn't take days, weeks, or months. It only took one blinding, breathtaking instant to realize that I was just a scientific barnacle, thinking I understood how a ship was built just because I was clinging to it, and that Ada was the shipbuilder. I had no way of peering into Ada's mind, because my own mind was so inferior by comparison. So I could be wrong about everything I've been speculating about."

"Except Ada told you that you were right," I said.

"Yes, she did," said Fielding, sounding resigned. "And now I'm left knowing only one thing for sure."

"What's that?" said Goldfarb.

"That I have now lived too long."

And with that, Lionel Fielding bit down hard on something that he must have put in his mouth when he went to get dressed. I didn't think it was cyanide, because there was no sign of pain or distress, no foaming of the mouth.

Michael screamed, "Dad!" one last time as he leapt out of his chair and ran to his father. Too late, he wrapped his arms around him. Too late, he cried, "Don't leave me, Dad." Too late, he whispered, "I love you," into his father's unhearing ear.

I tore my eyes away from the scene that was too difficult to watch, thinking of all of my unanswered questions, and then I lifted my eyes to the massive window, as if waking from a terrifying dream. When it had happened I'll never know, but the sky was suddenly clear, and the sun was out. Lake Cayuga shimmered in azure serenity. The storm had ended, and no one had noticed.

CHAPTER TWENTY-NINE

L OOK," said Detective Goldfarb, "why don't you let me take care of this? It doesn't require the two of us, and someone has to get Beth home."

Surveying the room, I couldn't disagree. People like Lionel Fielding don't die every day, and the room was swamped with state and local police, not to mention local and even national press. Andy Pilcher had quietly disappeared. I'd have to thank him later.

I went and talked to Beth, and she didn't give me a fight, even when I told her that I'd be doing the driving. We took one last ride down the cable car and got back onto Route 96. The midday sun and the upstate New York snow plowing crews were doing their usual heroic job, and before I knew it I was driving on clear roads.

I knew Beth had a lot of questions and a lot she wanted to talk about, but she was exhausted, and I don't think we'd driven ten miles before she fell sound asleep. She didn't budge until we pulled into my driveway right about dinnertime. I was worn out myself, and I hadn't been able to make myself think about anything other than staying awake and on the road. It was probably just as well that way. It wasn't until I saw the Christmas lights shining and the tree glowing in the front window that I remembered that it was Christmas Eve, and that I still hadn't gotten Doreen a present.

We got out of the car, and as we approached the front door, Beth looked at me and said, "Give me the keys."

"What?" I said.

"Just give me the car keys."

We walked into the house and found everyone in the living room putting final decorations on the tree, the colorful lights casting the entire room in a festive glow. Someone had dug up an old "Christmas Favorites" CD, and Bing Crosby was singing "I'll Be Home For Christmas," as everyone turned to greet us. But before anyone had a chance to say a word, Beth marched over to Cal, grabbed him by the front of his shirt, and gave him a long, hard kiss, then she took him by the arm and started marching him toward the front door.

"Where are we going?" I heard him say.

"Christmas shopping," said Beth, and without breaking stride she turned her head to look at Doreen and said, "Don't hold dinner for us." And with that, they were gone.

"I guess we all know what Cal's getting for Christmas," said Doreen's daughter, Laura, smiling.

"What was that all about?" said Doreen, looking at me with an uncharacteristically puzzled expression.

"Long story," I said. "Let's just say that I think Beth's bucket list is about to get shorter."

"Cal's, too, from the look of it," said Donnie, looking at my daughter, Emma, with an expression that I wasn't sure I was comfortable with.

"Okay, okay," said Doreen, "dinner's on." Then she looked at me and said, "You look pretty much all in. Maybe you should go and lie down. I'll keep a plate warm for you."

"I was hoping you'd be keeping you warm for me," I said, loud enough for the kids to hear, making Doreen blush. "I guess you're right," I said.

Everyone else went into the kitchen for dinner at the big round table while I took myself off for a quick shower and a nap. I honestly don't remember climbing under the covers.

*　*　*　*　*　*

I slept for twelve straight hours. It was still pitch black out at 6 AM, but I was wide awake, and I knew that I wouldn't be going back to sleep. I also knew that I wouldn't be seeing anyone else for a while. I remember when the kids were young we were lucky if we kept them in bed until five o'clock on Christmas Day, but these days they all stay up late, exchanging gifts with each other and chatting and eating snacks well into the night.

But I guess I wasn't surprised when I smelled the aroma of brewing coffee as I got downstairs, and saw that the light was on in the kitchen.

"Good morning, Mr. Hunter," said the small form curled up on the sofa at the end of the kitchen.

"Good morning, Beth. You want me to freshen up your coffee?"

"That would be great," she said, holding out her cup to me. She was wrapped in one of Doreen's bathrobes, and I guess she must have seen the question on my face. "Cal and I got back around midnight. Cal wanted to be back here for Christmas morning, and I couldn't stand the thought of waking up in my apartment alone, so he invited me to stay the night here. I slept on the floor in Laura's room, and Doreen lent me one of her bathrobes. I don't think we're going to see anyone else for a while; we were up pretty late. I know we're not going to be seeing Cal for a while."

I didn't know how to react to that, or even if I should.

"What has you up so early?" I said, as I refilled Beth's mug and filled up my own.

"I slept all the way home yesterday, so I had a tough time sleeping last night. And I guess I have a lot on my mind, and I was hoping you'd be up so we could talk."

"There's a lot to process, isn't there," I said as I sat down on the other end of the sofa. The coffee tasted good enough to make me think that life was worth living after all. "Is there anything in particular you want to talk about?"

"Oh, I don't even know where to start," said Beth. "I guess my first question is, do we really believe Lionel Fielding? Do you think he actually murdered Ada, or do you think he made that confession and killed himself just to cover for his son?"

The coffee suddenly began to go down hard. I put my mug down on the table.

"Well," I finally said "we have a problem, don't we?"

"What's that?"

"The problem is that the only two people who can tell us that for sure are both dead. And if Michael Fielding, Paul Janssen, and Justine Tan have any brains at all, they'll keep their mouths shut forever, whether they're guilty or not. So I guess the easy answer is that we'll never know. All I can tell you is that, speaking personally, I believe Lionel Fielding's story, word for word. It's the only plausible explanation for the murder scene, and, frankly, I just don't believe that any of the others are clever enough, devious enough, or cruel enough to have pulled something like that off. But you're going to have to make your own mind up about that. I'm thinking, though, that that's not what you really want to talk about, is it?"

"No," said Beth, looking down at her coffee cup. "I guess it's not."

"You want to talk about all that time and space stuff, right? You want to know if Alice Sterling really *was* Ada Danforth. You want to know where those letters came from as much as I do. You want to know why everyone, *everyone*, said the same thing about Ada, about how she was there but never there. And most of all, you want to know if Lionel Fielding was right: that Ada Danforth really had discovered cracks in space and time big enough for a human being to walk through."

"Yes, that's what I want to know. All of that."

"Have you ever read much Shakespeare?"

"What? Not really. I guess I read what I had to read in high school, and then I took a survey of English literature in college where I had to read a couple of plays, but that's about it. Why?"

"That's kind of what I've read. I went to John Jay, and they weren't really big on English literature there. But I remember reading *Hamlet* at some point in my life. I didn't get most of it, but there was one line that always stuck with me. It goes: 'There are more things in heaven and Earth, Horatio/ Than are dreamt of in your philosophy.' And I guess that pretty much describes where I am on all this. I'm not a genius, and I'm not a scientist or a philosopher, but I'm pretty sure there's an awful lot more that we don't understand about this world than we do understand. Maybe Ada could have told us more if she'd lived, but that wasn't meant to be, because she, and Lionel Fielding, chose to die so that we wouldn't find out. And now, Ada's murder case is closed, her body's been cremated, and I don't think anyone is going to speculate any more about that stuff."

"But what about those letters? Nobody has even come close to explaining them."

"No, they haven't, and now they never will. I'm pretty sure Steve Goldfarb is going to say that there's a rational explanation somewhere, but now it's time to close the case and move on. And I don't blame him. You know the work load you guys have. He has to move on, and so do you. And you know, he may be right: Maybe there is a practical explanation that we haven't been able to come up with yet. So, as lawyers would say, that question is now moot. All that's left to do is clean up a few practical matters."

"Like what?" asked Beth, looking either resigned or relieved; I couldn't tell which.

"I have to go and talk to Ada's family, that's the most important thing. I also want to talk to Richie Glazier. And somebody has to tell me who burned my poor Accord to a cinder."

"Oh," said Beth, "a report came in on your car yesterday afternoon. You won't be surprised to learn that it was Jeremy Carter. He decided to blame you for the fact that he was fired from his job."

"Why me, for crying out loud?"

"You're just lucky, I guess," said Beth, with a smile.

"So, Beth," I said. "Turnabout is fair play, you know."

"What do you mean?"

"You asked me about the letters and all the other stuff. I didn't give you much of an answer, but I did my best. So now it's your turn. What do you think?"

"I guess I'm with Shakespeare."

"What does that mean?" I asked.

"I guess it means I buy the whole thing. I think Ada was the real quantum child; she left those notes on your desk, and I believe her brother saw her in two places at one time. And, yes, I believe that she and Lionel Fielding are Michael Fielding's parents. I know that sounds crazy, and I don't intend to tell anyone but you that that's how I feel. But I've tried and tried to come up with some Sherlock Holmes-type rational explanation, and I just can't do it. And, besides, there's this."

Beth walked over to the kitchen table, where her satchel was sitting on one of the chairs. She unzipped it and pulled out a small item wrapped in a couple of tissues. Then she walked back to me and handed me the tissue-wrapped item. I opened it up.

"Beth, isn't this the photo that was hanging on Ada's wall in her house?"

"It's the same photo, but it's a different copy."

"Where did you get this?"

"After I got up from the bed in the guest room of Lionel Fielding's house and got dressed, I made a wrong turn when I left the room. I guess I was still feeling a little out of it, and I didn't know the layout of the house very well. So, anyway, I found myself in Lionel Fielding's bedroom, and this was on the nightstand next to his bed. I know I shouldn't have taken it, but I was just about sure that it was the same picture that was hanging on Ada's wall. It is, isn't it?"

"I'm pretty sure it is," I replied, as I stared, mystified, at the photo. I hadn't looked at the photo on Ada's wall since the night of the murder, and of course at that point I hadn't met Lionel Fielding. But now I looked at it long and hard. It wasn't a very good photo. It was black and white, and small, and it was clearly taken by an inexperienced photographer with a camera without a very good lens.

It was taken in some kind of a park on a sunny day. In the background was a parking lot, and the first thing I noticed was that all the cars were 1950's vintage. There were also a couple of other people in the background of the photo, and they all were wearing clothes and sporting hairstyles that made them look like extras from an episode of "Ozzie and Harriet."

But it was the two young people who were the subject of the photo that truly grabbed my attention. One of them was shockingly easy to recognize, despite the poor quality of the photo. He was a big man, about six feet tall, with a thick head of dark, well-combed hair. His face looked like it was carved from granite, with a prominent nose, a strong jaw, and a stubborn-looking chin. But his most remarkable feature was his eyes, which even in the old, indistinct photo, sparkled with intelligence. Despite the ravages of time, Lionel Fielding hadn't changed all that much. The other person could have been Ada, looking perhaps a little younger than on the day she had come to my office, but it was a tough call. I'd only actually seen her that one time, and there are a lot of small brunettes in this world. It could have been Alice Sterling, based on Fielding's description of her, and maybe he was attracted to a type: Maybe he found Ada attractive because she resembled Alice. But if it wasn't Ada, why did she have that photo hanging on her wall? And why did Lionel Fielding lie about it? There were probably a lot of possible answers to those questions, but I wasn't ready to think about them, not yet.

I turned to Beth, who was staring at me with frightened eyes. But any further conversation would have to be postponed as we heard footsteps descending the stairs and loud voices approaching the kitchen door. She silently took the photo from me and slipped it back into her bag.

"Another time, another place," she said.

I couldn't have said it better myself.

THE END

TO MY READERS

My writing is a constant work in progress, and I am always looking for feedback and advice whenever and wherever I can get it.

If you have just a few moments after you have finished reading *The Quantum Child* – whether you loved it, hated it, or anywhere in between – I hope you will please take the time to tell me what you thought of it.

The best way to do this is to give it a review on Amazon or on *Goodreads*. You should also feel free to contact me at charlesw.ayerjr@gmail.com. I'd love to hear from you.

Thanks you for reading my story, and thank you in advance for your feedback.

Chuck

Made in the USA
Las Vegas, NV
13 February 2022